THE DIRECTRIX

By the same author

The Quiet War of Rebecca Sheldon
Brief Shining

THE DIRECTRIX

Kathleen Rowntree

St. Martin's Press
New York

Library of Congress Cataloging-in-Publication Data

Rowntree, Kathleen.
    The directrix / Kathleen Rowntree.
      p. cm.
    ISBN 0-312-05414-9
    I. Title.
    PR6068.0935D57   1991
    823'.914—dc20   90-48995
                                                            CIP

First published in Great Britain by George Weidenfeld & Nicolson Limited.

First U.S. Edition: April 1991
10 9 8 7 6 5 4 3 2 1

THE DIRECTRIX

PART ONE

1

'I am very tired,' said the Prioress.

Margaret darted forward – an extra cushion, a reviving cup of tea?

In her haste to refuse these comforts, the Prioress's teeth became dislodged. Fortunately, her tongue sucked them back into place with well-practised aplomb, but not without a temporary loss of dignity. As Margaret and Catherine turned tactfully away, the Prioress was seized with resentment. She saw herself as they had seen her and, as she flinched, sciatic pain shot through her back and legs so that she almost cried out in protest. For she was not as that image suggested – feeble, muddled. A truer indicator of the state of the inner woman was her voice, youthful and steady; indeed, when she was amused (as, for example, at the sight of Sister Hope fleeing from a dangling spider, clutching her skirts and screeching as if it were a monster after her with rapacious intent) her laughter rang out in the cloister clear and true as the matins bell. Yes, in heart and mind she was lively still. 'Sit down,' she commanded when her mouth felt reliably under control.

Margaret and Catherine sat in two hard chairs placed distantly across the dusty rug.

The Prioress looked from one to the other; from Margaret, pink and glowing with eyes the blue of forget-me-nots, to pale, brown-eyed Catherine. 'Sister Mercy will not recover,' she announced. 'Something will have to be done. I have discussed the matter with Sister Mercy, who understands her position – that she can never succeed me, that she must prepare to obey a sterner call . . . More to our point, she can no longer be responsible for the day to day business of this Priory. She wishes, in fact, to resign.'

Noises of sad protest sounded faintly in the vicinity of the hard chairs.

The Prioress sighed and examined her knobbly hands. 'I am afraid the protracted illness of poor Sister Mercy has resulted in a rather serious state of affairs.'

Prominently in the minds of all three women was the thought that even in health Sister Mercy, as Directrix, had allowed things to get into a pretty parlous state. Income from the Priory's once famous dairy herd, from the vegetable garden and bee-hives, had dwindled, and there were fewer orders for the sisters' once celebrated needlework. The place had become shabby; important visitors seldom came on retreat. Commissions for the sisters' prayers were few and far between, for the reputation of Albion Priory was no longer high in the world.

Margaret craned forward. 'How very brave of Sister Mercy . . .' She stopped herself, recalled the advice of Beatrice, her friend and lieutenant ('You've got to develop "bottom", Mags, and that awful squawk of yours just doesn't help'), then continued in the deep, measured tone she had been practising of late. 'How *very* generous, and how typically *selfless* of poor, dear Sister Mercy. Things have indeed deteriorated, and I do so agree that they cannot be allowed to slide further. I know I speak for every one of us when I assure you, Reverend Mother, of our robust support.'

'Mmm.' The thought had slipped into the Prioress's mind – and she wondered if it had also occurred to her guests – that since it was she who had named Sister Mercy as her successor, and as a consequence made her Directrix of the Priory, her own judgement deserved a measure of blame.

But Margaret's thoughts had cleared this hurdle and were racing over more profitable ground. Since Catherine had also

2

been invited here this morning, and, since Catherine, as Mercy's assistant, was already a member of the Priory's hierarchy, Margaret could not jump to any flattering conclusion. She longed to prompt the old woman, but steeled herself to be cautious. 'I imagine it is a difficult task deciding on her successor.'

'Have you considered raising the status of the Council?' Catherine enquired, speaking for the first time. 'I wonder whether the task ahead requires the skill of more than one individual.'

'Aha, an interesting thought . . . But the Council is over-whelmingly composed of Sister Mercy's contemporaries. No; I have decided to skip a generation. You younger women have the energy and the fresh ideas we need. Now then – by common consent you are two of the more outstanding younger sisters – let me hear your views. Tell me, Sister Margaret; how would you proceed?'

Oh heavens! The moment had leapt on her without warning – the moment they had hoped and plotted for – she, Beatrice, Agnes and Joan. But they had banked on several more years; in fact, they had thoroughly bemoaned the time that must elapse before their chance could come. One matter they had forecast correctly, however: Catherine was to be the opposition. Margaret steadied herself; she was more than a match for Catherine. She pulled in her chin, flexed the muscles of her throat, invoked her new deep voice.

'We have here' – she threw out her arm as if to include the farthest field in the Priory's demesne – 'a priceless jewel. Think of the history, of the artists drawn by the beauty of the place, of the generations of sisters who have dedicated their lives to preserving and enhancing the reputation of Albion Priory . . .'

Already the Prioress's mind had strayed from the words – which made her impatient, for they told her what she already knew – to contemplation of the speaker: an arresting, person-able figure whose manner of utter confidence would calm many an anxious heart. As indeed it had. A deputation of the senior sisters responsible for the Priory's accounts had begged the

3

Prioress to pay heed to Margaret's ideas. Apparently, she had drawn up sheets of figures which were nothing short of revelatory. The Prioress hoped to do her duty without recourse to the figures . . .

'And what do we see? Shabby, scruffy interiors. Crumbling, decaying exteriors. Slip-shod ways, a pervasive air of defeat. Even' – and here Margaret's voice trembled – 'the Albion Tower declared unsafe.' She screwed up her face in disbelief – 'The Albion Tower in danger of collapse?' – then drew herself up and roared: 'The Albion Tower is known throughout the world. It is a symbol – it *stands* for something.'

'Not for much longer, m'dear,' thought the Prioress grimly, 'not unless you really can come up with something.'

'We must rethink the ways in which we seek to earn our living. Subsistence agriculture and horticulture will not restore the fabric, nor will a tapestry here or a nicely illuminated prayer there. Too many people, I'm afraid, engage in activities which are, frankly, a waste of time – worse, distract us from fruitful endeavour. I know this is not a popular view, but the world does not owe us a living. It is absolutely vital that we discover what things we can provide for the world that the world is prepared to pay for. Nothing in the sad saga of the last few years has so offended against the spirit of this place as the sight of Sister Mercy scurrying to the Church with her begging bowl. How humiliating – the Albion Priory dependent upon handouts. Never again, if I have anything to do with it!'

The Prioress shifted in her chair and jarred her sciatic nerve. Sharper than the shooting pain in her legs was the thought that Margaret had a knack of honouring the office of Prioress – her deep curtsy, her virtuous solicitousness – while managing to convey contempt for the incumbent. It was that bossy tone of voice, that steely glint in her eye . . . 'This is all very well, but we're waiting to hear what it is you would actually *do*.'

Margaret put her head on one side and smiled as if reproving an inattentive child. 'I think I did state what our first priority should be. We should seek to discover services we can provide that will bring us a satisfactory income. Of course, we can take advice on this from many sources, but some of us have been thinking along these lines and have come up with an idea – backed up with figures, let me hasten to add, which I am sure will interest you.'

'Yes, yes . . .'

'You see, it is *rarity* that makes a commodity valuable. Can we provide the world with a rare commodity? Indeed we can. We can provide *tranquillity*. And – more rarely still – we can give that tranquillity an aura of spirituality. Peace and quiet in an uplifting atmosphere. The setting is perfect – acres of privacy, glorious buildings, our music, our art, our daily religious observance. We can provide a refuge from the world . . .'

'Really!' cried the Prioress. 'Is that it? Your great plan? But we have always taken visitors on retreat.'

'The wrong sort of visitor,' Margaret snapped. 'I'm talking about the wealthy visitor. We need to attract powerful, important people, successful people able to pay handsomely for our hospitality. The thing would have to be done properly, of course; everything geared towards it. Superfluous, counter-productive activity would cease. We must free resources to service our new endeavour . . .'

'Well, thank you, Sister . . .'

'I realize this may take some getting used to, but I assure you, once you have seen the figures . . .'

'Quite. But now . . .'

'And if it seems a rather radical proposal, do bear in mind, Reverend Mother, that radical measures are required if we are ever again to hold our heads high in the world.'

'I'll hear Sister Catherine now.'

Catherine smiled.

At once the Prioress's heart softened. How right Catherine looked in her habit, her face neither diminished nor thrown into cruel relief – the sad fate of so many behabitted sisters. Rather, her beauty was dramatized by the white and grey frame. She wore coif and veil as natural appendages; she was all of a piece like a sculptured, robed madonna. Now, talking with evident strain and hesitation, her calm gravity made the woman

5

listening at her side appear the more active partner. Margaret craned forward to miss not a word, her eyes darted to keep pace with her thoughts, her arms curled into her body as if restraining a pent-up force. Was Catherine intimidated? Her words came haltingly.

'But when I remember the purpose of our community – that we should live a good life to the glory of God and share all that we have in the common good – I cannot think we have strayed far from our goal. We are a loving, caring community. By and large, every member is happy and fulfilled . . .'

Bless the dear girl! She was her heart's choice. Mercy's choice, too. How often had she and Mercy stood at the great oriel window watching Catherine below in the garden? They had nudged one another and confided: 'There she is. Yes, Catherine's the one.' In less complicated times there had been no doubt about it. To observe her in Council smoothing feelings, creating compromise; to hear her glorious *mezzo* giving the anthem at Evensong; to feel the better for her wide, warm smile was to know that she was special, that in due course she should succeed.

'I'm worried by Sister Margaret's talk of activities being unprofitable. Profit is not the only yardstick. These activities define what people are – people would be lost without them. And they are part of the fabric of this place, we relate to them. Some of the riches of our lives – music, art, writing – flow from them. I admit the need for some change, for we are certainly up against it at present, but it must be change with safeguards for all the good things we have built over the years. You talk about freeing resources. Please remember you are talking about people. And you spoke harshly about Sister Mercy's management of our affairs – with which I, as her assistant, am associated. But many of the difficulties we have been discussing are due to matters beyond our control, to changes in the world outside . . .'

Margaret could hold back no longer. 'Exactly! And we, too, must change if we are to survive, for it is from the world that we seek a living.'

'I'm sure there is a lot in what you say, Sister. Perhaps your ideas do contain the answer – I have admitted that something must be done, and I am not sure what, beyond improving the things we do already – but so long as we never lose sight of our purpose.'

'There can be no purpose higher than that of restoring our beloved Priory to its rightful place in the world.'

'But the Priory is *us* – we sisters. And I'm not sure we can claim a right to any particular place . . .'

'It is more, much more, than that. It is those who have gone before, those who will come after – more still: it is an *ideal*, a thing in its own right . . .'

During this exchange, the Prioress, as she afterwards recounted to Sister Mercy, was visited by the Holy Spirit. Suddenly, blazingly, she was enlightened. She saw clearly what it was she was called upon to do, which was to choose neither of them, but both of them. Plainly, both were needed. Catherine had admitted she had no practical solution, and Margaret was so sure of hers that she seemed to have lost sight of those precious things which Catherine had remembered to value. Their gifts – Margaret's practical drive and Catherine's spirituality – were complementary. 'I have it!' she cried, nearly ejecting her teeth.

This time her guests were too full of suspense to feign blindness. They stared frankly while the Prioress struggled with her mouth behind her hand. 'You are both to be Directrix. You will help one another – it's a big enough task. That way, all sides will be considered, nothing overlooked.'

'But which of us. . ?'

'Who will be. . ?'

'Don't even think about the succession,' the Prioress cried airily. 'There's plenty of time for that. I'm sure God intends me to endure this pain for many years yet; I've hardly begun to come to terms with it. Later, when the time draws near, I shall name my successor. In the meantime you are both joint Directrix. I wish you to devote all your energies to restoring the well-being of our community. Take advice and assistance from

7

Council; if necessary, appoint new members. I leave it to you. And now – kneel.'

Exhilarated, the Prioress gabbled a blessing. Not only had she come to a decision, she had been innovatory, for never before had the office of Directrix been held by other than the nominated future Prioress. She had excelled herself this morning, and had earned, she considered, a restorative measure of elderberry wine.

2

Margaret went at once to the chapel.

'Dear Heavenly Father,' she prayed.

Always in her private devotions she began thus – 'Father, Heavenly Father' were marvellous words, comfortable and redolent as any words can be to a daughter who knows she pleases. Her earthly father, though modest in his calling (a small-town grocer in fact) had been famous for his strict adherence to the virtues of prudence and thrift and for striving to establish their practice in civic matters through his position as a local councillor. The good shopkeeper had lived to see his daughter become as passionate an advocate for sound house-keeping as he. Satisfaction beamed from his face as he beheld her. 'Dear Father,' she murmured, observing his emotion; and later, sensing a loftier paternal approbation: 'Dear Heavenly Father . . .'

When she had completed her communication she got off her knees, and walked briskly from the chapel and through the corridors.

'Brr!' she cried, bustling into Agnes's room, the cold adding impetus to her customary haste. She sat on the edge of the bed and surveyed the waiting ones.

On the rug lay Beatrice, sprawled on her stomach, propped on cushion-pillowed elbows. Her violet eyes under straight brows, her prominent cheekbones and jutting chin proclaimed strength – rather attractive strength, Margaret acknowledged with affection and with a small, stifled sense of misgiving. She forgave Beatrice her boisterous affectations, and she forgave her in ignorant advance for whatever it was she made Margaret secretly uneasy about, because Beatrice, as well as possessing great charm, showed herself time and again to be a first-rate tactician. If she was a little – 'exotic' was the word Margaret's rather limited imagination invariably settled on – never mind; Beatrice had an unequalled nose for strategy.

Agnes, too, was a considerable strategist – certainly in her own estimation; but Margaret felt her value to be somewhat diminished by an uncertain temperament and a repulsive countenance. Sitting now at her desk, her sallow skin drawn into a scowl over half-moon spectacles, her lined mouth pulled sulkily down, she had an almost saturnine appearance. There had been occasions when their careful plans, nursed along by painstaking and artful reasoning, had very nearly blown sky-high in an intemperate public outburst from Agnes. And sometimes she gave unnecessary offence by referring disrespectfully to the Prioress. Agnes, sound as a bell on matters of policy, lacked a reliably politic manner.

Joan – dear, wild-eyed, tortured Joan sitting tensely in the easy chair – was their theorist. Such a nervous, highly-strung thing – but quite brilliant; able to produce a legitimizing Biblical reference or historical precedent at the drop of a hat, the possessor of a dazzling facility for matching strategy to goals and for conferring high-minded authoritativeness on mundane expediency. Unfortunately, Joan's talents required a degree of ideological sophistication to be appreciated; her handicap was that of many an intellectual: it was only to the already initiated that she could communicate.

At this point in a consideration of her colleagues, Margaret became blindingly aware of her own worth. They had honed their ideas and developed their plans as equals, but gradually it had become clear that if they were to win others to their cause, Margaret must be their front woman. Equals they may be, but Margaret was indisputably first among them.

'For pity's sake,' cried Beatrice, seizing Margaret's ankles and making a play of sinking her teeth into them. (Margaret smiled, but nevertheless primly removed her feet.) 'Hurry up and tell us what happened.'

'Well, our information was correct: Sister Mercy's resigned.'

Their gasps were fierce as snakes' hisses.

'And the Reverend Mother has appointed me – and Catherine – joint Directrix.'

'Joint?'

'Both of you?'

'But which . . ?'

'She declines to name her successor for the moment – she reckons there's plenty of time before it becomes an urgent consideration.'

'There probably is – the tenacious old bat.'

Margaret, recalling how, barely an hour ago, the old bat had been good enough to elevate her, said: 'I'd rather you didn't speak disrespectfully in my hearing, Agnes. I am now Directrix of this Priory.'

'*Joint* Directrix, for Pete's sake. How exactly did that come about? She had both of you closeted with her – was she trying to choose between you? Were you and Catherine in competition?'

With raised eyebrows and lowered lids, Margaret began a sweeping perusal of the floor – which was a sure sign that she had embarked upon rapid thought. 'No-oo. I wouldn't say . . . As a matter of fact, the Reverend Mother gave no indication of having any motive other than that of seeking advice. It is probable that were it not for Sister Veronica having pressed her to see me, Catherine alone would have been summoned there this morning. Catherine, I understand, was with the Reverend Mother at Sister Mercy's bedside yesterday evening.'

'Yes, I had Sister Hope watching her,' Beatrice confirmed.

'There you are. For all we know, the Reverend Mother was about to appoint Catherine and suggest that I merely advise her.'

'So you think you did sway her. In which case there *was* an element of competition.'

Margaret's eyes were now wide open; they seemed to jut towards her inquisitor as she boomed: 'I think my words swayed her – yes! She was very, very impressed. Whatever her plans had been prior to that interview, she made a decision then and there to include me. There was no doubt whatsoever that I advanced our position. I presume you would not have wished me to turn down the opportunity?'

'Perhaps,' mused Agnes, not in the least intimidated, 'you ought to have held out. Insisted on being sole Directrix – with Catherine to advise you if need be.'

An unpleasant redness rose in Margaret's cheeks; but:

'Too risky,' Joan protested. 'She might have lost everything.'

And Beatrice, with an air of closing the discussion, said: 'In any case, Catherine will present no problem. The important thing is, from now on, our hands are on the wheel. Any hands found to be pulling in the wrong direction will simply be dislodged.'

Margaret smiled gratefully. 'Catherine was awfully vague – quite out of her depth. "More of the same only done a bit better" seemed to be her solution.'

'Catherine will present no problem,' Beatrice repeated, then rolled on to her back to gaze at the ceiling. 'We must find a way of packing the Council with our sort of people.'

'Absolutely. We can't waste time arguing. At last we've a chance to accomplish our dream of a truly great Albion Priory. Joan, come to my room and help me with my speech, will you? Got to get all the facts and figures off pat.'

'Never mind the facts and figures, Mags. Give 'em one of your rousing turns – throb on about old Albion.'

Margaret hesitated then decided to smile. (Beatrice was a tease – but *staunch*.) 'Come along Joan,' she called pleasantly.

The silence following their departure held for some minutes. Agnes stared at her desk, Beatrice stared at the ceiling.

'Well, I'm off,' Beatrice decided at last, and hauled herself to her feet. But at the door she looked back. 'Oh – Ag?'

'Urh?' Agnes said suspiciously.

'Do guard your tongue in public from now on, sweetie. Margaret will want us to raise the tone.'

A mean look came into Agnes's eyes. 'Thanks for the advice. Perhaps I can reciprocate. You'll probably find this hard to understand, but Margaret's an idealist; she's not in this just for the power. But the trouble with idealists is they can't stand being let down by people they trust. Know what I mean? Let's say a close associate turns out to have a sordid side which could become public knowledge. Now that would be really upsetting. If I were you I'd watch my step from now on.'

Having listened carefully, Beatrice turned the door handle and slipped softly from the room.

3

It had begun to snow when Catherine sped through the cloister. Moonlit flakes spat in through the open archways. Head down, keeping close to the solid wall, she hurried to the Chapter House door, grasped the great iron ring with two hands, turned, pushed, and thrust herself inside. On her right was the lobby giving on to the Chapter House. Briefly, the scene there of this afternoon's Council played again in her mind's eye, intensifying her dread that what she had always taken to be firm ground was but shifting, crumbling dust. Skirting the lobby, she hurried along a vaulted corridor to the hospital.

Sister Luke came to meet her. 'She's asleep. But come in and wait. She was asking for you earlier, hoping you would come.'

In a narrow bed at the far end of the room lay Sister Mercy. Catherine sat in a chair drawn close to her bed. Peering through the gloom, she met the eyes of another patient who inclined her head then looked away. The small obeisance was for her newly conferred status, Catherine understood, with a renewed spasm of misery. The other beds were unoccupied. At the head of the room Sister Luke sat at her desk. Glare from the desk's lamp illuminated her jowly, coiffed face so that it seemed to float unattached in the darkness. Then a hand rose and jabbed the end of a pen into the mouth (Sister Luke bit on the pen and frowned in thought) and at once the face became anchored to an invisible whole.

14

Sister Mercy was thinking: 'She's here. I must tell her, I must speak.' But though the need was urgent and the words formed ready on her tongue, the effort defeated her. 'In a moment she will go. They will decide I have settled for the night,' she told herself, becoming panic-stricken. Her body was a great weight and her feet were frozen. 'Have patience. I'm trying . . .'

Catherine's thoughts had spun out of control. She had been led to expect, her mind ranted, yes, hints from Sister Mercy, Sister Cecilia and Sister Anne had led her to expect that the Prioress would soon appoint her. Awed, apprehensive, honoured, she had vowed to dedicate every scrap of energy to the task ahead. She had summoned her faith, gathered the resolution and confidence to believe that one day she would restore the well-being of Albion Priory. Apparently she had been naïve. It was not possible, no. Without immediate, radical alteration, the Priory was beyond saving: that was the proposition put forward so forcefully in the Prioress's room this morning and in Council this afternoon. '*There is no alternative*,' Margaret had bellowed – and it must be so, for it had been believed. For a moment, the heady atmosphere in the Chapter House had made her almost believe it herself – perhaps her understanding of the matter had been inadequate, and nothing short of revolution would suffice. But then, rising to reply, a stubborn residue of former conviction had led her to protest: 'We have the promise of further funds. We have so much good will, a wealth of advice to call upon. Why hurry? Let us accept help gratefully, restore what we have to the best of our ability and live accordingly. Above all, let us have faith in our traditions.' But this had not answered their mood. Margaret's picture of a glowing future had dazzled them. Shakily, Catherine had asked: 'What about those who cannot change; your solution will accommodate them, I trust?' 'We must all learn to adapt,' Margaret had replied coldly, and a sense of foreboding had seized Catherine. It was Margaret the Council had empowered to act. Nothing was asked of Catherine other than her presence at Margaret's side. 'I am to be a sort of symbol,' she thought; 'I am to quieten doubters, reassure the anxious, legitimize the new regime'; and then, wildly: 'I must extricate myself!'

Seeing Catherine shift in her chair, Sister Luke put down her pen and came softly along the aisle between the beds. 'Yes, I should go now. No point in waiting any longer. I don't think she'll stir before morning.'

'Wait!' Sister Mercy cried inside herself and made a supreme effort to break through the heaviness.

'I think she's waking. But she's cold. Sister, she's shivering.'

Sister Luke snatched a blanket from an unoccupied bed. 'Put this on her. I'll get a hot water bottle.'

'Don't try to talk,' Catherine murmured, pressing the blanket around Mercy. Pitiful sounds broke from the trembling mouth.

'Darn it – darn!' Mercy had known this would happen, that if she managed to speak, her words would be sabotaged by willfully chattering teeth. It was because she was so dreadfully cold . . . At last a hot bottle was placed against her feet. Warmth stole through her. 'Ah . . !' she sighed in a long exhalation. 'I knew you were here. I've been trying . . .'

'It doesn't matter,' Catherine soothed.

But it did matter. She had to say it. 'I'm so sorry. It's all my fault. If I hadn't made such a mess of things Reverend Mother wouldn't have asked Sister Margaret . . . It would be you – just you.'

'No, no. It's not your fault. It's just that things are far more difficult than we supposed.'

'I can hardly bear it – knowing how hopeless I've been – having to take that with me.'

Catherine was silent for a while. She decided she could not insult her old friend by dissembling. 'It takes courage to know what we are. And I imagine even greater courage is required to take that knowledge with us, honestly, without flinching from it.'

'Courage,' whispered Mercy. Then: 'That's something, I suppose.'

'A very great thing. Rare.'

Mercy closed her eyes.

'Goodnight,' Catherine whispered, kissing her.

Returning through the cloister she was oblivious of the snow now massing through the arches. One thought obsessed her. She had singled out a virtue, made a present of it to the dying Sister Mercy. Could she summon a sufficient measure of it herself?

* * * *

By morning, the snow lay thickly. On their way to chapel, the sisters hurried through hushed, dark corridors, clutching their cloaks closely round them. Prayers were offered in voices thick and cracking, yawns stifled behind decently clasped hands. Then, in a shuffling press through the doorway, they nerved themselves to face the working day.

There was a small commotion.

'Excuse me.'

'Really! Do you mind?'

'I do as a matter of fact. One of my lay sisters is in bed with the 'flu.'

It was Sister Mary John, the senior herdswoman.

'I'll come and give you a hand,' Catherine called.

Margaret caught her arm. 'Here is one aspect of our religious observance you might usefully attend to – if that is to be your province. This shuffling in and rushing out of chapel is quite disgraceful.'

'Oh, yes. But I must go and give a hand with the milking. They're short-staffed this morning.'

Her spirits soared at the prospect of a few hours in the cowshed. In the cloakroom she hitched up her skirt, pulled on wellington boots and a waterproof cape, then set off through the snow.

Steam hung over manure mounds in the yard making the first light ghostly. Reeking ammonia cut the air.

'Why – Sister Catherine!' exclaimed a lay sister. (There were many lay sisters attached to the Priory, specialist workers whose freedom from spiritual obligations allowed work to continue without interruption.)

'Right. What do you want me to do?'

The lay sister was embarrassed; she had expected more lowly assistance. (Sister Catherine had often tended the cows – she would set her hand to anything – but now she was Directrix!) 'Sister Mary John!' she called.

Mary John raised her head from a cow's belly. 'There's the hay to be put out, and the sluicing.'

A cowshed is the cosiest place, thought Catherine, pitching hay into mangers, shaking each forkful to make it airy and appetizing. Dust flew, heady-sweet, mingling with the milk smell and the pungent steam from the cattle. The rhythm of the place – the throbbing machinery, the chewing cud – went as steadily as heartbeats beneath intermittent clanging, spattering, swishing. She tossed pailfuls of water across the floor and drove the broom in short, sharp thrusts, exhilarating in the pleasurable stretching of cramped limbs. When she rested briefly on a bale of hay, a tabby cat came mewing and wove sinuously between her ankles. She caught it up and tucked its head under her chin, played its tail through her fingers and felt its contentment reverberate against her throat.

Afterwards, she did not go with the others to breakfast. Her labour had refreshed her. She set out along the broad tree-lined path to the woods.

The way ahead rose steeply. Here and there, spray misted through the trees like isolated snowstorms, and small avalanches of sun-warmed snow fell in thick clumps from the highest branches. A mass of snow struck her shoulder and splintered softly over her cape. Suddenly, a shot rang out, then another and another; but the retorts were only the sounds of snow clumps landing on the slush-covered planks of a foot-bridge over the brook. As she passed through the wood, snow beat spasmodically on her head like the patting of friendly hands.

Soon she came to a wicker gate. She let herself through and entered a meadow – a sea of snow, its rippled surface gleaming with crystals, crusty on top, soft and yielding below. It was a flawless expanse. She hesitated, reluctant at first to set foot upon it, then scrunched briskly across to a five-bar gate in the hedge on the opposite side. She swept snow from the highest rung, climbed up and sat down.

To her left, Albion Priory lay spread in the valley, its ancient stones yellow-warm against the whiteness, its twisted chimneys grouped like conspirators about the gleaming roofs. From the old chapel the famous tower bore a statue of Our Lady heavenwards through a dazzle of light. The place was beautiful, she thought, and Margaret's passion to save it commendable.

Her eyes watered; she lowered her head, and a wave of the previous night's agony rose over her, stale as a shameful dream. The thought came to her that hurt pride, as well as scrupulousness, had spurred her heart-searching.

Across the meadow, her footmarks came to meet her. She sprang down and began to make the returning set with clean, strong strides.

4

In the Sewing Room, Sister Cecilia put down her work, pressed together the tips of her long fingers and sighed – signals that she was about to speak and anticipated attention.

Sister Monica obediently turned from the tapestry frame and peered over her spectacles, and Sisters Anne and Elizabeth, who continued to wrestle with a completed tapestry they were stretching over damp cloths on the floor, ('Pull!' – 'I'm pulling!' – 'Blow! Lost the drawing pin now.') managed to convey, nevertheless, that they were all ears.

'I do wonder whether the Reverend Mother has done the right thing.'

'But you agreed with it, Cecilia. You voted that Sister Margaret be allowed to get on with it.' (At the mention of Margaret, Cecilia raised her fine eyebrows and screwed up her papery face.) 'Whereas I had the good sense to abstain,' Monica added triumphantly.

'My thinking was – after such a catalogue of woe: let the gel do what has to be done and then we can get back to normal and have Catherine as Directrix as we always supposed we should. That is why I gave the proposal my blessing. However, I have misgivings, I must confess.'

'At least the Reverend Mother forbore to name her successor.' (The clarity of Anne's observation was hindered by a drawing pin clenched between her teeth.) 'By the time she gets round to it, Sister Margaret, one fervently trusts, will have outlived her usefulness.'

'Oh, there's no question of *that* one for the succession,' Cecilia said with the air of one privy to Authority's thinking. And her friends accepted this implication, for it went without saying that no one did anything at Albion Priory without first consulting Cecilia. One of her ancestors had founded the community; bequests from later ancestors were a source of support; a great-aunt had once been Prioress; indeed, the present Prioress was a childhood friend of Cecilia's mother, and Mercy, who had been chosen to succeed her, was a distant cousin. Cecilia, though technically without power, had high status in the Priory, a receiver of confidences and a generous giver of advice. Generally, Cecilia and her intimates were not resented for their always knowing best (they especially knew best for the lowlier sisters) because they were famous for their compassionate good sense. Their very loftiness, it was felt, preserved them from the self-interested manoeuvrings which so detracted from the weight of lesser sisters. Those whom they took up flourished, and from her days as a novice, Catherine had been their particular pet. 'Mercy, then Catherine,' they had decided with regard to the succession. But Mercy, it now appeared, had rather let them down.

'Well, it's done now. It is to be hoped that this gel Margaret really does know her stuff. Veronica seems to think she does,' said Monica, turning again to her rather tricky piece of work.

'Sister Veronica is inclined to take too much upon herself these days. And I fear she has a tendency to get things out of proportion.'

'Speaking of things out of proportion: have you seen the way Our Lady is leaning from the Tower? I happened to look up yesterday as I came through the courtyard, and she gave me quite a turn. For a moment I thought she was about to topple down on me. It really is shocking, you know. A bit of a gale . . .'

'Yes, they ought to do something about the Tower.'

'And the east wing. Have you seen the state of it? I don't know; things really are in a bad way.'

Cecilia hugged her spare body. 'So long as the boiler doesn't break down. I nearly died that time last winter. I can stand most things, but not the cold.'

'Oh, I'm the same. Starve me, deprive me of every convenience, but please not the heating,' Monica cried with the complacency of one who expects to retain all her comforts.

'I do so agree,' said Elizabeth. 'I can cheerfully do without food, but I must have warmth. Look, if I pull here, can you stick a pin in between my hands?'

With a sigh, Cecilia took up her embroidery ring, but then she recollected the point she had been leading to. 'It was something Catherine said in her speech – more of an impression I gained, really. I wonder if Sister Margaret's a bit of a bully?'

'A bully?'

'Oh, surely . . .'

'Well, we'll have to watch out. We can't have her pushing the poor things about.'

'Certainly not. The lay sisters, for instance; they do such splendid work.'

'A thoroughly decent bunch of women.'

'We must make sure their position is safeguarded in all this. After all, they have no say . . .'

'But they've got us to speak for them. We've always dealt with that sort of thing.'

'And there's Catherine.'

'Of course. Things can't go far wrong with dear Catherine.'

They lapsed into a comfortable silence, which was eventually broken by a squabble between the tapestry stretchers whose knees and backs had begun to ache and whose thumbs, violently imprinted with the tops of drawing pins, were by now very sore.

'Drat!' Elizabeth, shuffling sideways on her knees, got caught up in her skirt and fell sprawling across the tapestry.

'E-*liz*abeth,' Cecilia tutted.

Anne was cross. 'You've wrinkled it. Honestly! I really suffered getting that bit straight.'

'Well, if you'd stop hogging the pin box . . .'

'And if you weren't so clumsy . . .'

'Sisters, sisters. The novices may come in at any moment.'

But when the door opened it was Margaret who came in, followed by Agnes carrying clipboard and pen.

'The Sewing Room,' Margaret announced, and proceeded to a thorough examination.

'Good afternoon,' Cecilia said severely.

Margaret appeared not to hear. Her eyes lighted on a pile of folded silk. She darted forward. 'This, I take it, is the altar frontal commisioned by Deveraux Abbey?'

Monica agreed that it was.

'And you are presently engaged upon – what?'

'Oh,' Monica said airily, 'this is a piece I've been doing for myself. Frightfully difficult, actually.'

Margaret walked over to the tapestry stretchers and circled their work with a deliberate tread. 'And this is?'

'For the Refectory. Reverend Mother thought it would cover that awful crack.' Elizabeth put her head on one side. 'We think it's turned out rather well.'

Margaret and Agnes moved to the window, each talking exclusively to the other.

'This is what we're up against. I mean, there are probably plenty of commissions to be had if only they'd get a move on.'

'Of course, the tapestry for the Refectory's a good idea – once the plaster's been attended to. We could do with lots more about the place, great big ones – they're so impressive.' Margaret looked over her shoulder and inquired of Monica: 'Where are the other needleworkers this afternoon?'

'Well you see, we can't get on with the altar frontal because we're waiting for more of that gold thread. So they've gorn orff somewhere . . .'

'Leaving you four with a nice cosy setup of your own, eh?' Agnes suggested rudely. She turned back to Margaret. 'What they *do* is all right – it's very good by all accounts – the trouble is, they lack direction. We're coming up against this problem again and again. Every area needs someone in overall control.'

'Mmm.' Margaret began to pace about. She came to rest beside Monica's tapestry frame and leaned her arm along it. 'You see,' she told the needleworkers patiently, 'this area of work will be expanded. We anticipate many, many orders for vestments and altar frontals. And our own Priory requires a great deal of embellishment. So you'll have to take on more help. Don't worry – you'll have plenty of people to choose from – several other areas of work are closing down. Now do you think you can deal with that?' Since they remained silent, she addressed her further thoughts to Agnes, and together they moved towards the door. 'So the first priority here is to put someone in charge.'

'Certainly. And that applies everywhere. We'll have to sort out some suitable people.' Agnes pulled open the door.

'*Our* sort of people,' Margaret murmured, sweeping through to the hall.

For a time the Sewing Room was still and silent. Eventually, without stirring, Monica said in a small voice: 'Did someone say something about a bully?'

Cecilia could not at once respond. It was being suggested, she slowly grasped, that *they* – not the lay sisters or the humbler *religieuses* – but *they*, members of *their set*, might be susceptible to bullying. 'Don't be vulgar,' she snapped.

*   *   *   *

Apart from the light in the organ loft, the chapel was in darkness. Catherine ran up a flight of stone stairs and slipped on to the end of the organ bench. 'Sorry I'm late.'

Angelica smiled and played on. The fugue went ponderously on solid diapason.

Watching the music, Catherine waited for the start of a new episode and just as it would begin, leaned forward and smartly changed the stops. Now the sound was high and fluting like the toy piping of a merry-go-round. The fugue began to build. Catherine pulled new voices into play, a round tone, a reedy tone, a low growling in the bass. For the valedictory statement she organized a blaze of sound, and when Angelica released the final chord it hung for a second among the rafters, then vanished abruptly leaving their ears straining after emptiness.

'Oh, John Sebastian . . .'

'The lovely man,' Angelica agreed. She studied her friend. 'You look happier.'

'I think I am. I've had a very good discussion with Margaret. Perhaps I've misjudged her. She listened carefully to everything I said, seemed to appreciate my anxieties and assured me she wants us to work closely together. We decided that I should be responsible for our religious observance. And of course, she's absolutely correct about the need for action. I'm determined to be constructive, Angelica. I'm determined to get on with her so that we can put things right without hurting people.'

'Well, you have changed your tune.'

'I just want to be fair. Many of the criticisms she makes are thoroughly justified – not just about the general decay – but about our slipshod behaviour. Take, for instance, the way we all push and shove through the door after Morning Prayer. And the way we leave the clergy to just wander in. The Reverend Mother used to make quite a ceremony of receiving them and bringing them into chapel.'

'It's her sciatica, poor thing.'

'I know. But one of us could do it. Look, I realize Margaret's got an eye to the impression we'll make on all these hoped for visitors, but even when no one is there to see us, we should still behave respectfully.'

Angelica began to search through sheets of music. 'Well, I'm glad you're feeling happier. But Sister Cecilia is far from happy, let me tell you. Apparently, Margaret and Agnes burst into the Sewing Room this afternoon and started to throw their weight around. Cecilia and Co. were not impressed.'

They laughed, and Angelica found what she was looking for.

'Here we are – the solo I had in mind for you.' She began to play.

Catherine, following the manuscript, listened and hummed. After a time she sprang to her feet. 'Right. Let's try it.'

' "As the hart pants for the waterbrooks, so longeth my soul for Thee," ' sang Catherine, her voice soft and intense over the beating hum of the organ, flute-like when the melody rose from its chordal bed.

A nun hurrying through the cloister below, paused to listen. She was still there, motionless in the moonlight, when silence came.

5

In the gleam from an unshaded light bulb, Sister Hope sat tensely on the edge of her bed, hands pressed between serge-covered knees, eyes fixed to a spot on the floor, ears strained, listening. Her heart's pounding made her feverish. She shivered, and the involuntary movement unfixed her eyes; they slid towards the uncurtained window, but the diamond panes of navy-blue glass revealed nothing. Her eyes returned to the floor boards.

Then she knew – though there was no light outside other than a pale reflection from the snow – that a figure had clouded the window glass. 'When you look,' she urged herself, 'please don't start.' She turned her head slowly: her mouth flew open, her heart leaped, but at least her screams were mute.

On the other side of the window, Beatrice grinned and thought what a simple matter it was to rouse pathetic little Hope to a state of sheer terror.

Hope rose to her feet and took a step towards the window. A hulking head and shoulders filled the window space. She took a further step and saw a face – Beatrice's face – grinning steadily, eyes watching her intently.

With trembling hands Hope undid the buttons of her robe. She untied the knot of her girdle. The girdle dropped to the floor; the robe, freed from her slight body, hung straight and loose. Now Hope pushed the robe over her shoulders and down over her arms and let it fall to her ankles. Next she loosened her coif, then snatched off coif and veil in a single movement. Standing in her shift, Hope raised hands to her head and explored soft clumps of hair. Her hair felt quite long now, five or six inches, though not, of course, as long as Beatrice's. She shook her head to loosen her hair and plunged her fingers again and again through sensuous silkiness. Hair, hair, she exulted, her fear quelled for the moment by a thrill of forbidden pleasure.

When she looked up, Beatrice had gone. She stepped out of her robe, drew a curtain across the window, went to the switch by the door and turned off the light.

* * * *

'Where the dickens is Beatrice?' thundered Margaret. 'It's too bad of her. Joan has come up with the most marvellous scheme and I wanted us all to hear about it. Well, we can't wait for her all night. Welcome, Sisters Veronica, Clare, Imogen, to our little group. Agnes will take notes, but our meeting is quite informal; it's an opportunity to try out ideas on one another, and to spark off new ideas, I hope. Joan's brainwave, for example – will you tell them, Joan, or shall I? Well, put simply, we sell the dairy herd. The dairy requires a great deal of investment if it is to be profitable, investment that is beyond our means, and, quite frankly, not an appropriate venture for our Community. We sell the herd and realize a much needed capital sum, but – and here comes the brilliant part – we let the pasture and cowsheds to the buyer for rent. In other words, we continue to derive income. And I'm pleased to report that we have already had several enquiries. Marvellous work, Joan! Now, Agnes: you were looking for means of improving the guests' accommodation.'

Agnes scowled and drove the point of her pencil along a groove in the tabletop. 'Haven't had time. I've been stuck on confounded room offices all week. I don't know who was supposed to do 'em last week but they didn't pull the beds out. There was dust half an inch thick.'

28

One of the sisters tutted sympathetically, otherwise there was silence.

When Margaret spoke, her voice was low and exasperated. 'This is nonsense.' She looked from one to the other. 'Don't you see? It's *sheer lunacy*. Inefficient. A waste of resources. You can't have someone like Agnes sweeping out rooms; clearing up after people who . . . Well!' She shrugged and left it to their imagination. 'These archaic practices stifle initiative.'

'It's supposed to be valuable,' Veronica pointed out. 'I mean, Jesus washed the disciples' feet . . .'

'Correct me if I'm wrong,' Margaret said kindly, 'but I don't think Our Lord made a habit of it. It was just the one occasion, I believe.'

Agnes chortled humourlessly.

Joan craned forward. 'I think Margaret has a valid point here. There are plenty of people to do the cleaning, but only a few who have the intelligence and imagination to make this place viable.'

'And as people become more productive and more specialist – the needleworkers and the artists, for example – they won't have time to do the cleaning, either. I can see we have a job of education to do. We must try to get as many people on our side as we can before a formal proposal is put to Council. Agreed? Right. Next I want Beatrice to . . . Oh blow it! Where the dickens *is* Beatrice?'

* * * *

Beatrice lay with Hope on Hope's narrow bed. Their bodies and Beatrice's streaming fair hair were silvered by ghostly light through the curtain cracks. All else was in darkness. They were perfectly still now, drifting sleepily.

Presently, Beatrice stirred and shifted her arm on which Hope was lying and which had become numb. They re-arranged themselves and settled comfortably. But now Hope's eyes were open and staring into the dark. Soon, fears and horrors began their familiar chase through her mind.

'What's the matter now?'

Hope screwed up her eyes and stuffed a fist into her mouth.

'Can't make you out,' Beatrice mused – not impatiently, but carelessly. 'I mean, you expected me this evening. You'd have been pretty disappointed if I hadn't turned up. I saw you waiting, but when you turned and saw me it was as if I were a ghost come to haunt you. For a nasty moment I thought you were going to yell out. Then I nipped straight down the corridor and into your room and blow me if you didn't start jumping and trembling all over again. Beats me. If I hadn't showed, you'd have sulked like anything. Go on, admit it!'

'I know,' Hope moaned miserably. But inside she was gloating: 'Fat chance of you not showing! You've no choice; you can't resist me.' It was a potent combination – her drawing power and her helplessness. She pictured herself, fearful and trembling, drawing strong, powerful Beatrice to her bed. And Beatrice, she recalled, had become more powerful than ever since Margaret's elevation. Margaret . . . A delicious new thrill formed hazily. She fluttered her fingers over Beatrice's stomach. 'You know, I've a feeling Margaret rather likes me.'

'Margaret?' Beatrice frowned. 'I'd be surprised if Margaret's more than vaguely aware of your existence. Oh, I get it!' She gave a low laugh. 'If you're thinking of extending your favours, I shouldn't bother. Take it from me, duckie, there's no call for it around here.'

'Don't be horrid. I wasn't thinking anything of the sort. You know I was totally innocent before you . . . before you . . .'

'Aw, shut up, Hopeless.'

Hope began to snivel. 'If you knew, if you knew the half of what I have to go through – my stomach leaping, my heart going mad . . .'

'But what *at*, for Heaven's sake?'

'Anything. Nothing.' She thought for a moment, then whispered: 'Things.'

'What things?'

'Things that are sudden, or . . . Oh, I don't know. Some are worse than others; I mean, one thing's so terrifying I can't even say its name. I daren't think about it. Sometimes I have a nightmare . . . There's this . . . this . . .'

Curiosity got the better of scorn. She encircled Hope in her arms and urged cooingly: 'Go on, love, you can tell me.'

'Can I?'

'Course you can. Now . . .' She leaned over Hope and blew languorously over her face. 'Tell me.'

'I can't say it. I'll spell it,' Hope whispered shakily. 'M. .i. .c. .'

'Mice?' Beatrice asked disbelievingly.

With a scream, Hope shot forward into a ball.

'Shh – idiot! Do you mean you've got some sort of phobia?'

'I don't know. But I'd go mad if . . . Once, when I had to go to the shed for potatoes, a – thing – ran over my foot. I screamed and ran and screamed and ran and . . .'

'Take it easy. Fancy being frightened like that, you poor duffer. Never mind. Come here,' she soothed, smiling contemptuously into the dark.

6

The Prioress pushed her teacup to one side. 'I know nothing of the sort.'

'That's because you've cut yourself off,' Cecilia said calmly. 'If you would leave your room for longer than it takes to attend chapel, if you would sometimes come to the refectory, if you would just stand about and *talk* instead of hurrying back here at the earliest opportunity, you would discover what I say to be true. People are quite wretched.'

The Prioress recalled that even Cecilia's mother had at times found Cecilia hard to bear. Her placid assumption of speaking for all sensible folk was very irritating. 'I dare say some of them are disaffected. After all, there have been changes . . .'

'Too many, too quickly, without – and this is the burden of my complaint – proper consideration for people's feelings. Take, for instance, the sisters who ran the dairy. They have been deprived of their role and are now merely at the beck and call of the bullies. And it's no use sniffing – if you don't like my saying "bullies" you should come and watch that officious Sister Imogen giving her orders. Imagine it. Sister Mary John, a respected senior sister, obliged to report to her daily and told to clean up after everyone else because we no longer take our turn to do the offices. It's outrageous. And because there is now no dairy interest to be represented on the Council, these sisters have lost their ability to speak up for themselves. They're not likely to get it back, either. Apparently, there are to be no new regular jobs. Something to do with "freeing resources", which seems to mean they are free to do the skivvying.'

'I dare say something'll be done for 'em. Rome wasn't built in a day.'

'The gardeners are in the same predicament. Their numbers have been drastically cut. From now on there'll just be the flower gardens and enough vegetables grown for the house. Such a pity. People came from miles around to buy Albion Reds; and Sister Martha's Purple Wonder . . .'

'Didn't pay. None of it paid, I gather. Besides, potatoes and purple sprouting don't give the right image.'

'Image? What do you mean "image"?' Cecilia asked suspiciously.

But the Prioress was not entirely sure. It was the word Margaret had used when she attempted to explain why bee-keeping, though not strictly profitable, was to continue whereas cow-keeping and the more robust forms of horticulture were to cease. 'You'll have to ask Margaret. I haven't time to go into the technicalities.'

'Mmm. Well, Sister Martha is making a terrible fuss. And have you heard the rumour about a plan to convert the east wing into accommodation for all these new paying guests they hope to attract? They won't get away with it. There's tremendous feeling. The lay sisters have always lived in the east wing.'

'I suppose they can live somewhere else?'

'As far as I know there's no indication of where they think the poor things might live. That's the trouble. These people do as they please and damn the consequences for those who are discommoded. I think you must do something, Reverend Mother. You must put your foot down before things get worse.'

The Prioress looked bleakly into her empty teacup. She was not entirely out of touch, she reflected, thinking of the sisters who had recently visited her sitting room. Some of them had lavished praise on the new regime. This very morning Sister Veronica had sat where Cecilia now sat and had given a confident account of the latest financial situation. Even Elizabeth, having first secured the Prioress's promise not to breathe a word of it to Cecilia, had expressed great satisfaction with the achievements of her newly expanded needlework department. On the other hand, the Prioress had glimpsed that good soul, Sister Mary John, wiping tears from her eyes during Vespers; and Catherine's strained face (paler than ever with bruised wells beneath her eyes) warned her of worry and trouble abroad. Catherine had already confided all that Cecilia now conveyed, though she had fallen over her words in a scrupulous attempt to be fair to Margaret. Well, Catherine had been accorded an equal share of authority. It was up to Catherine to fight her corner. The Prioress wagged her head vehemently and thought it too bad that, having made an arrangement calculated to achieve the best of all worlds, still more was expected of her. For she was tired, quite beyond it . . .

'Reverend Mother! Are you in pain?'

The Prioress scowled. Did the idiot imagine it a painless condition to be twisted and bent as an old hawthorn? 'Just tired,' she growled.

'Some fresh air might buck you up; it's awfully stuffy in here. Come outside for a while – take a turn round the cloister. Do come. It's spring!'

'The air's still sharp.'

'No, it's quite mild today. Look, I'll go and fetch Monica. She and I will take an arm each, then you'll feel perfectly safe.'

The Prioress pictured herself shuffling round the cloister between Monica and Cecilia. She found she did not care for it. 'Not today, I think.'

'Will you come and see Mercy, then? She's a tiny bit better. Yesterday she sat in a chair for an hour.'

'It won't last,' sighed the Prioress.

* * * *

Mornings were the worst, thought Sister Mary John, kneeling in her pew. By evening, fatigue permitted the comfort of a few weak tears. Impossible to weep in the harsh void of early morning when desolation gripped her and her body functioned in a state of shock so that her movements were slow, her breathing laboured and her heart beat fractionally too late. In the days before the blow had fallen, her thoughts had been no more engaged by the early morning service than they were today; they would slip to the task ahead, to the medication she must prepare for the cow with mastitis, to the cart she must dispatch to the barn for fresh hay. Recalling this now, she saw they had been the thoughts of a satisfied woman. It had not occurred to her to treasure the mundane routine of her life – but she should have done, oh, she should! As Morning Prayer proceeded, the half-heard, familiar canticles worked treacherously on her mind, conjuring a lost rosy world. 'I am bereft,' she mourned.

She craved the touch of warm creatures. Throughout her life there had been some animal at hand to stroke and fondle and melt life's troubles away. As a child she had nursed her cat by the fire, had curled up with the dog basking on the doorstep. Cats, dogs, cows, taking life as they found it, showing contentment with the fire, the sun, the hay, had drawn her into a stream of well-being never seriously penetrated by hardships and irritations. Whatever the calamity, she had only to put out her hand and know that life was fundamentally good.

Perhaps her worst moment had come when the herd's new owners had experienced staffing problems. The Community could assist, Sister Joan had decreed (of course, for a price). But only the lay sisters had been directed there. Religious sisters were to concern themselves solely with matters endorsed by the new regime. The memory of her dashed hope returned so sharply that she was obliged to clutch the prayer book ledge for support. And then she saw that the pews were almost empty. The service was over.

She struggled to her feet. Sister Imogen would make life even more uncomfortable if she were late reporting for her allotted office of the day.

A hand on her arm detained her. Looking up, she met the

eyes of Sister Catherine. For some seconds they held one another's glance.

'Are you all right, Sister?'

Mary John could not reply. She disengaged her arm and hurried from the chapel.

Catherine watched her go, then ran up the steps to the organ loft.

'Got pencil and paper?' she asked Angelica who was putting sheets of music away in a cupboard. 'Right. This afternoon's meeting. This time we're going to win.' Her voice was fierce. 'This time it's clear we've got the majority on our side. But we won't take chances. We'll play it their way and do a canvass. Make a list, put down every single sister who might support us. Because over the east wing issue, Angelica, I'm determined we're going to win.'

*　　*　　*　　*

Beatrice was the last to arrive in Agnes's room. She closed the door and leaned back against it, thinking: Our first setback, so it is just the four of us again. We have come to lick our wounds.

Their bodily attitudes gave much away, she decided, observing each in turn. Joan was sitting forward with her head in her hands, her fingers stiff and spread. 'How impossible it all is,' her posture seemed to bewail, 'for however brilliant, however neat the idea, human beings are bound to muck it up.'

Anger rather than despair held Agnes in thrall. She was hunched over her desk, doodling in the margin of a sheet of notes with hard, short pencil thrusts. Her free hand was clenched. She was brooding vengefully, gathering herself for a scrap.

Margaret, too, was angry. She sat on the edge of the bed with her knees and ankles together and her hands folded in her lap; but her prim posture was betrayed by bulging brows beneath which her eyes darted ceaselessly. She was going over it, Beatrice knew, recalling every word uttered at the meeting, on the lookout for a loophole that might yet yield some advantage.

36

Plainly, they required release from their fruitless ponderings, and who better to free them than Beatrice (who secretly did not care a fig one way or the other, but would chase any thrill capable of charging her veins with adrenalin – a state as easily achieved by the drama of failure as of success)? She stepped forward and snapped her fingers. When they had frowningly focussed a portion of their attention on her, she said, 'It was a setback, that's all. Let's keep a sense of proportion. Think of everything we've achieved.'

'But we had only just begun,' Joan moaned.

'You're such a defeatist, Crackling . . .'

'Don't call her that,' Margaret said hastily, fearing a repetition of the row that always followed this abominable reference to Joan's sainted namesake, 'it's not nice. However,' – but she, too, had been annoyed by Joan's use of of the past tense – 'I agree we can't be diverted by one setback. No, I've been thinking . . . The east wing issue can be set aside for the time being.'

'It can't, you know. The roof leaks, the timbers are full of rot,' Agnes objected. 'The question is, do we patch it up for the lay sisters or completely refurbish it for paying guests? The decision may have gone against us, but something'll have to be done.'

'I said, leave it,' Margaret snapped. 'Let 'em stew for a bit.'

Agnes narrowed her eyes and decided to trust Margaret's thinking which had evidently jumped well ahead of her own. 'Right you are. I've been trying to work out why we lost this afternoon.'

'Possibly because the majority were against us?'

Agnes ignored Beatrice and went on. 'You know, I doubt whether we've ever commanded a majority of opinion. We've just made a better job of presenting our case. The new thing is the opposition's woken up. They've taken a leaf out of our book – Catherine and Angelica were canvassing in the refectory. I'm afraid they're not going to be such pushovers in future.'

'And some of the young ones are quite bolshie. Yes, we've got a problem. We must all *think*.' Margaret's glare indicated the ferocious degree of cerebral activity required.

'What we need,' Agnes reminded them to ensure that the thinking proceeded along the right lines, 'is a way of controlling opinion.'

Beatrice sighed, pulled a pillow from the bed and threw it to the floor then arranged herself, stomach down, on top of it. After a time she sat up and hugged the pillow to her chest. 'I think I've got it.' She began slowly. 'The trouble with Council is, we can't control it. So let's establish regular open meetings for the whole Priory. Ostensibly they will be briefing meetings to explain what we're doing, what our aims are and so on. We can make a show of asking for suggestions and comments. But our purpose is to plan the introduction of each new issue so that it shows in the best possible light.' She was speaking quickly now. 'Yes, and we can plant our people strategically in the audience having told them beforehand what questions to ask and how to react to criticism and encourage support for the right line. We can even divert attention to side issues if necessary. The point is: we'll be in control and Catherine will always be on the defensive. And Council will feel constrained to bow to popular opinion. What do you think?'

Margaret, who had been sitting very still, magisterially nodded her head. 'Yes, I think it will do very well.'

'You do think up some good schemes, Beatrice,' Joan conceded, cheered into forgiveness now that her theories would live to fight another day.

'We must keep this entirely to ourselves. We may take our people aside from time to time to explain what is required, but we must treat them singly and in strict confidence; none but we four are to know that the whole thing is stage-managed. You know, it really is a brilliant idea.' Margaret shook her head in appreciation. 'We can drop suggestions about certain people, for example . . .'

'Oh yes, we can cook Catherine's goose,' said Agnes.

Margaret bounced to her feet. 'I'm going to leave it to you' – she waved a hand towards Agnes and Joan – 'to work out the details; what to call the meetings, for example, and how often to hold them.' She turned to Beatrice. 'Come on. I need some excercise. Let's walk.'

Beatrice clambered to her feet and strolled after Margaret who had already left the room.

* * * *

Catherine and Angelica came running down the path from the wood. They leaned recklessly into the wind which held them like a firm hand until it dropped, sending them staggering and laughing at their helplessness. 'What?' yelled Catherine, seeing her friend lurch and shout. But nothing could be heard above the wind's rush and the flapping of their streaming veils.

Behind a tall yew hedge bordering the garden, they found shelter. Panting, searching in their pockets for handkerchiefs to mop dripping eyes and noses, they flopped on to an iron seat and spread their legs out straight. The blustering wind had added zest to their excitement following the afternoon's success. Now they basked in the sunny calm and thought how good it was to know that right and reason prevailed – and how amazing that they had ever doubted it. The dislocation and pain of the last few months could now be viewed in perspective: simply, an over-reaction to the alarming financial situation. Catherine even allowed that Margaret's new broom had worked to some good effect, but from now on, she promised, its sweepings would be inspected to ensure people's feelings were not cast aside. There would be no more innovations unaccompanied by mitigating measures, for progress was empty when the well-being of individuals was sacrificed.

Angelica was still savouring their victory. 'The best moment was afterwards, when that group of young sisters came up and grabbed our hands. I'd always thought there were people who felt as we did, but I hadn't understood how passionately.'

'It surprised me, too. After all, a lot of people have done well out of the changes. They love not having to take their turn with the chores. Being waited on makes them feel valuable and important. I'd begun to dread that people's support would depend on whether they stood to lose or gain.'

'That's hardly fair; take Sister Cecilia . . .'

39

'Oh, I know. Even so, Cecilia may have done well as a needleworker, but in terms of prestige you would count her as a loser, with Elizabeth being put in charge of the Sewing Room.'

'You've become cynical, Catherine.'

'This afternoon they proved me wrong. I happily admit it. No one had a thing to gain by sticking up for the lay sisters.'

* * * *

In another part of the garden, Beatrice and Margaret were battling with the wind.

'This weather alarms me,' cried Margaret. 'I wish we'd the money to go ahead with the tower. We must make it a priority. It would be an utter tragedy if the statue came down.'

'Don't worry. I went up and fixed it. Roped Our Lady to the buttresses.'

Margaret came to a halt. 'You went up? Out on to the top of the tower?'

'Good job I did, with this wind.'

'But the tower's unsafe,' Margaret roared, evidently angry.

'Make up your mind. You said the statue's of paramount importance – a symbol of the Priory.'

'So it is. But let others see to it. You're indispensable. What an idiot thing to do, Beattie! How'd we get on if you'd killed yourself?'

Beatrice grinned, showing her even white teeth.

Margaret's wrath dissolved. Beattie's such a charmer, she thought, and suddenly the reason for Agnes's nasty little hints and imputations came to her. The woman was jealous of Beattie, being herself so frightfully plain. In the middle of being put out over another matter, Margaret was pleased neverthe-less to mentally tick off this item, for she delighted in tidiness. 'It was rather splendid of you,' she said forgivingly. 'But don't ever do such a risky thing again.'

Beatrice was still grinning. 'Confess, Mags. Which would be the worst calamity: losing the statue or losing me?'

Margaret's lips, which had been parted smilingly, now came together in annoyance.

Beatrice swung away, laughing so uproariously that Margaret was obliged to call after her, 'Shut up, you fool.' But Beatrice had already become quiet, having caught sight of Catherine and Angelica on the garden seat. 'The opposition's over there. Maybe we should go back.'

Margaret examined the flowerbeds, then became decisive and walked briskly towards the startled seated ones. 'Just the person. Sister Angelica!'

So full of embarrassed surprise was Catherine at the approach of her adversary – her vanquished adversary, she endeavoured to recall, inwardly shrinking before the eagerly inclined head, the avid blue eyes and the china complexion wind-whipped to a sparkling rosiness – that some moments elapsed before she made sense of what Margaret was saying.

'These endless arguments put it clean out of my head, but I've been meaning to suggest it ever since Evensong on Sunday. Tell me, what was that delightful piece you played at the end?'

'Oh – the Fauré . . .'

'*Mar*vellous! Well, it came to me then, that an organ recital after Sunday Evensong would be just the thing for our Visitors' Programme. What do you think? You could plan a series of recitals in advance. Sister Prudence could make some nice little programmes with a few notes about the music and so on.'

Angelica, going red in the face, got out that she thought it an interesting idea and wondered if Sister Catherine agreed.

'Oh – absolutely.'

'And Sister Catherine, of course, has such a fine singing voice,' Margaret informed Beatrice. (Beatrice, who already knew this, said nothing but continued to smile amiably.) 'One does hope that all the argument and debate we seem stuck with lately doesn't overtax it – the human voice is a delicate instrument. Perhaps Sister Catherine should sing a solo at some point during the recital? I'll leave it with you, Sister Angelica. Draw something up and let Sister Beatrice have it.'

She had moved out of earshot. Too late now for the clever,

softly spoken phrase putting them on an equal footing, thought Catherine, furious with her tongue-tied meekness. Her fury turned rapidly to self-disgust that she should care.

'What do you make of that?' Angelica asked anxiously.

'She has recognized what a good musician you are and has had a clever idea.'

'It was rather sporting of her, wasn't it? I mean, she didn't have to come over, never mind say something nice.'

'Magnanimous, indeed.'

'I must say, I'm very attracted to the idea.'

'So am I,' said Catherine, smiling brightly so that her friend would not guess that her newly-found confidence had unaccountably taken a blow.

7

In the top greenhouse, Sister Martha (she of Purple Wonder fame) was busy propagating *Begonia rex* from leaf cuttings. She was ruefully observed from the potting-shed doorway by Sister Lazarus. (The name 'Lazarus' was a mark of gratitude to God who had restored her after a desperate illness.) By tradition these two sisters were close friends, Martha the senior vegetable grower and Lazarus the chief flower gardener; but when vegetable growing on a large scale ceased and Martha became redundant, their friendship entered a testing phase, for Martha refused point blank (and there was an immovable quality about Martha) to consider any occupation save gardening, and it was not unnaturally assumed that her services would be welcome in the extended flower garden. Unfortunately, Martha had grown accustomed to directing others and reserving her own energy for the more interesting tasks. And herein lay a difficulty, for the propagation of *Begonia rex* was one of Sister Lazarus's particular joys; it was a treat she saved up for herself during the June rush with rose and lily spraying, with bulb lifting and staking out and weeding in the borders.

'It is not that we don't need the extra help, but that she is the wrong sort. We need more strong girls to weed, rake and mow,' Lazarus told a faceless, imaginary friend, aware that the friend to whom she would normally confide was the very subject of her complaint. Lazarus bit her lip and turned back to the bulbs that required cleaning and storing in stacking trays.

Taking a razor blade, Martha severed a prominent vein junction on the underside of a large leaf. She worked slowly and deliberately, making an arc of judicious cuts, then pinned the leaf with half-hoops of wire on to a dish of peat and sand. In her mind's eye arose a specimen of *Begonia rex* hitherto unknown, its leaves spotted orange and silver – 'Sister Martha's Spotted Beauty', perhaps? She was full of optimism as she sliced and pinned; her rage at the slighting of the Purple Wonder a dead thing, only dimly and infrequently recalled. 'For that's me all over,' she liked to tell herself whenever she thought about it: 'quick to blow up, but quick to calm down, and then there's no one more easy-going.' Not that she was ashamed of her outburst and fiery-eyed refusal to work anywhere but the flower garden – not likely! Catch her eating humble pie and meekly going wherever Sister Imogen had it in mind to send her – like poor old Mary John, for instance. But then Sister Mary John was a fool; she, too, should have taken a stand.

All in all, Martha thought comfortably, things had turned out rather well. It was companionable working with Lazarus, and the flower gardens were beautifully sheltered – unlike the exposed acres where Purple Wonders were sown. 'Oh, it's you, Laz,' she commented, looking up as someone opened the greenhouse door. 'I thought it might be't lass wi't coffee. What's up wi'em, this morning, d'you reckon? We had to stand kicking us heels waiting for breakfast, and now there's no elevenses. It's all right for them inside, helping theirselves when ever they feel like it, but for us stuck out here working in all weathers, well, yer get peckish . . .'

Martha settled into a sprightly 'us and them' talk, while Lazarus, who usually supplied the 'Mmm' and 'I'll say!' accompaniment to this theme which had so deliciously bonded them over the years, remained resentfully silent. Lazarus ran her eyes over spilled peat and sand, over tools encrusted with old dirt, over a coffee mug with a ring round its inside and soily fingermarks and dried-on drips on its outside. That any

44

gardener should behave so uncleanly in a greenhouse was beyond her. She tried to recall the state of the vegetable greenhouses, and then remembered that Martha had always wandered down to the shelter of the flower gardens for one of their cosy chats. And then I cleared up after her, thought Lazarus, picturing herself carrying two dirty coffee mugs back to the house. 'I came in to ask if you'd mind giving Sister Barbara a hand with the weeding,' she suddenly blurted.

Interrupted in full flow, Martha blinked and said reproachfully, 'But I'm busy in here. I'm doing the *Begonia rex* for you. Anyway, I couldn't face all that stooping today,' she added with a certain look to indicate a certain condition.

Prickly heat broke out over Lazarus. Martha had a nerve . . . If anyone had a right to claim indulgence it was Lazarus. But no one ever heard Lazarus complain, in spite of recurrent painful attacks of pins and needles in her limbs. Yet here sat Martha, fat and complacent, assuming a sufferer's part . . . To relieve her feelings, she stooped to search under the bench for dustpan and brush. Having found them, she vigorously swept up the spilled peat, emptied it on to waste paper and rolled it into a tight parcel. Then she stood, twisting and kneading the paper, and imagined herself confronting Sister Imogen with a demand that Martha be exchanged for a more compliant sister. Only – and at this point she almost dropped the parcel – how would it be if Martha put up a fight and it somehow fell out that she, Lazarus, were the one removed from the garden?

'You're not listening to a word I say! What're yer doing with that paper? What's up wi'yer this morning, Laz?'

'I need that coffee. I'll go and see what's happened to it.'

*　*　*　*

The kitchen had encountered setbacks. The place was in turmoil, and it was all due to Sister Mary John, Sister Lazarus discovered when she stepped in at the scullery door. A sister scrubbing potatoes at the sink described in breathless undertone how Sister Mary John had been astonishingly clumsy from the moment she had begun work this morning. At this very moment Sister Imogen was within, deciding what was to be done with her.

It was thought, it soon became clear, that Sister Mary John would wreak less havoc outside. The chastened one came into the scullery and began to hunt for a yard broom. 'Excuse me, Laz,' she said shamefacedly to her old friend who was standing in her way.

Lazarus, seeing Sister Imogen watching from the kitchen doorway, affected an offhand manner towards Mary John, thus shielding herself from any association with that luckless sister's fallen status. 'What's happened to the coffee?' she called brightly, pretending, in Imogen's presence, to a confidence she did not feel.

'Just coming,' someone called.

'Good-oh. I'll take mine and Sister Martha's with me, then. Not that I'm desperate; it's Sister Martha. "Can't tackle another leaf without me coffee," she declared; so I thought I'd better come for it. Got to keep the workers happy,' she added daringly. But Sister Imogen had her sharp eyes on Mary John and evidently did not hear.

Lazarus noticed an unpleasant taste in her mouth as she bore two brimming mugs to the greenhouse. Perhaps she was out of sorts. 'Here you are,' she said, handing a mug to the solid woman at the workbench who seemed to have more the appearance of an enemy than a friend.

'Great. Find out what the delay was about?'

'No.' Lazarus gulped her coffee and hoped it would clear the thickness from her mouth.

'Well, it's good and hot, I'll say that for it. Couldn't half go a bicky, though. Have we got any, Laz?'

'No.'

'Ah well. Grateful for small . . . I say, I was thinking while you were gone. When I've done the begonias I might try me hand with the african violets. Same method, after all. You can get some amazing colour variations . . .'

'When you've finished your coffee I'd be glad if you'd help

46

me with the bulbs – that is, if you're still too delicate to lend a hand with the weeding.'

'I told you, Laz . . .'

'Right. Drink up, then; I want us to finish the bulbs today.'

Martha stared thoughtfully at her over her coffee mug.

'Finished?' Lazarus asked after a while. She stood up and waited pointedly.

'I'll just . . .'

Lazarus opened the greenhouse door. 'Come on.'

Closing the door behind them, she found her hands were trembling. A great longing for someone to talk to stole over her, as in the old days she had talked to Martha.

*   *   *   *

Margaret and Catherine were doing the rounds of the Priory in the company of a surveyor. They had already studied his report; the problem now was to decide on priorities. Margaret could have done very well without this excursion, for she had already settled on the immediate restoration of the Albion Tower, but Catherine was more worried about the danger to the lay sisters in the east wing, and the surveyor was inclined to agree with her. The kitchen area, its sculleries and outhouses, also required attention, particularly in view of an anticipated influx of visitors. It was a matter of what could be afforded, Margaret reminded them whenever they paused to examine stonework, suck in their breath, and refer worriedly to the report.

Sister Mary John was sweeping the yard. She drew their eyes as they paused there to discuss the outhouses. The head of her broom refused to go neatly into a dirt-stuffed corner. Fascinated by Sister Mary John's ineffectualness, Margaret stared and listened and detected that Catherine and the surveyor seemed already to have forgotten the requirement to bear in mind what the community could afford. She was preparing to remind them of this – for she had no shame in constantly repeating herself – when her patience snapped, and

47

she marched forward and snatched the broom handle. 'Like *this*,' she boomed, getting down to it.

Sister Mary John seemed to shrink. Catherine watched as Margaret deftly cleared the corner then, with an air of contemptuous exasperation, held out the broom for Mary John to retrieve. A look of sullen stupidity now covered the face of Mary John; the look, Catherine recalled, adopted by habitually unsuccessful schoolchildren.

Catherine went forward, took the broom and propped it against the wall. 'Sister, I don't think you're up to this today. You need a rest. I'll finish the sweeping, later. Is there anyone here who can help us?' she called towards the scullery door, and when a sister appeared drying her hands on an apron, continued, 'Take Sister to her room. Make her lie down – oh, and open her window so that she breathes good fresh air.' To Mary John she said, 'As soon as I've finished here, I'll be along to see you,' and she squeezed her arm and pushed her gently away.

Each of Margaret's cheeks bore a bright red spot, Catherine noticed, turning again to the matter in hand. 'Now where were we?' she prompted the surveyor.

*   *   *   *

The moment she was left alone, Sister Mary John rose from her bed and went to sit in her chair by the open window. She was sitting there, breathing calmly, when Catherine came in. Having got her breathing under control, she was reluctant to speak, so smiled instead and put out her hand.

'You're looking better; more like your old self,' Catherine commented, retaining the hand and kneeling on the rug beside the chair.

Quietness grew, friendly and easy. A breeze lifted one of the curtains. In the distance, voices called.

Catherine studied the hand in her own. It was large and rough, stringy-veined and scarred; an industrious, turn-to-anything hand. It was not that Sister Mary John worked

48

unwillingly at her present chores, but rather that she was encumbered by a heavy heart, Catherine all at once understood.

'Do you know, I've really missed the farmyard? – the cattle, and the cats. We've been so busy reconstructing this place there's been no time for normal things – like taking a summer evening's stroll, for instance. Let's go for one tonight after Evensong.'

An emotion – fear, was it? – clouded Mary John's eyes.

'What's the matter?'

'I don't know whether we're allowed . . .'

'Allowed? It's still our land, you know. They only lease it. Really, I ought to keep an eye on it. I shall go tonight and I'd like you to come with me. And then, perhaps, I can ask you to make a regular inspection?'

'Oh, yes.' The eyes had cleared.

'Meet you after chapel, then?'

Mary John nodded.

Catherine rose. 'I'd better go and do the sweeping.'

'Oh, I'd rather you didn't. I'm better now, I'll finish it myself.'

'Nonsense. Stay where you are. The rest is doing you good.'

But Mary John grew flustered.

'I don't understand,' Catherine said slowly. 'We've worked side by side over the years. I've often helped you to muck out, to cart the feed. It's not out of the way, surely, for me to sweep the kitchen yard?'

'Things are different now.'

'How "different"? We're still Sister Catherine and Sister Mary John, members of the same community. We help one another. No one here is above the rest.'

Mary John looked unconvinced.

'It's true. That's how it is.' Catherine's voice had become shrill. She tried to soften it as she hurried to correct any misleading impression she herself had created. 'I know I don't do as much around the place as I used to, but that's because

I've so many new things to do these days. But perhaps you're right. Perhaps I ought to do more.'

'No, no. I didn't mean . . . You do enough as it is,' cried Mary John with a rush of motherly feeling. 'Don't take any notice of me. I only understand dairying – I can't get the hang of this new routine. But it'll come.'

'Well, it'll be nice poking about the farmyard this evening.'

'Oh, it will!'

Having negotiated emotional, if not intellectual understanding, they parted, comforted.

* * * *

From up the bank on the far side of the hedge, the sound of vast nostrils snorting in the grass; then a monstrous tearing sound and breathy mastication – hot breath, dew rising, the heady scent of bruised meadow grass: amiable cattle savouring a summer evening.

And Catherine and Mary John – strolling along the track, ears full of birdsong, eyes on a sky turning yellow and pink.

At the gate they pause and lean.

Soon the curious ones arrive, abandoning their cud to push and nudge and become transfixed. Their eyes, innocent of deceit, offer a frank exchange from the living to the living. They will go on watching for ever.

At length, Catherine and Mary John sigh and heave away from the gate. The cattle watch them go.

It is still warm from a day's basking in the farmyard, but new sunless air creeping in between the buildings casts a chill. A cat and her kitten come running. The women bend low. 'She has had five or six kittens,' thinks Mary John, exploring the cat's empty flap of a belly; 'but at least they have allowed her to keep this one.'

The cats squirm under their hands, raise their heads and give stabbing, plaintive yowls. Catherine says, 'We should have brought something for them. Next time we will.'

Stealthy shadows deepen. Sniffing night, the cats become distant, widen their eyes and stalk away.

Catherine and Mary John part in the cloister and drowsy and peaceful go to their beds.

8

'Oh, my *head*,' cried Cecilia, pressing three stiff fingertips to her temples. 'Open the window, someone. It's so close, I can't breathe.'

But when Anne opened it, a ferocious wind darted in, dashing curtains to ceiling, sending paper patterns flying from a worktable. Anne promptly closed the window and began to gather up the patterns.

Monica seized one of them and began to flap it in front of Cecilia's face. 'Lie back and I'll fan you.' (Cecilia tipped her head as far as possible from the crackling paper.) 'Or would an aspirin do you more good, do you suppose?'

'Possibly . . .'

'Oh, I'll get her one.' With an air of resignation, Elizabeth removed her spectacles, laid them down on an open record book, and marched from the room.

'That gel is so disagreeable,' Cecilia marvelled through her nose. 'Thank you, Monica, I think that'll do.'

Monica and Anne exchanged looks. By 'disagreeable', they understood Cecilia to be referring, once again, to Elizabeth's unfortunate elevation. The new regime had put her in charge of the department because of her superiority as a needlewoman. Naturally, this had offended Cecilia who was, by general consent, the most innately superior of their little band of superior personages. What one could *do* hardly came into it.

'I'm not sure that having to write everything up in a book really suits her,' Monica said, sending a reproving glance towards the record book. 'I rather think it is gone over with a fine-tooth comb by certain people. Life is not entirely hunky-dory for those who have recently enjoyed preferment. The strain on Elizabeth is beginning to tell.'

'Mmm. I happen to know . . .'

'Yes?' prompted Cecilia, suddenly alert, for Anne was closer than any of them to Elizabeth.

'You know she had tea today upstairs?'

'Yes, yes?'

'Well, apparently it emerged over the Royal Worcester that the Reverend Mother is at last thinking seriously about the succession. A deputation of young sisters called on her yesterday and complained vigorously about Margaret. Soon afterwards, the Reverend Mother made an impromptu visit to the east wing – and we know what the poor things there are having to put up with . . .'

'Yes, we do know,' Cecilia confirmed, thinking of damp and draughts, of wormy beams and crumbling plaster.

'I have a feeling – from what Elizabeth told me of the Reverend Mother's reaction – and bear in mind, this does not give Elizabeth pleasure – that the experiment may soon come to an end.'

'Well! Though I must say, Margaret has become thoroughly unpopular lately. I know we never liked her . . .'

'But now they all seem to detest her. People are fed up with the changes. They've gone too far.'

'Quite. So I shouldn't be at all surprised . . .'

But Cecilia got no further, for just then Elizabeth returned with a glass of water and aspirins.

'Thank you, dear,' murmured Cecilia with unusual tenderness.

'My goodness, the wind has got up,' Elizabeth reported.

'Shouldn't wonder if we have a storm. Good job too – clear the air. Has anyone seen Catherine, by the way?' Monica wondered.

No one had, it was agreed thoughtfully between Monica, Anne and Cecilia.

'Why?' Elizabeth asked sharply.

'Just wondered, dear, just wondered.'

*　*　*　*

Martha was holding forth in Lazarus's easy chair. 'Don't get me wrong,' she said, raising a hand and an eyebrow, evidently addressing the crucified Christ on the wall above the desk. 'I'm not still hurt or owt, it's just my heart bleeds for all them poor folk as can't get their Albion Reds. It's the flavour, yer see; quite unique. Baked in their jackets, yer can't whack 'em – lovely waxy earthy-tasting flesh and the skin all crisp and toasty . . . Properly cooked, mind you. We know a few cooks as could manage to ruin a simple baked spud wi'out really trying – don't we, though, Laz? No, as I were saying . . .'

'Is it coming back? Oh God, don't let it come back!' Lazarus prayed, staring down at her hands. 'Don't be ridiculous, woman,' she countermanded, 'you've had this numbing sensation before, and it always goes as quickly as it comes.' She willed herself to be calm. She would set herself a test and then she could laugh at her fears. She would put out her hand, now, and deftly turn a flimsy page of the prayer book lying open on her bedside table.

Her hand went forward. It wobbled a little, but not significantly. Her fingers met the page, tried to take hold, but became thick and fumbling as though clothed in gardening gloves. A wodge of pages mounded up, refused to separate. 'It *is* coming back,' Lazarus cried silently, terror-struck.

'Something on your mind, Laz?' asked Martha with a coy glance at the prayer book. 'You can talk to me, y'know. Or perhaps y'ought to see Father Dawson. Meself, I swear by Father Dawson. Remember that time I had scruples over the slugs?'

Will I ever forget? Lazarus groaned to herself, thinking of hours spent listening to Martha on the subject. But then, striving to be fair, she recalled her own fascination: it had seemed a delicious dilemma and she had followed every twist of the argument eagerly. Why, she wondered, was she now so keen to stoke up resentment against her friend? Martha had not changed, neither had she. It was the Priory that had changed and turned Martha into a threat. For if her paralysis were indeed returning . . .

Lazarus tucked her hands in her skirt and began to hunt through a plethora of gardening jobs, panicking at the thought of the fiddly ones, dwelling hopefully on those suitable even for the cack-handed. But would she retain her authority? Once, a tradition of respect and consideration would have made it certain. Sister Marjorie, for instance, their most talented illuminator of sacred texts, had continued to be revered as the senior artist even when her sight had failed. It had been done with delicacy and tact. And then Sister Mercy, the Directrix, had fallen sick . . . Ah, yes; that had been the start of it: deference to an ailing Sister Mercy had precipitated their present troubles. Even so, by putting things right in a harsh and uncaring fashion, they were changing the very nature of the community. And people had not been consulted about *that*.

No, there would be no crippled Head of the Flower Garden, Lazarus thought grimly, looking hard at the garrulous one whom she imagined succeeding her. Suddenly, she knew how very much the position meant to her. It was not that she was bossy or proud, but that her life had meaning and dignity; above all, that she was respected. Yes, that was the thing. Loss of respect would be insupportable. The thought made her jump. 'Look, Martha,' she cried urgently, 'as a matter of fact, I would appreciate a bit of time to myself. To be quiet, you know.' And she looked meaningfully, and untruthfully, towards her prayer book.

'Right y'are,' Martha said easily, getting to her feet. 'By gum, hark at that wind! I should stuff rug under t'door, if I were you – ain't half a draught. I'm right sorry for them poor souls in t'east wing tonight. That reminds me. Did you hear about Reverend Mother paying 'em a visit?'

'Yes.' Lazarus opened the door and the draught made it swing in violently.

'Whoops! Y'all right? Well – 'night, night; sleep tight . . . Though how any of us'll get a wink with this racket . . .'

'Goodnight, Martha.'

* * * *

Mary John could not sleep. She lay staring at her agitated, shadowy curtains, listening to the wind battering her window. She could not sleep because she dreaded to wake, for mornings had become more desolate than ever. Waking on the morning following her evening stroll with Catherine, the cowshed and the meadows had called her with such haunting insistence that by denying them she seemed to drown. And then the psalm at Morning Prayer ('Save me, oh God, for the waters are come in, even unto my soul') – her heart turned over to think of it.

And now, of course, she was obliged to assume a false brightness before Catherine, who meant well, who was anxious on her behalf. She had taken to avoiding Catherine.

Suddenly, Mary John sat up. She listened attentively, measuring the wind's new ferocity. Then she climbed out of bed, removed her nightrobe and began to put on her clothes.

* * * *

'I suppose,' Beatrice said, 'I really ought to go.'

Hope whined complainingly.

Just then, a wind blast shook the building. Beatrice bounded out of bed. 'D'you hear that? I hope the tower's still standing.' She began to pull on her clothes.

While Beatrice was sightless with a skirt over her head, Hope slid her hand to the floor and felt for an item of clothing which she secreted under her body.

Soon: 'Where's my girdle? Drat! Where is the blessed thing?'

Hope gave a squeak.

56

Beatrice promptly seized and raised her and retrieved the girdle. She gave Hope a clout.

'Ow, that hurt!'

'Serves you right for messing about. I suppose the damage this wind might be doing hasn't occurred to you. Just listen to it. Damnation! To think we were all set to make a start on the tower!'

'Shall I come too?'

'Please yourself.' Beatrice knelt to tie her shoelaces. 'Though you'd probably be a liability. I mean, if the tower does come down there'll be hordes of homeless bats . . .'

Hope yelped and stuck her head under the pillow.

Beatrice put her foot against the door to prevent it from opening too suddenly; pulled, listened, looked; then stepped out, closed it, and sped away.

9

'Where have you been?' Margaret roared.
They had met – collided almost – in the cloister;
Beatrice running from one direction, Margaret, Agnes, Joan
and several others rushing from another.

'Is it the tower?'

'The tower's all right – apart from some fallen masonry –
but . . .'

'The statue's wobbling. The ropes have come free.'

'If it falls, that'll be the end of it – it's so fragile.'

'The statue will *not* fall. We can't allow it.' Margaret, the
moonlight on her face, seemed to summon more than earthly
determination. She would defy the inevitable, forestall the work
of the elements . . .

'Better take a look,' said Beatrice.

They gathered in the courtyard below the tower, a continu-
ally enlarging group of grey-veiled sisters, their robes driven
like bunting. Wind-sped clouds over a brilliant moon cast
alternating blackness and shine. For long moments the light
revealed her dazzlingly, Our Lady of Albion on her platform at
the top of the tower, framed by four open arches rising from the
corners to meet at the middle point above her head. She
watched over the courtyard; her outstretched arms invoked a
blessing upon the sisters about their daily duties below. For
some months she had leaned precipitously, and Beatrice had

made her temporarily secure with anchoring ropes attached to the arches. Now, gazing upwards, holding veils from their faces, they strained to count the flailing ropes. 'They're all loose,' Beatrice said at last, and a groan went up.

Suddenly, during a particularly ferocious wind-gust, the watchers saw the statue move. There was an instinctive flinching and averting of eyes – but not for Margaret. 'No,' she yelled, charging forward, hands raised against the invisible destroyer. 'You shan't!' When she turned back to them, she seemed to have come more vividly alive. Her eyes glittered, a clenched hand pounded the air and rendered her words emphasis – 'We can't allow it. That statue is known throughout the world. If we let her fall, we might as well pack up and go. Sisters, the spirit of Albion is under attack. What are you going to do about it?'

Gasps, shuffles, cries.

'It appears not everyone is bothered,' Agnes shouted witheringly. 'At least half of 'em are messing about in the east wing.'

'The *east wing?*' Margaret could not believe it.

'Yeah. Trying to evacuate it.'

'You hear that?' Margaret screeched. 'Half of our members are more concerned with their creature comforts than preserving Our Lady of Albion! Fetch them. Go on. Tell 'em to come here. Now!'

The sisters looked at one another. Imogen and Clare slipped away.

Beatrice went forward and put her mouth to Margaret's ear. 'Don't worry about them. I'm your woman. I'll get up there and fix the ropes.'

'You . . . will . . . stay . . . here.' A stiff finger jabbed towards the ground. 'You're the only one with knowledge of the conditions. You must direct operations, but from a safe place. I've told you before – you're indispensable.'

'Steady on, Margaret,' Joan warned, catching her arm. 'I don't know what you've in mind, but for Heaven's sake be careful – our stock's low enough as it is.'

59

Margaret jerked her arm free. She, too, was haunted by their waning popularity; indeed, the imminent loss of the statue seemed to presage their downfall. But if Joan imagined caution could ward off an already beckoning defeat, she, Margaret, knew better. This was the moment to chance all. Audacity might yet secure victory. 'Aha!' she cried as the party arrived from the east wing. 'I see we've managed to rouse the comfort-lovers. Sorry, you lot, but your arrangements'll have to wait. We've got a crisis on our hands.'

'There's nothing we can do about it, surely?' Catherine shouted back. Having been brought urgently from organizing an evacuation of lay sisters from the east wing, she still clasped a bundle of bedding. 'The tower isn't safe. No one can go up there.'

There were murmurs of assent. They drove Margaret wild. She examined the white-faced creature with her homely bundle and almost spat her contempt. 'Yes, we might have expected that from you. You never have been able to grasp anything beyond the safe, the ordinary, the pedestrian. "But we always do such-and-such so we had better go on doing it for ever, even if the place is crumbling about our feet, because we haven't the wit to think of anything else." ' Abandoning her mock-mimicking tone, Margaret became bullish: 'Well, I say there *is* something we can do about it. I say the sisters of Albion are not cowards, they will do their duty gladly, without flinching. I say the sisters of Albion are proud of their reputation in the world; they will give their all to defend it . . .'

Many of her words were drowned by the wind, but there was no mistaking their message. A particularly ferocious blast sent the sisters staggering and colliding. When it relented there was an anxious peering towards the top of the tower, but for the moment Our Lady of Albion held her ground.

'The wind'll beat us to it if we don't get on with it. Tell us what needs to be done,' Margaret roared to Beatrice.

'Well, as I said, she has to be roped again to the arches. But it's a bit dodgy in the tower – missing stairs, lumps out of the wall . . .'

'Who'll volunteer?' shouted Margaret, silencing Beatrice with a glare. 'Surely some of you feel as passionately as I do?'

'Why don't you do it yourself if you feel passionately?' one of the younger sisters screamed. (One of the bolshie ones, Margaret noted.)

'Let me assure you, Sister, were it not for my onerous duty – that of running this community – I wouldn't hesitate. In fact,' – the wind charged, and she darted an anxious look over her shoulder – 'I am sorely tempted.'

Her ardour was palpable. They believed her.

'Me! I'll do it!' cried Mary John.

They turned their heads.

As Mary John met their eyes, she felt herself swell and grow. For many months she had been unable to meet another's glance, and this phenomenon she had observed in others of her kind; it was an affliction of the redundant, a leper's bell warning those with their self-respect still intact to keep their distance. Glorious, now, to stare brazenly and watch amazed confusion dawn in the face of Sister Imogen.

'Sister Mary John!' proclaimed Margaret, as if conferring a sainthood. 'Let her pass.' She reached out and caught Mary John's hands.

Agnes began to clap. General applause broke out.

'Wait!' cried Catherine. 'Have you all gone mad?' But Agnes, in her eagerness to cry, 'Who else?', jostled Catherine and caused her to lose her balance.

'Me!' a lay sister cried, catching the mood.

'Me!' 'Me!' The cries, abrupt as firecrackers, were each swallowed by applause.

'Wonderful. Come forward,' Margaret beckoned. 'Yes, you, you . . . Well done!' In an aside to Beatrice, she snapped: 'Take 'em off and tell 'em what to do.'

'You mean, with this lot?'

'Stop fooling and get on with it.'

Catherine was pushing through the group. Finding Mary John gone with Beatrice, she rounded on Margaret. 'You're putting their lives in danger. You've no right. And to save what? A lump of stone? A bit of metal?'

'To save our reputation.'

'Nonsense!'

'Sister Catherine's right.' Some rebellious sisters crowded round, arguing, shouting Margaret down.

Catherine turned away. 'I must catch Sister Mary John.'

'I shouldn't bother,' one of the dissenters said in Catherine's ear. 'If she's fool enough to get herself killed it might even do some good.'

'Good?'

'There'd be a scandal – it'd put a stop to *her*.'

Horrified, Catherine pushed through the crowd, but Agnes and Imogen were barring the way to the tower.

She began to run in the other direction.

'Where are you going, Catherine?'

It was Angelica pounding after her.

'To fetch the Reverend Mother . . . and Cecilia and Monica . . . why aren't they here?'

* * * *

It was some time before Catherine discovered the Prioress. She was with Cecilia, Monica, Anne and Elizabeth, at Sister Mercy's bedside. As Catherine entered the hospital room, Sister Luke drew her aside and hissed: 'The end's very near.'

Oh, Mercy, thought Catherine. What a time to choose.

She hesitated, thinking of the peril facing Mary John and her companions, looking towards the bed where one of the little band of friends would presently die. Impossible to disturb their vigil. On the other hand, only the Prioress could prevent a probable catastrophe. Undecided, she slowly approached the bed.

Monica saw her and smiled. Cecilia followed her friend's glance and shuffled to one side, touching the bed to signal that Catherine should join them. Obediently, Catherine knelt between Monica and Cecilia, closed her eyes and unsuccessfully attempted prayer. When she looked up, the women on the other side of the bed – Elizabeth and Anne kneeling, the

Prioress in a chair – smiled at her sadly. Cecilia, who was holding Mercy's hand, took Catherine's and wrapped it round the nearly lifeless one.

Awe in the presence of death, her companions' expectations, her fatal lack of certainty: all three combined to make her incapable of action. She continued to kneel there, strong for neither Mercy nor Mary John.

* * * *

'Dear God, what a *shower*.' Beatrice used the term with feeling, for her fears concerning the volunteers' competence had proved well founded. 'We'll have to bring her down; she's blocking the way.' ('She' was a fallen sister who had failed to negotiate a gap in the staircase.) 'I warned them,' Beatrice complained to Agnes, who was keeping her company at the tower-house door. 'I said, "Watch out just after the sixth window." Can you hear me up there? – have you got her? Well, get a move on – and *keep away from the wall*.'

Now and then when the wind dropped, Margaret's voice came across like a foghorn through mist: '. . . all pray.' 'Our brave sisters . . .' '. . . inspiration to us all.'

Agnes, her political acumen as sharp as ever, went off to warn Margaret to remain with the main group in the courtyard so that she would not be obliged to reconsider the operation in the light of an accident.

With much heaving and panting, the rescue party emerged. Imogen bustled forward to examine the moaning injured one.

'How many are still up there?' Agnes, returning, wanted to know.

'Three. And not one of them's arrived on the top. If they had, they'd have been spotted from the courtyard – Joan's on the lookout. The thing is, Ag, it's all very well for Margaret to make stipulations, but she doesn't seem to realize the need for someone with a bit of savvy up there. I think I should go up –at least I can find out whether they're still functional.'

'Perhaps you'd better. I'll keep her out of it,' promised Agnes.

* * * *

Mary John, nearing the top of the tower, began to whistle her milking tune. Danger had exhilarated her. She had clambered over one inert sister, evaded the clutching hands of a fear-stricken other; she had negotiated gaps, scrambled over rubble, ducked from falling masonry, and when sucking draughts came at her through gaps in the wall she had laughed and pushed on. The skills acquired in her tomboy youth had come into play as naturally as if she had never ceased from their daily practice. Now she was ready for the summit.

Moonlight flooded. She blinked, stood upright, gazed around.

The night was wild and wonderful – gold-streaked indigo, a rushing river of air – and the show brilliant – delirious snakes leaping and slapping beneath the outstretched arms of a ringmaster, a spotlight swinging gleam and dazzle, then closing her in a booth of black velvet with the noise pounding, growing louder, until ('yes, here it comes . . .') brilliance flooded again. Enchanted, she moved over the floor, Beatrice's warning ('And when you get to the top, watch out for rotten boards; keep to the outside.') gone cleanly from her mind. When the boards gave way and she plunged downwards, her strong arms encircled a beam and she threw herself with a tree-climber's ease on to firm floor beyond the statue. 'My, my!' she spluttered. 'Whatever next?'

* * * *

On the dark stairway, Beatrice had stumbled across the unconscious sister. 'Oh, God, not a corpse,' she prayed. 'I'm not sure we could weather that.' But at once a vision came to mind of Margaret announcing a martyr for the cause, and the prospect became tenable. She stepped over the inert form and

64

climbed on. Her skirt became a nuisance; she pressed against the central pillar and cautiously raised herself until she could blouse it through her girdle. For good measure she tore off her coif and veil. Should have done it sooner, she thought; and then: What a peculiar row!

It was the frightened sister successfully avoided by Mary John. She was huddled in a corner by a gap in the wall through which the wind licked spitefully. Her hysteria had reduced to a manic whimpering.

'Get hold of yourself, for Pete's sake,' Beatrice urged, stepping warily round her and continuing on her way to the top.

Like Mary John before her, Beatrice crawled from her dark confinement and emerged, slowly unfolding, into windswept, moonlit space. The vista took her breath away – swelling waves, racing smoke, and the brilliant bobbing moon. She threw out her arms and felt the wind in her sleeves; it streamed her hair and as she tipped up her face and whooped, rushed warmly to fill her mouth and throat. The joy-riding clouds cast a funfair mood – speed, thrills, damn tomorrow! Nothing could bring her down, not even the discovery that half the floor was missing and poor old Sister Mary John was marooned on the other side. Well, good for Sister Mary John, she had actually made it. What's more, she appeared to be enjoying herself. 'Yoo-hoo, Sister – quite a night isn't it? You're in a bit of a pickle. But don't worry, we'll think of something. Tell you what, I'll swing over on a couple of ropes. We'll tie one to the statue and swing back on the other.' She struggled to catch the nearest tossing rope.

Mary John heard not a word.

Once, when still a child on her father's farm, she had wrestled her half-drowned body from a bog. And down there, from where she had just hauled herself, was a mire of deepest pitch. She would never go back. She would remain in this gaudy tent playing a medley of the best moments of her life. One evening long ago her father took her to the circus. Afterwards, she rode bareback on her pony and taught her terrior to jump through a hoop; she turned somersault on a tightrope plank and flew through the air on a tree-borne trapeze . . . Oh! – Mary John clasped her hands beneath her chin and gasped, for here, now, through the spangled night, with her moon-coloured hair and her pink and white laugh, flew the trapeze lady!

('Damnation – missed! Hang on, Sister – better luck next time. Right – one, two, *three–ee*.')

And here she came again. But now Mary John saw that it was not the trapeze lady. It was . . . (because, look at her hair, her *golden* hair, and the wings billowing from her shoulders) it was the angel of the Lord! God had sent his angel for Mary John. Such care, such love – Mary John had never imagined this reception. Overcome, she hurled herself forward towards the angel's arms.

* * * *

In the area of the Albion Tower, time entered three dimensions.

For the watchers in the courtyard below there was no time between the moment when the fall began and the moment of impact upon the ground. There was no point when they could say, 'The body is there, then there, now there,' for time was too swift for their cumbersome perceptions. Later, they would imagine the form's flight. But were it not for the *smack* upon the ground, repeating again and again in their inner ears, the form – so eternally still – might never not have been lying there.

Beatrice wrestled with time. She crouched against the parapet clasping the rope and willed time to play over again. 'Come back, you idiot. Stay put, *stay* . . .' Her mind recovered Mary John, set Beatrice flying again . . . but though she struggled to right the moment when her feet struck and launched Mary John, it remained unchanged, slipped further away, evaded her straining grasp.

Time has become infinite for Mary John. She floats smoothly on to where time has always been drawing her. Old friends turn their heads; gaze tenderly. They will go on watching for ever.

66

10

'If she's fool enough to get herself killed, it might even do some good – put a stop to *her.*'

These words, so shocking to Catherine when they were spoken, rose obstinately from the back of her mind during the aftermath of the Albion Tower incident. And this was not surprising, for their sentiment – less brutally expressed – echoed constantly in discussions around her. Many of her associates felt that Margaret had miscalculated and could not survive.

There were two bodies of opinion, one viewing the incident as a triumph, one as a disaster, and neither side appeared to notice the inability of the majority of sisters, still dazed and confused by the affair, to decide one way or the other. Catherine's supporters made a further misjudgement: they doubted the sincerity of Margaret's camp, supposing their strident confidence to cover secret guilt.

Margaret, in fact, was buzzing with an inner glow she would never have permitted herself were not self-congratulation in order. Her conduct of the affair had been magnificent, she judged. No one but she, not Beatrice, not Agnes, could have summoned the sheer guts necessary to see it through, aware throughout of snapping dogs at her heels – failure, scandal, ignominy. With the fall of Mary John the stakes had rocketed; but she had kept her nerve. It had been a bad moment – the body on the ground, Catherine sent for, the weeping, the beginning of recrimination – but in the nick of time Beatrice had completed the task attempted by Mary John, thereby defying a particularly vicious wind-gust and affording Margaret the opportunity to declare Mary John's death well vindicated. The crowd had cheered despite the recent tragedy. Massively relieved, Margaret had turned on her carping critics: 'The statue is safe. Rejoice about *that!*'

It had shut them up. But even then she had been obliged to keep her wits about her. Joan, for instance, had become quite hysterical over some aberration she imagined concerning Beatrice's headgear. Agnes had rushed off to ensure that when Beatrice reappeared she would be decently attired. And it had been mildly annoying to discover Beatrice's disobedience; though, in the circumstances, she could hardly complain. Beatrice was a heroine – so too was the fallen Mary John. Margaret's mind became busy with plans for celebrations – a service of thanksgiving, and later on when the Tower had been restored, a procession to the courtyard and a service of dedication, the scene presided over by a newly gilded Lady of Albion. Imagining it, Margaret was full of honest pride. It was a fitting way, she told herself in the rallying language she favoured, of announcing to the world that the Albion Priory was back on its feet again.

In the meantime there was work to be done. They had won a marvellous victory: it should, it must, be sustained. With Mercy dead the Prioress would feel more than ever obliged to consider the succession. And the succession could not be allowed to go the wrong way, Margaret thought grimly, deciding to go and talk the matter over with Agnes at once.

Similar thoughts occupied Agnes. 'This mood of mourning,' she said, drawing a tombstone in the margin of her notes, 'it's gone on long enough, and it's not doing *us* any good. As soon as we've buried Mercy and Mary John, I suggest a change of atmosphere – call a meeting, then have a good rousing service.'

'I suppose it'll have to be a Council meeting,' Margaret said regretfully. 'Catherine will insist.'

'I've thought of that. No. Our line is, that in view of the momentous happening, we think everyone should be there. After all, Sister Mary John wasn't even a member of Council – not since we sold her cows. We think her peers should have a say.'

'Mmm. I should think that'll work, so long as we pack it with punch.'

'Right. I mean, we come on *strong*.'

Margaret pulled in her chin and bellowed: 'This is a moment when the entire Community must draw together . . .'

'You've got it. Now, according to reliable sources, the other side assumes we're on the defensive. They're all set to put the skids under us. So this evening we'd better get together and plan every detail.'

'I've been thinking, Agnes. Why not bring in one or two more? Imogen, for instance – I'm enormously impressed with Imogen. And Veronica's sound. That spunky little Clare – one of us, wouldn't you say?'

'Oh, certainly.' Agnes began a new, spikier doodle. 'But . . .'

'Us four plus those three.'

'Just Imogen and Clare,' countered Agnes. 'They're younger – got the right idea. Veronica's useful, but I don't see her grasping the finer points of, you know . . . strategy.'

'Perhaps you're right. Just Imogen and Clare, then. Now . . .' (Margaret carefully removed a speck of fluff from her habit) 'I suppose – mm – I suppose Beatrice is all right? The limelight's going to be on her rather, from now on.' (Agnes's drawing changed course again, became an impression of a female head with a spectacular mane of hair.) 'We'll have to put all we've got into the Beatrice aspect, to counter the Mary John effect.'

'True.' Agnes paused. 'Yes, Beatrice'll be all right, I should think. Perhaps a pep talk from you: explain that she's our trump card – people'll be watching her – got to live up to it. You know the sort of thing.'

'Quite. But you would tell me, Agnes, if there were anything I ought to know.'

'Absolutely, Margaret.'

* * * *

Sometimes Catherine thought over the events of that night, lest she should overlook her own culpability. But she did not delude herself. Margaret's new rule had been the cause of Mary John's fatal despair. For the sake of others in Mary John's position, she steeled herself to work for Margaret's defeat. It was time to put a stop to her.

She prepared for the meeting – or 'briefing' as the opposition liked to call these occasions – with confident composure. The sisters were horrified by Mary John's death and the injuries sustained by her colleagues. They would back her. It could not be otherwise.

* * * *

'Now, I'd like you all to take a look at this.' Margaret waved a yellowed card before the noses of those occupying the front seats. 'An old print of the Albion Tower. And do you know where it came from?' She paused, craned forward and showed her teeth to say: '*Italy*.' The card was put down and a book taken up. 'And here again.' She held the book open at an illustration. 'Our Lady of Albion. You can read all about it in here – in *Russian*.' (Her audience duly reeled.) Soon, Margaret went on to predict, the world would thirst again for news of the Albion Priory, would clamour to visit. If all went according to plan – and Margaret did not foresee any delay – the visitors' programme would come into effect this very autumn. 'That is why it was so vital to save the statue. Imagine an empty space at the top of the tower. Hardly the way to show we're back in business again. But thanks to our brave sisters the world can have no doubt of it – the Albion Priory is back on its feet again!'

Applause spread like flame through tinder. Even to some of the unconverted members of her audience, Margaret's words gave meaning to Mary John's death. She had prescribed a more comfortable memorial than one suggested elsewhere – that her death was a useless disgrace.

But some sisters were still angry. They waited hopefully for Catherine to speak.

Her musical voice came out evenly. 'I have a question for Sister Margaret. Has she described to us the *means* by which these great things will be accomplished? I think she has not. Will she please tell us plainly what they are? I ask because when her original proposals were put to Council she did not explain that many sisters would be deprived of their way of life; she did not explain that these sisters would then have no function other than that of cleaning up after others; she did not explain that those unfortunate enough to bear the burden of these "improvements" would lose their voice in Council and thus any means of countering their distress. She did not explain that some of us would become less than others . . .'

Oh, thought Lazarus. My thoughts exactly! That is what happened. They asked us whether we wanted our affairs to be put in order. They did not explain that it would change the way we live with one another – no one asked if we wanted *that*. A part of Lazarus resolved to speak out in support of Catherine at the first opportunity. She shuffled to the edge of her seat in readiness. But another part of her pulled back, shrank from the idea. If only she were strong and whole; if her position were not under threat . . . As it was, her mouth had gone dry, stabbing pains were attacking her joints. When she slumped down, shamefaced, in her seat, she knew herself to be doomed.

'It would not be so bad if it were frankly admitted that some sisters have been placed at a disadvantage. Then we could make sure they were compensated. That would be the honest, the moral thing to do. After all, it is no one's fault, it is quite arbitrary, that some forms of work are now found to be more profitable than others. Perhaps we should reconsider our support for the new proposals. Let us hear Sister Margaret again and listen critically for her answers.'

Agnes smirked. Beatrice grinned. Margaret heaved a sigh of

71

relief. What a novice Catherine was, playing the ball back into her opponent's court!

Margaret rose; inclined her head, raised her eyebrows. 'Sisters, I confess to a certain disappointment. Was that *really* the carping tone we expected to hear this afternoon, so soon after our triumph? And, yes, we *have* had a triumph. For goodness' sake let's rejoice about it.' She lowered her eyebrows. 'Now, to answer the points raised by Sister Catherine. "Some of us have become less than others"?' she quoted with disbelief. 'Less than others? Because of a change of work? Look, I believe Sister Mary John was one of those whose working life had changed. Is it seriously proposed that Sister Mary John could have acted as she did, believing we did not value her? What nonsense! Sister Mary John *knew* she was a valued member of this Priory; that is why she gave her life for it. It is true, some people are doing work they were not used to. Well, times change. The world has changed. We must change. I tell you, sisters, *there – is – no – alternative.* Are we frightened of change? I say to my critics, *you* may fear the challenge of change, but please don't stifle our initiative. Please allow us our vision.' She craned forward, preparing to make things plain even to halfwits. 'You see, it was *vision* that inspired Sister Mary John. It was *vision* that inspired Sister Beatrice.' She threw out a hand towards the heroine. 'Sisters, many of you watched Sister Beatrice on that terrible night, risking her life for our beloved statue. If everyone of us here can summon a small portion of that fearless spirit, between us we shall save our beloved Priory!'

Beatrice smiled her widest smile. So overcome was one sister in the front row that she darted forward to kiss the hem of the heroine's robe. 'Sisters,' Margaret cried, shooing the emotional one, 'I think it would be fitting if Sister Beatrice were now to lead us in prayer.'

Oh help! thought Beatrice, looking wildly round.

Joan, never at a loss for a suitable text, handed her a book and pointed to the place.

' "Stir up, we beseech thee, O Lord, the wills of thy faithful people . . ." ' (My goodness, this goes rather well, thought

Beatrice, much taken with the sound of her voice, stealthy and ripe in the bated-breath hush as a dove's on a summer evening. She lingered voluptuously over the more enjoyable words.) ' " . . . that they, plenteously bringing forth the fruit of good works, may of thee be plenteously rewarded . . ." '

Cecilia, peeping under her brows, was similarly impressed. What a charming voice the gel has, and such a nice, frank smile. And so plucky . . . Pity's she's in with that awful crew. Think I'll take an interest in her from now on . . . 'Amen,' she intoned sonorously, deciding that the needlework room should entertain Beatrice to tea.

'Amen,' Catherine said hastily, wondering whether to try again.

But Margaret was too prompt for her. 'One hardly likes to add a word,' she said apologetically. 'However, Sister Joan wishes to bring a matter to your attention. Sister . . .'

Joan, pressing fingertips to forehead as if to calm an exquisite pain, began hesitantly. 'Mmm, ah, the bulletin. I thought – well, several of us did really – it'd be a nice idea to keep everyone *au fait* with all the changes and so forth. So we thought we'd bring out a regular bulletin and pin it up outside the refectory. Anyone with something to communicate to the rest of us can get in touch with me. Oh dear . . . I think that was it. Yes, thank you.'

Margaret was already halfway to the door, mouthing 'Hellos', reaching to touch hands lightly with her own.

Two sisters rushed to Catherine's side. 'She didn't answer. Why didn't you pin her down?'

'Perhaps it was not quite the right occasion,' murmured Cecilia, overhearing them. 'Wasn't Sister Beatrice splendid?'

Angelica began to steer Catherine to the door. 'You're white as a sheet. Let's go to the chapel. We can practise the anthem.'

'Anthem?'

'For tonight. I've found a really joyous setting of "O sing unto the Lord a new song".'

'Are you mad? We buried Mercy and Mary John less than twenty-four hours ago.'

'But Sister Theresa specifically said that psalm. And I thought a new setting would be a change. After all, it's a special service tonight, a service of thanksgiving.'

'Look, tell Sister Theresa from me: all due respect, but I'd like her to think again; thanksgiving by all means, but in a context of remembrance – yes, and contrition, too. Do it for me, will you, Angelica? I'm going for a walk. I need to think.'

Angelica went doubtfully to the Precentor's office, recalling the Sister Precentor's uncompromising manner when she had handed Angelica tonight's order of service. She sighed. Perhaps, if Sister Theresa remained adamant, she could satisfy Catherine by finding a chant that would moderate the psalm's triumphant tone.

* * * *

'What d'you mean, "camped it up"? I put heart and soul into that prayer,' Beatrice protested indignantly.

'I thought you read it beautifully,' soothed Margaret. 'No time for arguing, Sisters. I need to know whether everything's in order for tonight.'

'The service? Oh yes,' said Agnes. 'I made our requirements crystal clear to Sister Theresa.'

'And I found just the psalm. "O sing unto the Lord a new song: for He hath done marvellous things. With His own right hand, and with His holy arm, hath He gotten Himself the victory." '

'Marvellous, Joan. By the way, when you write up the bulletin you will try and slip in how very much faster we'd all get on if it weren't for all this carping and whining.'

'How about a catchy postscript – like "Moaning minnies sap our strength"?'

' "Moaning minnies" is good. It's got a ring to it.'

'If it doesn't do the trick, we can go for something stronger later on.'

'Perhaps not so much stronger, as suggestive,' Beatrice said thoughtfully.

74

'Plenty of ideas, anyway. That's what I like to hear. Now, Beatrice – I'd like a chat. Let's go and chivvy those gardeners.'

* * * *

The low sun beamed towards the sanctuary, removing those in its dazzle-paths to a different plane, haloed, blind, divorced from their shadowy sisters. In the chancel, the sun singled out Catherine, and beyond her, on the gilded altar frontal, a lamb bearing a cross. By Catherine's side, the Prioress squinted at the sun-spashed page of her prayer book as though she did not know by heart every word of the liturgy. To the left of the Prioress knelt Margaret, apparently rapt in prayer.

Margaret was thinking what a dismal start to the service it had been; the organ muted, the responses half-hearted. She looked forward to the psalm, though it was apparent from the lack of music on Catherine's desk that no anthem was to be made of it. How small-minded of the woman, she thought scornfully. She, Margaret, had achieved a success, so Catherine must sulk and decline to lend her *mezzo* to the celebration. Well, people would draw their conclusions . . .

The congregation rose to say the Gloria. The organ gave out the chant.

Soon, a red spot dawned in each of Margaret's cheeks. In the nave, Beatrice stole a glance at Joan and grinned to herself, for Joan, finding her intentions sabotaged once again by human incompetence, had thrust a clenched fist to her brow. Unnoticed at the back of the chapel, Agnes slipped quickly from her pew.

Angelica, keeping a careful eye on the psalm's pointing, was thinking how clever she had been to find this blameless little chant in F-major. It had just the right air of innocent cheerfulness, and voiced by the light, bright stops she had selected, conveyed nothing of a thumping victory. Catherine would be reassured. Fondly, Angelica pictured her in the chancel singing with a clear conscience and a light heart.

When a hand appeared from nowhere and snatched out the

eight-foot diapason stop, Angelica almost fell from the bench. 'What y'doing?' she hissed, fighting to control her suddenly dithering fingers.

'Just keep playing,' Agnes commanded in her ear.

'Get out, you fool. You shouldn't be here.' Angelica steadied herself. If she were not careful, she would lose her place and make a mess of things. 'Don't. Please go,' she frantically whispered when Agnes not only remained but pulled further stops into play.

'Come on, put a bit of life into it. This isn't a funeral.'

'You must be mad.'

What would people think? What would Catherine think? Angelica ploughed on to the end.

'I don't know what you thought you were doing, but you'd better go now.'

'What have you got for the Magnificat?' asked Agnes, unmoved.

Angelica turned the pages. 'Will you please *go*?'

Agnes, who could not read music, regarded the chant with suspicion. 'Mmm. Well, make it loud and lively.'

Below them at the lectern, a sister announced the end of the first lesson. It was Angelica's cue. There was no choice for her but to play.

'Better,' murmured Agnes at the Magnificat's close.

'Look, I suppose Sister Margaret sent you. Well, Sister Catherine's going to be pretty annoyed, and I daresay the Prioress . . .'

'Shh.' Agnes put a reproving finger to her lips, then sat down on the end of the organ bench. 'How's that pupil of yours coming on?' she asked in Angelica's ear. 'Sister Laura – that's her name, isn't it? I hear she's rather good. If you've lost your appetite for this work, perhaps she's ready to replace you. Pity, though, 'cos Sister Margaret was really taken with the idea of your Sunday evening recitals . . .' She glanced down and whispered, 'Nice capable hands you've got, Sister Angelica. I bet Sister Imogen'd be glad of your help in the housekeeping

76

department. Think about it . . . Now, what's next?' She peered at the music. 'Ah, the Nunc Dimittis – well that's always a quiet one. But see what you can do with the hymn. "Now thank we all our God" – I'll expect something really rousing for that.' She slid from the bench and disappeared round the side of the organ.

Angelica's immediate resolve was to put Agnes's words out of her mind. She played the chant warily; but the words undid her. 'Lord, now lettest thou thy servant depart in peace . . .' Tears like rocks stood in her eyes. An end to music-making – she tried to imagine it and saw that it would mean more – an end to the only achievement worth striving for, an end to those supreme moments when she and the sound were locked together on their lighted island in a vast listening darkness. This last picture overwhelmed her; she battled against it, but the image came again and again in waves of piercing desolation.

The hymn. It was almost time for the hymn. She blew her nose, found the right page in the hymnal, pulled out every stop, wedged open the swell box. They would have noise, would they? Well, let the noise blast them!

At the end of the service, Catherine hurried to the organ loft. She waited for the last brilliant notes to die. Then: 'Whatever got into you?' she demanded. 'It was going so well; then all hell broke loose. Did you have a brainstorm, Angelica?'

Angelica pushed home the stops, removed her music and closed the console doors.

'Answer me.' Catherine seized her friend's wrist, but Angelica avoided her eyes.

Catherine released her and watched as Angelica stacked the music away in the cupboard. Suddenly, she sat down on the bench and put her head in her hands. 'What's going on?'

Angelica hesitated. 'Sister Agnes came up.'

'Up here? During the service? You mean, she made you play like that?'

'Please, Catherine, don't make trouble.'

77

'Angelica . . .' She put out her hand. It was ignored. 'Oh, dear God,' she whispered.

11

'I do get tired . . . and rather stiff,' admitted the Prioress. (They tutted sympathetically.) 'However, *inside* one is tireless – vigorous, even.'

The words seemed to hang in the air. She turned her head to gaze irritably at a jug of red ox-eye daisies, but they made her think of Sister Lazarus and feel crosser than ever. Lazarus had brought the flowers this morning, had insisted upon making them into 'an arrangement'. As she worked, she had twittered nervously and incessantly (and largely unintelligibly). When she had gone, the Prioress found a mess of green slime on a favourite tray cloth. Why could the woman not have moved it? the Prioress wondered for the umpteenth time. She hauled herself out of her chair and lurched across the room to poke at the cloth which was soaking in a bowl of cold water on the table.

Margaret coughed discreetly behind her hand. (The Prioress peered at her severely, but Margaret chose to ignore this.) 'Aren't you delighted with the refurbished refectory, Reverend Mother?' she asked brightly. 'The tapestries are splendid, they lend such a wonderful atmosphere. I'm sure it will prove a most attractive room for our visitors.'

'Mmm, very nice.' The green stain did not appear to be lifting. She pushed the cloth back under the water, then dried her hand on her skirt.

'Yes, it's all coming along splendidly. The kitchens and

79

outhouses are nearly finished. Next week we start on the tower.'

The tower. The Prioress frowned. What a shocking thing that Sister Mary John business had been; and even more shocking was the way it had all turned out. She had expected an uproar, a laborious enquiry – but not a bit of it. Evidently, a great thing had been done, and Margaret, the escapade's instigator, was proclaimed a marvel. 'Seems a rum thing to me,' she muttered, thinking of the stream of people to her door all bursting to lavish praise on the woman. Even Cecilia seemed to have lost her head over the tall girl who had survived the incident – what was her name – the one with the eyes and the grin? 'Sister Beatrice,' she told herself out loud.

'Sister Beatrice?' Margaret repeated. 'Did you expect her? I thought it was just to be myself and Sister Catherine.'

'Yes, yes.' Arriving back at her chair, she lowered herself into it gingerly. 'You see, by now I had hoped . . .' Her eyes dwelt reproachfully on Catherine. She found she could not complete the sentence.

No need. Her guests understood perfectly.

You had hoped, thought Margaret, oh yes, you had *hoped* to be naming your precious Catherine your successor. Well, we can all *hope*, only some of us prefer to roll up our sleeves and set about creating our own destiny. How furious the Prioress must be to have been let down by one of her own select little band. And how full of chagrin at the prospect of making Margaret – not one of *them* – her successor . . .

'But I've decided there's no hurry. With so much going on you both have your hands full and have quite enough to think about without an added responsibility hanging over you. No. As I said, I may get tired, but I am still a vigorous woman . . .'

You can't bear to do it! Margaret thought angrily. It really goes against the grain. Well, we shall see, but I rather think you'll come to it, m'lady. In fact, now I see how the land lies, I shall make good and sure of it . . .

'Reverend Mother, you must do as your conscience tells you. Don't think of my – our feelings.' Looking into the hurt, disappointed face, Catherine was full of shame. Dimly, she understood that the Prioress felt obliged to ignore the Spirit's promptings and back Margaret, for that was the advice she was undoubtedly receiving from almost every mortal here. So she had decided to hang on . . .

Once the financial recovery is assured, things will change again, the Prioress was promising herself. This made sense. Margaret was more suited than Catherine to money-grubbing and fabric mending. Catherine's qualities were spiritual: they had been noticed by the Prioress and her friends when Catherine was a mere postulant. Of course, Catherine's mother was Anne's first cousin – or was it Elizabeth's . . ?

'Well, if that's your decision for the time being . . . Look, I'm afraid I must go. Tremendous amount of work to be done down there.'

Automatically, the Prioress dangled her fingers from her sleeve. Gravely, for she prided herself on her formal manners, Margaret lowered her lips to them and dropped a curtsey. 'Goodbye, Reverend Mother,' she murmured, then bustled away.

'You see,' Catherine burst out when the door had closed, 'I'm not sure I'm going to do any better. Things seem to slip from my grasp. I'm not sure what's going on. Words don't mean what I think they mean. For instance, Sister Margaret's having a great campaign to re-establish our traditional values. Wonderful, I thought. But it turns out to mean that people shouldn't run or talk in the corridors, but walk with their heads bowed and their hands together; and that we shouldn't chat during supper but listen to readings from Scripture – that sort of thing. Things to impress the visitors, I couldn't help thinking – but perhaps that's cynical of me. *I* want us to remember that we are all equal in the sight of God and get back to treating people with care and consideration.'

'Have patience. As soon as our affairs are in order people will discover Margaret's limitations.'

'But I rather fear, Reverend Mother, that by then our community will be irrevocably changed.'

81

'Nonsense. How could that be? Really, Sister, you had better buck up. That reminds me: will you call in at the needlework room and ask one of them to come up? There's a nasty green mark on my cloth and I don't know how to get rid of it. Monica or Elizabeth, I should think; they're awfully clever about stains and so forth. If I don't shift it quickly, I'm worried it may take hold.'

PART TWO

12

'About the arrangements for tomorrow,' Sister Luke said, catching Sister Joan's arm.

Joan jumped, and squinted at her clipboard. As the chief organizer of the ceremony to mark the restoration of the Albion Tower, she dreaded the escape from her attention of some small but essential detail.

'Obviously, the paraplegic – Sister Brenda – will be wheeled along in her chair,' Sister Luke continued confidently. 'Thinking it over, it might be sensible if the other two were put in wheelchairs. They are able to walk, it is true, but Sister Ellen cannot stand for long with her hip, and poor Sister Grace is so unpredictable I think we'd manage her better in a chair; perhaps we could strap her in – for her own protection, of course. And they'd look more of a piece, don't you think, the three injured ones in three wheelchairs? I suppose you'll want them near the head of the procession?'

'Sister Joan,' called Margaret, who, passing by, had stopped to catch the gist of this. 'One moment, Sister Luke. Sister Joan will get back to you, but I must borrow her for a moment; the memorial tablet has arrived . . .' She led Joan from the cloister and the ever-present danger of well-meaning but time-wasting interruption (it had always puzzled Margaret why such a draughty place should attract the lingerers and gossipmongers), through the great vaulted hall and out into the autumn sunshine.

Their shoes scrunched on the gravel. By the creeper-clad wall a sister hunted for leaves fallen since the previous day's tidying.

'Over my dead body,' Margaret said in fierce undertone.

Joan clutched herself in fright. 'Oh, you mean the wheelchairs,' she gasped with relief, suddenly comprehending. 'I thought they sounded a bit off, myself. They'd draw attention . . .'

'I mean the injured. I won't have them anywhere near the ceremony. Make sure they're shut away somewhere for the afternoon. In fact, not to put too fine a point on it, Joan, I'd prefer it if they were shut away pretty well most of the time. I'm sick to death of the way they're handed around like overgrown babies. Sister Luke and her lot are always at it. They remind me of those ghastly mothers who imagine they've given birth to a miracle and the rest of us are busting to jiggle the thing on our knees. Do you know, I was actually invited to congratulate the revolting dribbly one?'

'Oh heavens! – you mean Sister Grace . . .'

'Grace!' Margaret scoffed. 'Yes, her. I was expected to make a fuss of her because she'd managed to tie her own shoelaces.'

'*Sickening*, Mags.'

'Can't a room be found for them?'

'They've got one – the old lumber room in the hospital corridor. It's been made very comfortable.'

'Then why on earth don't they stay in it? But as for tomorrow – not a hint of an injured nun, not a glimpse of a wheelchair. Have I made myself clear?'

'Perfectly.' Joan scribbled on her clipboard. 'Did you say the stone had arrived?'

At once Margaret's face cleared and her voice became tender. 'Over here. Come and see. They're going to lay it this afternoon and drape something over it until the ceremony. There.' From the finely etched script and the immaculate surface of the polished stone, she drew deep satisfaction. "In memory of Sister Mary John, who gave her life for this Priory . . ." she read lovingly for the second time that morning.

'Very nice.'

'Nice?' Margaret frowned.

'Fitting.'

'Inspirational, Joan.'

'Oh, absolutely, Margaret.'

* * * *

The pain, embedded like a chisel in the left side of Catherine's brow, very slowly turned. Her lips parted; she moaned mutely, for every sound, but particularly that of her own voice, intensified in ripples to fill the vast hollow of her skull. She closed her dry lips and breathed carefully, minimally.

'Not another migraine?' Angelica had exclaimed in dismay, discovering her in bed in a darkened room. Calculating with the aid of past experience, she had added: 'I suppose this means you'll miss the ceremony – oh, Catherine! And my recital.'

Through her eyelashes, Catherine had observed upon the face of her friend the arrival, dismissal and obstinate return of an embarrassing conclusion. You wonder whether this migraine is self-induced, she had silently, and correctly, guessed. The assumption was understandable. She had suffered from these headaches in her youth, but never as a member of the Priory until two or three months ago. The proposed ceremony of dedication at the foot of the Albion Tower had filled her with disgust; perhaps, after all, her illness was a protest, an excuse to preserve her from taking part. As she peered into her motives, lights flickered beneath her eyelids. Her stomach moved sickeningly and she instantly decided that, given the conscious choice, she would prefer any humiliation so long as she could stand upright and free from pain.

The lights beneath her eyelids converged to form a stream. The stream gathered momentum. It surged, lapped at her. She resisted weakly. The stream became a flood tide of gloating and glorifying, rushing towards the Albion Tower. Everyone here is swept away, she thought; then: no, not everyone, not Sister Luke who had the care of those injured by the derring-do, not young Sister Christa, not Angelica. (But Angelica had developed a trying habit of qualifying every critical remark as if Sister Agnes had hidden herself in the organ loft on purpose to eavesdrop: 'Of course, it's very pleasant to see the place looking so much smarter', or 'Though I do think the Albion Tower espisode restored people's pride'.) Why were they so witless about the saving of a statue? What real good had it done? Catherine could see only the harm. But she knew, because the stream dazzled her, that there had been a great welling of bright emotion; it had swept them beyond reason's reach; it had changed their perceptions. (Vainglorious hymns, once sniggered at or avoided, were sung these days with passion; and the old custom of arguing for a change of mind or an alternative proposal had become sacrilegious.)

Alone with her headache, she was tempted to abandon the struggle, to turn her face from the plight of those sisters forced to bear the burden of the Priory's recovery. Perhaps they deserved their fate; were despicably meek and accepting. But this line could not be held for long. Soon it came rushing in upon her that a large number of the disadvantaged were lay sisters, and although the Community had taken pride in good and gracious behaviour towards them, membership on a footing equal to that of the *religieuses* had always been withheld. So the evil of the present had roots in the careless snobbery of the past, for the very existence of a lesser class provided today's elite with a ready dumping-ground.

A rapping on the door sent shock-waves through her. Sister Christa came in and leaned over the bed. 'So it's true – you are ill,' she conceded grudgingly. 'I thought you were copping out. Anyway, may as well give you the latest: I've just heard from Sister Luke that they've banned the injured from taking part in the ceremony.' When no word, no movement came from the bed, she demanded, 'You're not asleep, are you? You did hear?'

Cautiously, Catherine opened an eye.

'What a time to get a headache! Can't you take something for it? We need help. Why should they get away with it? The injured, above all, have a right to be there. They *ought* to be there, to remind everyone of the cost.'

86

With her one eye, Catherine observed that anger made no lasting impression upon the youthful face. Deep lines creased the brow, then fled. Lips pursed, then became shiny and unshrivelled as ripened fruit. Heat from pent-up youthful energy wafted to her. She shivered at her own enervation and was overcome by nausea. Now she was obliged to swallow, to gulp, to cry feebly: 'Water!'

'Where? Oh, come on then. Shall I hold your head?'

Catherine sipped, then let her head loll against the supporting arm. When she regained the pillow, only the headache tormented her.

'You all right? Well, sorry; suppose I shouldn't have . . . Better leave you in peace.'

The door opened, then softly closed.

* * * *

'One hardly knows whether to laugh or cry,' Margaret mused. 'Our guests will be spared the sight of her doleful face, and for that one is grateful; but for the joint Directrix to give in to some trifling indisposition at such a solemn moment in the Priory's history . . . well! It's hardly the stuff of leadership.'

'She's a bad loser. That's the long and short of it,' Imogen declared; thus earning the indulgent smile with which Margaret acknowledged support of a robust but impulsive nature.

Beatrice, who had pictured herself being honoured before an audience of enemies as well as admirers, felt some of the zest had gone from the occasion. 'I'm fed up with her attitude.'

'We can use it,' Agnes said.

'Ah.' They became thoughtful.

'Each of us – not Margaret, obviously – but the rest of us should make a point of confiding in one other person. Pick the person carefully – someone who can't keep a thing to herself. The line is: "Catherine is licking her wounds, which is understandable, but unfortunately reflects badly on the Priory." Get it? Our concern is that she is letting the Priory down. Say it in a burst of anxious confidence. It'll spread like wildfire.'

'Good thinking, Agnes.'

'Bit tame, though,' Beatrice commented. 'No more than our usual stuff. And I reckon it's such a snub, she deserves something more dramatic.'

'Such as?' Agnes demanded.

'Don't know yet, do I? But I'll think of something.'

'Good. But we mustn't waste time. Agnes's plan is well worth implementing. Let us know what you come up with, Beatrice. Come on, everybody: there's work to be done. I want everywhere to be absolutely immaculate by tomorrow.'

* * * *

'You've got a smashing little bum, Hopeless,' said Beatrice with calculated flattery.

'Oh, do you think so? Why?'

'It's round and downy . . . like a strongly indented peach.'

Hope was entranced, but quickly recalled her manners. 'Yours is pretty good, too.'

Beatrice agreed absently. 'Hopeless, pet,' she went on, 'I wonder if you could do something extra specially clever.'

''Course I could.'

'How's your Welsh accent? Can you do one?'

'A Welsh accent? – indeed to goodness!'

'Mmm. Well, I've thought of a rather good plan.'

As Hope listened, it became clear that here was no ordinary scheme. More, much more, than simply spying, eavesdropping or asking a cunning question was required. She could start thinking in terms of a larger than usual recompense. 'I'm sure it could be done – if you're quite sure that's where she'll be.'

'I'll check it out about an hour before the ceremony. It'll be simple enough to go outside and see whether her curtains are still drawn.'

'And no one else will be about?'

'Everyone will be in the procession, except for one Sister remaining with the invalids in the hospital wing.'

Hope drew her fingers through Beatrice's long, fair hair. 'It'll take some nerve, but I'd do anything for you, Beattie.'

Beatrice took note of this and sat up.

'You're not going?'

'Got to. I'm on show tomorrow. Need my beauty sleep.'

'Not yet. Stay a bit longer.'

'Look, tomorrow night it'll all be over. I'll stay for hours tomorrow. Now, have you got every detail in there?' she asked, seizing Hope's head and shaking it.

'I won't let you down. And by the way, Beattie: you're in with Sister Clare, aren't you? Ask her to make Sister Prudence put me in charge of the souvenir prayer cards. I'm the best artist in our group, but they never let me be in charge of anything. It's not fair.'

'Do a good job tomorrow, and I'll see what I can do.'

* * * *

Catherine was feeling a little better; the nausea under control, the headache less dwelling. Sister Monica had been with her, had fed her with soup, cake and tea. Afterwards, she had helped her to the bathroom and put fresh sheets on her bed. So long as she could lie perfectly still between cool sheets with the air coming softly through the curtain crack, all would be well. Soon, very soon now, she would drift into sleep.

How good was Monica, with her coddling, motherly ways sustaining as manna to a would-be convalescent; and how intrinsically wise, for she could persuade the most painwracked and done-for of sufferers that life, after all, might be worth the candle. Catherine was almost ashamed to think that she proposed to harry the good soul, to make her thoroughly uncomfortable with intimations of something rotten in the state of Albion. Soothed and peaceful, she felt herself shrink from the idea. Strange how, on the morning after, even a nightmare supported by reason faltered a little, put its head on one side and suggested: 'Ah, go on – not worth it is it? – not the end of the world. Bit embarrassing, y'know – all this fuss you're making.' Cosy to give in, to take the best life had to offer – friendship, worship, beauty – to drink so deeply of these that the senses were sated, could absorb nothing further. Tea in the needle-work room – always a dainty occasion – with the Rockingham china, and Cecilia pouring, of course . . .

Catherine slept.

* * * *

When the bell summoning the sisters fell quiet, Hope stepped from her room. She gathered her skirts and ran through empty corridors until she could mount the flight of stairs leading to a wide landing overlooking the courtyard. Then she waited, her heart's drumming the only sound, only the dust moving in sunlight pouring through the glass of a stone-carved window. Below, the visitors were waiting on a patch of ground near the foot of the Albion Tower – covering the very spot, she thought idly, on which Sister Mary John had fallen. They waited, orders of service in hand. Hope waited, tingling with readiness.

The faint singing of a canticle reached her, and then came into view a simple cross borne by a sister; next, a smattering of visiting clergy, then the main body of women, their silver-grey robes flowing like smooth water, their pristine white coifs and cuffs startling as unblemished snow. Now, she raised her eager hands to the window catch. Stealthily, she released it and pushed the window wide.

The scene was set. Gathering her skirts, she raced to retrace her steps.

In the south wing, she thrust open a door, crying, 'Sister! Are you awake? I need your help, urgent now.'

Catherine woke with a start and as the voice penetrated her consciousness, turned her head towards the door.

Squinting through the dimness and seeing that Catherine was roused, Hope gabbled out the important information in her hastily practised Welsh accent. 'Sister Grace has got out. I found her on the landing over the courtyard – the ceremony caught her eye, I shouldn't wonder. Leaning out of the window she was. I tried to pull her away, didn't I? – but she won't budge. And I've Sister Ellen taken terrible poorly; I shall have to go back. Will you go to the landing for Grace, Sister? There's no one else here I can ask.'

'I'm . . . coming.'

Hope fled.

Catherine pulled on her robe, tied the girdle, and fastened the first button of her veil over her coif. She did not wait to put on shoes. Lurching through the corridors, she might have been at sea – levering herself from the walls, fighting for balance. 'It's just weakness,' she reassured herself. 'The headache has virtually gone.' Going upstairs, she hauled on the banister rail, and nearing the top, cried, 'Sister Grace, Sister Grace.' But the landing, when she arrived there, was deserted.

Her heart leaped as she took in the open window. She rushed to it and leaned out in dread, then raised herself on tiptoe to crane further; but no crumpled nun lay sprawled on the grass below. Across the courtyard the ceremony was in progress. A voice intoned ringingly. Squinting, she saw Beatrice – who could miss her? – and Margaret, and . . . yes, there was Angelica, sharing her order of service paper with Theresa. Then a nun, who had inclined her head confidingly towards her neighbour, suddenly looked up and stared at Catherine. It was Sister Agnes. And her neighbour, who was also staring up, was Sister Martha. It was an unreal moment, containing only that silent, long-held stare. When the bright light sickened her, she stepped back and fumbled with the catch to close the window.

Unsteadily, she went on – through the gallery above the cloister and into the corridor leading to the hospital. Her vision swam. Her head swelled with returning pain. From behind a door the sound of an easy voice reached her. She turned the door handle and staggered into the room.

Sister Luke was encouraging Sister Grace with her knitting. The knitting, which was to become a dishcloth, was done in string and was executed on very large pins. 'Over . . .

round . . . and through. Good girl! Why, it's Sister Catherine. I thought you were unwell, Sister. Whatever. . . ?' Sister Luke rose and hurried to the swaying figure in the doorway.

Catherine held her off. 'Where's your assistant? The Welsh nurse?'

'Sister Megan? Oh, I let her go to the ceremony. Thinking it over, I found I preferred to stay up here.' She sent an affectionate glance to the far end of the room where Sisters Brenda and Ellen sat with their sewing. 'Did you want something, Sister Catherine?'

'No,' Catherine said as blood rushed from her head.

Sister Luke caught her as she fell.

*   *   *   *

'I were sharing me order paper with Sister Agnes' – Martha mentioned this fact casually, but it was the most exciting feature of her story, for she had been tremendously flattered to find herself on chummy terms with so powerful a figure – 'when she suddenly whispers in me ear: "Can that be Sister Catherine at t'window?" And – d'you know? – it were 'er – staring down at us, cool as a cucumber. Or bold as brass you might say, seeing as how she'd made out she were too ill to gerrup for t'ceremony.'

A most satisfactory gasp erupted in the potting shed.

*   *   *   *

At that moment, in one of the laundry rooms, several sisters were clustered round Sister Maud. 'Honestly, if you don't believe me, ask Sister Imogen,' she was saying above the hiss and pop of a steam iron. 'It was Sister Imogen first saw her. She was so surprised, she gave me a nudge. "That surely can't be Sister Catherine looking out of the window," she whispered. I looked up and saw Sister Catherine as plain as I'm seeing you now.'

* * * *

Over the washing up (and there was plenty of it – over a hundred visitors to tea, not to mention the two dozen guests in residence), Sister Virginia was explaining how she had been diverted from the prayers of dedication that afternoon and found herself staring up into the face of the joint Directrix. 'Sister Clare was beside me. She suddenly gave this gasp. I followed her eyes, and there she was – Sister Catherine, leaning half out of the window. I could hardly believe it, because when Sister Monica came for her tray this morning, she said Sister Catherine was so poorly she had to lie still and keep her curtains closed . . .'

* * * *

Beatrice had slipped into the Art Room. She leaned over Hope's easel and murmured: 'Nice work. I've just had a word with Sister Clare about your promotion.'

Hope gazed up, thrilled.

Mouthing 'See you later' over her shoulder, Beatrice left.

* * * *

In the hospital, Sister Luke was applying a compress to Catherine's brow. 'Any better?' she asked anxiously.

Catherine could not reply.

93

13

After all, this is very pleasant, Anne thought, taking a japonaise finger from the dish. With her lips standing delicately from her teeth, she bit off the end of the cake. Sugary crumbs showered over her chest and lap. She noted where the larger crumbs fell so that later a moistened finger might convey them to her mouth. Cecilia, she recalled, had been sniffy about her coming here this afternoon, peeved, no doubt, because it was Anne whom Elizabeth had invited rather than her good self. Cecilia purported to despise the Blue Sitting Room. (Having no official right to enter it, she had made an inspection, nevertheless, the moment the room had been declared ready for use. 'So vulgar, my dear – all velour and tassels and deep pile carpet.') 'Well, I think it is delightful,' Anne imagined herself telling Cecilia later on. 'The chairs are the last word in comfort, and the colour scheme – keeping strictly to blues – is most restful.'

That the Blue Sitting Room should be restful was the precise intention of its creator. Elizabeth had explained Margaret's thinking. 'You see, the pressure of work on we Heads of Department is so great that a special place had to be set aside for us to relax in. The greater one's responsibility, the greater one's need to unwind in comfort, so that one is refreshed and able to continue performing effectively. And if the Heads of Department work well, the Priory as a whole benefits.' It had made sense to Elizabeth, and now, sampling the facilities, it made sense to Anne, too. Her view was reinforced by Elizabeth's recent confidence that she had decided to make Anne her deputy, thus conferring upon her the right to make free and grateful use of the sitting room.

When she had finished her cake and raised most of the crumbs from her habit, Anne licked her fingers daintily and reached for her teacup.

'Can I top you up, Sister?' the attendant sister hurried to ask.

'You may,' Anne kindly corrected her. 'Thank you.' She took her cup and settled back to sip its steaming contents.

It had been decided that the heads of the larger departments should appoint deputies to assist them with the increasing work-load. This had provoked lengthy and sophisticated deliberation. The likeliest candidates were not automatically chosen, for the coming of privileges had bred in those who enjoyed them a fierce desire to preserve them for their own use. Even Elizabeth, who in the early days of her elevation had wondered whether it was worth all the work and worry, now desired above all else to safeguard her position. A hardworking deputy was one thing; a challenging deputy quite another. Anne was a comfortable choice and would surprise no one, for Anne was her closest friend.

Surveying the occupants of the Blue Sitting Room, Anne was surprised to see one or two who were present on the same terms as herself. She was not surprised to see Sister Martha – on the contrary, it was always a jolt to recollect that Sister Lazarus and not Sister Martha was the Head Gardener; but she was surprised to see Sister Prudence of the Art Department with Sister Mark in tow, for Sister Mark was a mousy little thing with hardly a word to say for herself; surprised, too, that Sister Veronica of Accounts had not chosen as her deputy someone with more about her than Sister Faith. And Sister Imogen's choice of bland Sister Joy seemed a trifle eccentric. Still, people were getting along very well together, and Anne supposed that a convivial atmosphere could only assist the business of relaxing. For her part, it was not just the right to wallow in all this luxury she found so pleasing (her attention at this point was caught by the handy placing in the walls of push-button service bells), not at all; it was knowing how useful she could be to dear Elizabeth who, until now, had been most frightfully overworked.

* * * *

'Look, there is Sister Beatrice,' breathed Cecilia, suddenly halting and causing the tray of scones she was carrying to slither on their plates. 'Let's ask her to tea.'

'I dare say she'll go to tea in the Blue Sitting Room – she's eligible, as Margaret's chief aide.'

'Well, she's not *in* the Blue Sitting Room. She's out *there*.' (Cecilia and Monica had come to rest before a window overlooking the garden.) 'Go and ask her.'

'You know Elizabeth asked us to stop having tea parties in the work room. It's forbidden. We're just ordinary workers.'

'Monica! Don't be so . . .grubby.'

'Dear one, I'm only repeating what is said . . .'

'Well, phooee! If you won't ask her, I will – only I'm carrying the tray,' she pointed out piteously.

Monica considered the tray.

'Oh darling, I must be able to swank a little when they come back from their horrid Blue Room tea. If I can say we had a party, too . . .'

This glimpse of her friend's vulnerability so appalled Monica that she hastened without more ado to call through the garden door, 'Sister Beatrice! Will you take tea with us in the needlework room?'

Beatrice, with her fascinating smile, came slowly along the path.

It was the way, when she smiled, her cheeks pushed up and emphasized her feline eyes, thought the waiting Monica, trying to assess the precise nature of Beatrice's pulchritude.

'How nice,' Beatrice agreed affably. 'I do hope we shall use that pretty china again.'

96

'The Rockingham? Oh yes, we always use it – when it's just our group, you know.' Monica laughed deprecatingly. 'It belonged to Sister Cecilia's mother – of course, strictly speaking, it now belongs to the Priory.'

'Strictly speaking,' laughed Beatrice.

Cecilia, who had gone ahead to fill the kettle, was putting out the china when they arrived. 'Hello!' she cried gaily. 'How kind of you to come when far superior comforts are to be had elsewhere.'

'But not presented with your élan, Sister Cecilia.'

'Sister Beatrice was saying how pretty she thinks our china.'

'Then she shall come and use it as often as she likes. One lump or two, Beatrice, dear?'

* * * *

The beneficence of the Blue Sitting Room was not universally effective. Sister Lazarus sat edgily in her chair. Thrice she had declined tea and cake. 'No, no; I never partake between meals.' Martha had paused just long enough in her peroration to overhear her and mouth an explanation to her neighbour behind her teacup – 'Wobbly hands, hates to show herself up' – which Lazarus had lip-read easily. Resentment flooded her. This was Martha's first visit and already she had the manner of a long-standing habitué.

With an effort, Lazarus removed her eyes from Martha and covertly examined others in the room. The Sister Precentor was breaking the rules by talking shop with Sister Angelica. Lazarus deduced this from their looking at a score, and thought, that's musicians for you. Sister Prudence of the Art Department was another offender. It was done surreptitiously; she retained her sociable smile, but her words to Sister Clare were more redolent of complaint than relaxation. ' . . . that funny creature, Sister Hope. I know you recommended her . . . upset the whole group.' And Sister Clare was not enjoying the exchange. Her eyes slid furtively to the corners of the room.

When Sister Joan came in, Sister Clare sprang to her feet. 'Sister Joan – take my seat; I'm just leaving.'

The sisters by the fireplace were trying out new personae – one would have to call them Blue Sitting Room personae, Lazarus supposed, for she had never known them adopted by these particular sisters elsewhere. She listened enviously to their clever, competitive talk.

'Have you seen the carpet samples for the north wing?'

'No, but . . .'

'*I* have. Sister Imogen brought them round. I do hope we go for sage green.'

'Perhaps khaki would be safer. The way some sisters barge in through the north door.'

'Oh, she means *dirt*-coloured – hee-hee.'

'At least they're pulling their socks up in the kitchen. Breakfast has been on time . . .'

'But the supper on Thursday! Whatever was that concoction?'

'Apparently, the poor dears are trying to be adventurous . . .'

There was a sudden hush as the door opened and Margaret came in. She glanced appraisingly round the room, appeared satisfied, then launched into a noisy fuss – for she knew herself to be the centre of attention – over which cake to choose. Presently, she sat down and spoke civilly to her neighbours; and, with half an ear to the great one's conversation, the Blue Sitting Room's occupants gradually resumed their own.

* * * *

In the scullery, tension was building. Sister Kirsty, one of the redundant sisters directed for the time being to labour in the kitchen – always an obliging soul – had this afternoon evinced obliging helpfulness to an almost unbearable degree. 'No, no; I'll take that from you, Sister,' she had cried, seizing the slop bucket; and on her return from the yard had all but hurled the bucket to the floor, so avid was she to substitute her own body for Sister Michael's at the top of the step-ladder. 'Mind yourself now, Sister. Do come down and let me reach for it – my arms are longer.' And at the conclusion of every chore, 'What next?' she cried breathlessly.

It was driving them mad. It disturbed their rhythm. It appeared to imply, Sister Ruth considered darkly, that some people were getting past it.

Sister Rachel put on her 'voice', signalling to those in the know some meaning beyond the sense of her words. 'Sister Kirsty, it's time we were doing the vegetables. Go into the shed and weigh them out.'

'Right y'are, Sister,' Kirsty cried eagerly, dropping a teacloth in her haste to obey.

'Now look.'

'Sorry. There – no dirt on it.'

'Into the laundry basket, if you please.'

'Right. I'll be weighing the vegetables, then. Shan't be long.'

'As long as it takes to do the job properly, I trust.'

But Kirsty had gone. They exhaled vigorously.

'Thank goodness for that.' Sister Rachel pulled in her chin and raised her eyebrows. 'She's trying to worm her way in.'

They considered this over the washing and drying of baking tins, their hands slowing to their normal pace.

'Well, I hope Sister Fortuity doesn't fall for it,' Sister Michael said. 'It'd be a mistake to start letting any of that lot in permanent.'

'Yes, 'cos say the number of visitors dropped off: they might cut down on the kitchen staff.'

'But not us. We've got years of experience.'

They worked silently for some moments, but it became evident that this had failed to be entirely reassuring.

'You never know,' Sister Michael said thoughtfully. 'After all, who's to say who they'd move?'

Sister Rachel dried her hands on the roller towel. 'I think we ought to put Sister Fortuity straight. I mean, Sister Kirsty likes to give a good impression – but take that teacloth business . . .'

'She's slipshod,' said Sister Ruth. 'We'd better get the others to back us.'

* * * *

Catherine paused outside the Blue Sitting Room. She disapproved of it strongly, this setting apart of the most powerful. And the reasoning behind it did not impress her. 'But we all work hard – according to our individual abilities,' she had protested when the idea was first mooted during a Council meeting. 'And we all have a need for rest and recreation.'

'Of course,' Margaret had agreed reasonably. Then, raising her voice, she had launched into a diversionary tirade – her usual response to any attempt to argue with her. 'But don't, please, talk to me about "we all". Some people are working incredibly hard – for the benefit of everyone else, I might add. Yes, they *are* being encouraged to rest. Yes, a place *has* been set aside for them, and I think it is petty and small-minded in the extreme to begrudge it. Instead of stirring up envy it's a pity these moaners don't look at what's *right* with the Priory for a change. My goodness, just look at the improvements. Just look at the change in morale. Let's stop trying to stir up trouble for the sake of it, and start thinking *positively*.'

It was impossible to argue with her, Catherine concluded, for she would never stick to the premise. Rather, she scuttled for safety to a premise of her own instantaneous devising and clung to it so belligerently that her opponents were left open-mouthed and reeling.

Catherine had resolved to cold-shoulder the Blue Sitting Room. The Prioress, when acquainted with her decision, took exception to it. 'Do you want to lose every vestige of your popularity? Because you're going the right way about it, Sister. People can't abide a sulky-sides – and from where I'm sitting, that's what you sound like.'

Now, her heart knocking unpleasantly, Catherine opened the Blue Sitting Room door and went in.

Immediate silence. But unlike the silence attending

Margaret's entry, this was short-lived, buried by conversations resumed animatedly as if to deny the least idea of anyone having entered the room.

Except for Angelica, who called in a pleased way, 'Sit here. I'll pour you some tea.' She half-pushed her friend into her chair and elbowed the attendant sister from the teapot. 'I'll get it for Sister,' she insisted in a low voice, knowing it would embarrass Catherine to be formally waited upon.

Sister Theresa, the precentor, was also glad to see Catherine. 'Look, will you sing the solo part in this arrangement of Sister Angelica's? It's charming, and bang in the middle of your range. I must have something new for Sunday . . .'

Catherine, with Angelica perched on the arm of her chair humming in her ear, studied the score. 'All right,' she agreed, mindful of the Prioress's advice, though aware that her voice was off-form these days. Angelica and Theresa chatted across her. Their proximity was sheltering. She sipped her tea and broke small pieces from the cake Angelica had put in her lap. Eating, smiling, sometimes interjecting, her attention wandered.

Eventually, murmuring that she would return, she rose. Across the room, Sister Lazarus looked ill at ease; no one appeared to notice her. 'How are you, Sister Lazarus?' asked Catherine, sitting in friendly fashion upon the arm of Lazarus's chair. When no answer came, she went on, 'I must say the chrysanthemums look splendid in the chapel – especially the big golden blooms . . .'

Lazarus could hardly credit her misfortune. It had been a terrible afternoon – but to be sought out by Sister Catherine! It was as if failure had recognized and claimed failure. Lazarus looked wildly round. Yes, they were all watching – pretending otherwise, of course; but their darting looks were like knife-wounds. She struggled from her chair and hurried from the room.

'Duty calls,' said Martha, stretching.

Elizabeth looked enquiringly at Anne. From long practice, they achieved a simultaneous rising. Elizabeth, passing the chair where Catherine still sat, said kindly, 'Come and see the St Peter's reredos. We've hung it in the gallery to check the weighting. It's turned out well – though we had doubts at first, never having undertaken a modern design before. It's a sort of seascape – fish and shells and seaweed – quite daring.'

'Yes, do come and see what you think,' Anne encouraged sweetly.

Catherine, in a dream, followed them.

14

Agnes was addressing the company in the Green Sitting Room, a facility brought into use soon after the opening of the Blue Sitting Room. An unprepossessing figure, Agnes was nevertheless a popular speaker here, for the Green Sitting Room had been her idea. It was a room where the second rank of workers, those who could boast of five or more years continuous service in one of the flourishing areas of work, could gather and exchange views in a convivial and comfortable atmosphere. Needleworkers would learn how the Art Department fared, cooks hear the thinking of accountants, and thus would be engendered a feeling of everyone pulling together. Those eligible to use the Green Sitting Room took pride in their membership, and Sister Agnes was their favourite visitor. They heard her respectfully, disposed to agree with every word in advance.

Agnes's mode of delivery was not exciting; her tone was flat, her choice of phrase homely. Yet her message often contained breathtakingly vindictive asides aimed at named persons. Sister Agnes did not mince words.

'I suppose,' she was saying, 'Sister Catherine feels an extra sympathy for those with no particular job because, in a way, she's got no particular job. She excused herself from taking one because she doesn't like hard decisions. She's afraid of responsibility, and that's her problem. But if she starts interfering with the rest of us who have to do the jobs she can't or won't do, then that could get dangerous. People understand what we're doing and they want us to get on with it.'

'Hear! Hear!' they cried, as Agnes sat down.

By the door, Beatrice, who had been commissioned by Margaret to keep an eye on what Agnes got up to, smiled and slipped away.

* * * *

In an anteroom off the Chapter House, Margaret was talking to the Forward Planning Committee. 'Beatrice shouldn't be long,' she announced, glancing at her watch. 'I want us to give her a nice hand when she arrives, because she's brought off a magnificent coup – two large gifts in as many months. She really is making a tremendous success of liaising with the visitors. But of course, she has charm, and they're so thrilled to be talking to the heroine of the Albion Tower incident; particularly the men – well, I suppose men do warm to bravery, and Beatrice has certainly got plenty of that commodity . . . Ah, here she is. We were just talking about you.'

'Well, don't stop.' Beatrice beamed, and they broke into gentle applause.

'Well done, Beatrice. We're proud of you. Now, as I was saying, our latest benefactor – the gentleman in room eleven by the way; please be especially gracious in your dealings with him – proposes to hand over the cheque this afternoon. I've got to go and brief the Prioress in a minute. She's giving him tea . . .'

'But I thought you said "never again" after her teeth dropped out that time.'

'I know,' Margaret sighed. 'I shall be on tenterhooks. But where else in this place can one find decent china? Imogen, make sure it's not rock cakes again.'

'Talking about decent china,' Beatrice said thoughtfully. 'That old trout Cecilia has got some really fine stuff. Keeps it in the needlework room for the exclusive use of the snobs. It was her mother's. Of course, officially it belongs to the Priory; she's got no business hanging on to it.'

They had listened with sharp attention. Now there was a pause, broken by Margaret. 'Most interesting. Thank you, Beatrice. One for Agnes, I think. Ask her to look into it, will you? Now where were we?'

'About the gift,' put in Imogen. 'If there's more money coming in, isn't it time we did something about the east wing? Those cracks in the ceiling are looking ominous.'

'No, I don't think so.'

They darted looks at one another. Margaret's perpetual refusal to discuss repairs to the east wing contrasted strangely with her keenness to tackle every other deficiency.

'Let's get to the problem of the old vegetable fields. Joan has come up with something.'

Joan clapped a hand to her head. 'Mmm. Yes. Well, I've found someone at last who might be interested, but only if we include the field where we grow vegetables for the house. But I think we could strike a good deal, and it occurred to me – whoops!' In her excitement, an expressive gesture sent her notes flying and further explanation was accompanied by a scrabbling over the floor to retrieve them. 'Why not let him – ah, thank you – grow the vegetables for us, rather like – excuse me; under your foot – the deal we have with the milk? I've got the figures somewhere . . .'

The figures were found and passed around.

Clare was always impressed by Joan's cleverness. 'Brilliant idea. Saves all the bother, gives us a good return, and releases a few more people for the general work pool. As Sister Margaret says, we've got to keep resources flexible.'

'And I really do want to swell the numbers attending regular devotions,' said Margaret. 'It gives such a good impression. Mind you, I'm not sure everyone is getting the message about bowed heads and grave demeanours. Catherine's supposed to be responsible for our religious observance – what does the woman do with her time? Perhaps we should put someone in charge of decorum.'

'Me,' Beatrice suggested.

Margaret considered the matter. Beatrice, sprawling about in private, could seem almost disreputable. But there was no one to touch her for grace and style in public. 'If you could perhaps demonstrate what is required – rehearse them.'

'My pleasure.'

'Now, I can't wait any longer for Agnes. Think about Joan's idea. I believe you're doing some follow-up work on it, Clare? Well, we'll discuss it next time. And remember, Imogen: nothing too challenging for tea.'

When she had gone, Clare drew Beatrice to one side. 'I know you think highly of that Sister Hope, but Sister Prudence is at her wits' end with the woman. At my request she put her in charge of the souvenir prayer cards, but she's just not suitable. Sister Prudence says she's a perfect pest. Sorry, but I told her to use her judgement.'

'Fine,' Beatrice said easily. 'I was just impressed with her work, that's all.'

'Oh, apparently she's a good enough artist, but she upsets people.'

The door opened and Agnes came in.

'Too late, duckie. Business all over. That was a nice little talk you gave the plebs.'

'Yea,' said Agnes. 'Noticed you lapping it up.'

* * * *

Sister Kirsty, weighing out potatoes in the shed, was suddenly taken by a great wave of wistfulness. She put down the bowl and took up one livid pink, pockmarked potato. A patch of black earth had dried on it – the very earth Kirsty had until recently tended. She raised the potato to her nose and sniffed, then touched the earth with the tip of her tongue. She stared into the gloom and imagined sunlight on the crests of rain-sodden furrows, and the squelch of her feet in muddy pools between; smelled the sharp, nourishing tang of the steaming earth and felt hunger stir inside her.

All behind her now, she recalled sternly, and tossed back the potato. No use sorrowing. Steam these days smelled of detergent and she had better like it.

Quick footsteps tapped across the yard. Kirsty peeped out. It was Sister Fortuity, and she was alone.

'Sister!'

'Oh, my goodness.' Sister Fortuity clasped her throat.

'Have you – you know – thought about it?'

'Thought?'

'About me being kitchen staff – regular. You said you'd see about it.'

Sister Fortuity's face fell. 'I'm sorry to disappoint you, Sister, but I had a word with Sister Imogen and I'm afraid it's out of the question. It's not policy to attach people permanently now. They want things to be flexible, so that whatever needs doing takes priority. Oh, don't look so devastated. Look on the bright side – at least you get plenty of variety.'

'You don't know what it's like, Sister, not belonging.' Kirsty grabbed a fold of her skirt and began to knead it rapidly. 'It's terrible being passed from pillar to post. Some don't want you; they get mad 'cos you don't know their ways. Then Sister Imogen says go somewhere else and they put in a complaint 'cos you didn't have time to finish a job. Everyone looks down on you. They stop talking when you come in. You've no friends. And it's terrible waking up in the morning, not knowing where you'll be. It's a really terrible feeling that – a sort of pain; you don't want to get out of bed . . .'

'Come come, Sister. Aren't you over-dramatizing? And in any case . . .' She was about to repeat Sister Rachel's complaint about Sister Kirsty's slipshod ways, when she changed her mind. 'I'm pleased with your work,' she finished lamely.

So there was a gleam of hope? 'Oh then, if they change their minds. . . ?'

'Most unlikely, I fear.'

'I see. Thank you, Sister.'

She watched Sister Fortuity go, then slowly returned to the shed. For a few moments she stood very still; then, as blood rose and sang in her ears, crouched in a corner and let her hot tears come.

* * * *

Night air ruffled the sycamores. Beatrice unconsciously shivered and pressed closer to the windowpane, watching without expression the striptease taking place under the light bulb on the other side of the glass. She bit into an apple: bit, munched, watched.

The apple, the first of the season's Orange Pippins, had a stimulating acidity; the striptease on the other hand was bland and predictable. Think I'm getting bored with Hope, she decided after a time. Was this because she had discovered a new diversion? The question made her suck in her breath, for the very thought of her discovery – her new 'game' – made her nerve-ends sing. In the room, Hope unbuttoned her shift. Beatrice chewed and watched, and because the spectacle lacked zing, played through the game in her mind. There she was, gliding silver and white towards her victim – the gentleman in room eleven, perhaps – beauteous, desirable, and for ever out of reach. With demure innocence, she extended her hand and uttered soft words of greeting – had the journey been exhausting? – it was her fervent hope that the visit would prove restorative (this last accompanied by a hand pressed anxiously to the bed's counterpane, testing for restfulness). Then a walk across the room to sniff the bowl of flowers on the table, a turn, a reminder that visitors were most welcome at the sisters' devotions, a smile to show how the fairest blooms paled beside her loveliness. And all the time the knowledge of eyes unable to leave her, of a heart quickening . . . It was a thrill more sweet than any conjured by Hope's writhings.

Beatrice tossed away the apple core and reflected that it was perhaps just as well she had Hope to fall back on, for the game's sting depended upon her own inviolateness, and one could not stay in the clouds for ever.

She went silently along the path by other (decorously

curtained) windows. At the heavy oak door, she turned the handle and stepped inside.

In her room, Hope had drawn the curtains.

'I think you're losing your touch. That performance left me quite cold,' Beatrice grumbled, sitting down on the side of the bed.

'That's 'cos you're in a mood – I can always tell. Come here.'

Beatrice shoved her off and bent half-heartedly to undo her shoes. 'And another thing: why'd you have to mess up the new job I got for you – chucking your weight around – getting up people's noses?'

'I didn't.'

'Yes, you did. Apparently, you're not fit to be in charge. Don't ask me to put in any more words for you. You're going to be demoted, by the way.'

Hope began to pummel the bedclothes. 'No! They can't. Don't let them . . .'

'Shut up, you fool,' hissed Beatrice, smothering her with a hand. 'Do you want to raise the house?' And when Hope still struggled wildly: 'I won't let go till you're quiet. Ouch!'

Hope had got her teeth into a finger. Beatrice let her go and examined the wound for blood.

'Don't let them, Beatrice. You can make them do as you say.'

'Of course I can't. And I'm not going to damn well try.'

'Right, then.' Hope sat up and looked grim.

' "Right, then", what?'

'I'll make trouble.'

'You can't. No one'd believe your ravings. You're a well-known hysteric.'

Hope looked at her with glittering eyes. Then: 'But wouldn't they love to hear how we tricked Sister Catherine, indeed to goodness?'

15

'Come and have tea with us,' Monica said, slipping her arm through Catherine's. 'It's ages since you did, and you're looking peaky. Isn't she Cecilia?'

Cecilia came tripping down the corridor. She had just waved to Beatrice across the cloister and received a dazzling smile in return. 'Isn't she what?' she cried gaily.

'Looking peaky. I've asked her to tea.'

'Oh good. We'll tell Anne and Elizabeth.' (If the joint Directrix sanctioned tea in the needlework room, who were they to object?)

When they reached the needlework room, Cecilia went through to the gallery where tapestries were weighted. 'Elizabeth. Anne. Come on. We're going to have tea. And don't pull faces – Catherine wishes it.'

A sister, overhearing this, looked furtively about, then slipped away in search of Sister Agnes.

In the main workroom, they arranged themselves in easy chairs. 'Are you run down, do you think?' Monica asked, taking hold of Catherine's hand and examining it as if it might yield a clue to her state of health.

Cecilia, setting out the Rockingham tea service, gave a tiny sniff. Privately, she considered Catherine to be suffering from a prolonged bout of nose-out-of-joint. Catherine had once been the Priory's star, but Beatrice, with her brighter beauty and her courage, had eclipsed her. Cecilia had mentioned this theory to the Prioress, and for once the tiresome old thing had not argued with her. She leaned forward and raised the lid of the teapot, inserted a silver spoon and stirred.

'Were they pleased with the reredos at St Peter's?' Catherine asked.

'Oh, delighted,' enthused Elizabeth. 'It caused quite a stir. The publicity's bound to do us good.'

'Our order book's full to bursting already,' Anne said, taking her cup from Cecilia. 'Thank you, dear. I must say, this is nice. Horrid cups in the Blue Sitting Room, almost as thick as the refectory ones.'

They were murmuring their contentment with the thinness of the Rockingham china when the door opened and Agnes came quickly into the room. 'My, this is cosy.' She smiled – always an unnerving sight – and sat on the arm of Elizabeth's chair.

'Do you want something, Sister?' Cecilia enquired frostily.

'Oh, don't mind me. Just carry on.'

'Perhaps Sister Agnes would care for some tea,' Monica suggested nervously. 'I'll fetch another cup.'

'Now that would be nice.'

An awkward silence fell. Only Agnes appeared at ease, waiting calmly for her tea, taking it, remarking in a mild voice on its acceptability. 'I didn't know you got up to such things in the needlework room,' she commented with heavy jocularity.

Elizabeth rushed to explain. 'Usually we don't – rather – that is to say – Sister Anne and I go to the Blue Sitting Room, of course, but as Sister Catherine . . .' Her voice trailed away.

'Well, well,' said Agnes. And then, holding her cup at arm's length as if noticing it for the first time: 'This is very unusual. Tell me about it.'

'Rockingham,' snapped Cecilia.

'Indeed?'

'It was my mother's.'

'Was it? How interesting.'

'It was left to me.'

Agnes raised an eyebrow.

Catherine, beginning to see how the land lay, explained, 'Sister Cecilia gave it to the Priory, of course; but I suppose it was felt there was no particular use for it. I must say, I'm surprised, Sister Agnes, if you haven't seen it before because Sister Cecilia has often served her fellow sisters from these cups.'

'Perhaps she didn't cast her invitations too widely,' Agnes suggested, her mouth smirking, her eyes baleful.

'I've used the china on many occasions, and I know I'm not alone.'

'No doubt. Still, it's a pity more of us haven't had the pleasure. Though I suppose it's very old and shouldn't be used too often.'

'Quite,' encouraged Monica. 'It has to be washed very carefully. You insist on doing it yourself, don't you, Cecilia?'

Cecilia, who had turned pale, said nothing.

'I've just had an idea.' Agnes held her cup and saucer to the light and moved her head to view them from several angles. 'Wouldn't the service look splendid in a display cabinet? In the visitors' sitting room, perhaps. And then, when Sister Margaret had to entertain an important guest, it would be there to hand. Do you know, I think it's even prettier than the Reverend Mother's service?'

Cecilia opened her mouth, then closed it. This was no time to disparage the Prioress's Royal Worcester. But thinking of the Prioress, she gave a sigh of relief. 'The Reverend Mother wouldn't hear of it. She has often sat here and had her tea from these cups.'

'I'm not sure it's up to the Reverend Mother. The china belongs to the Priory; we shall have to see what the sisters in general think about it. Well, pleasant as it is sitting here chatting, I shall have to get on. Some of us have work to do, you know.'

Catherine hurried after her and detained her by the door. 'It is only a small thing. Is it worth causing distress?'

'Distress? Now why should it cause distress? Really, Sister Catherine, you seem to see distress everywhere these days.'

* * * *

Catherine and Cecilia were in the Prioress's room. Cecilia was too good to cry, and fearing herself in danger, ecshewed speech. Her forbearance impressed upon her companions the severity of her pain.

Catherine doubted whether her own presence could help matters. She had always viewed the inveterate tea ceremony with amusement, as an enjoyable little vanity of Cecilia's; but between these two old friends, she guessed, lay a deeper understanding; for them the tea parties stood for something – background, family, the past. Besides, it seemed she had lost favour with the Prioress, so her opinion would be of scant value. She pitied the Reverend Mother, who would not care to be publicly associated with a breach of their vows, however venial.

The Prioress, having had the difficulty explained to her, sat in disgruntled silence. Then: 'Never did like the cut of that one's jib,' she growled (the Prioress's father had been an admiral), and when her companions frowned enquiringly, barked, 'Sister Agnes.'

They considered this, each summoning a vision of Agnes's unpleasing features, and finding themselves no further forward, sighed.

'I don't know. Suppose they'll be after the Royal Worcester, next.' The Prioress spoke as if it were a progression in ascending order of merit.

Cecilia felt for her handkerchief and fiercely blew her nose.

'I suppose you haven't any bright ideas, Sister Catherine?'

'Only that you might appeal to Sister Margaret.'

'On what grounds?'

'You might broaden the question – beyond that of the china, I mean. Ask her to consider whether ends are always justified if the means cause distress. Plainly, the china is of limited importance to the Priory as a whole, compared with what it means to Sister Cecilia. But I think it would be wrong to limit an appeal for tolerance to this one case. There is also the issue of

113

some people being treated cavalierly, as if they are of less consequence than others. Could you get her to consider taking things more slowly, even modifying her objectives to mitigate unhappiness? She might consider whether so-called successes are just that, if they are bought with people's suffering. If only it could be admitted that people *are* suffering – it compounds the wrong done them to deny it. If we are all resolved to care about one another, we could find other paths, perhaps less direct, but wide enough to take us all.'

'We seem to be getting away from the china.'

'It would be encompassed by a more charitable attitude all round, without begging favour for one case. Do you see?'

The Prioress was not sure she did. But plainly an attempt must be made to explain the subtleties of life to these people. 'I suppose it comes down to what you've been used to,' she imagined herself saying patiently. 'When you're used to drinking from nice thin china, tea doesn't taste right in that thick stuff. I daresay there are people who feel just as strongly the other way round – who prefer something substantial . . .'

'Will you talk to Sister Margaret, Reverend Mother?'

'Oh, *will* you?' begged Cecilia, twisting her hankerchief.

'I suppose I must,' the Prioress conceded.

* * * *

'Come in.'

Fussily, Margaret closed the door, then came across the room with a businesslike air. The downward tilt of her head which obliged her to peer upwards, gave her a look of penetrating watchfulness – though, as the Prioress had noticed on previous occasions, she tended to avoid direct eye contact.

'Oh, how pretty,' Margaret remarked, extending a hand in passing to some rather nasty mauve chrysanthemums arranged in a vase this morning by Sister Lazarus. (The Prioress had spread old cloths extensively before allowing Lazarus to commence.) She took the chair indicated to her, having first pulled it nearer to her hostess's side.

How healthy the woman looks; she quite glows, the Prioress thought enviously, and at once her opening line ('I know Sister Cecilia can be a bit of a fuss-pot') flew out of her head.

Margaret took prompt advantage. 'I've brought something to show you.' She passed over a large, marbled notebook. 'Council Meeting minutes.'

'But . . .' began the Prioress, who had been present at many of the meetings.

'I want you to look at the past dozen or so voting figures. I've pencilled stars in the margin to guide you. Do look; you'll find them revealing.'

Dully, the Prioress turned the pages.

'A most striking consistency, don't you find?'

'Oh, very.'

'Every proposal passed without exception by a thumping majority. And the same tiny number voting against on each occasion. This does bring home the almost universal support I – er – my measures enjoy; have enjoyed for many, many months. The support for Cath – for the other side has been virtually negligible. In view of this, Reverend Mother, is it not time to come to a decision about the future? People do rather feel there is a quite unnecessary question mark hanging over it. A decision now would underline our success. And I am sure you agree we have been quite astonishingly successful?'

The Prioress clapped shut the notebook and handed it back. The woman had a nerve – instructing her to pronounce on the succession, no less! 'There are also religious considerations, however,' she said coldly.

'Of *course*,' breathed Margaret. 'I'm so glad you brought that up. It's something I hoped to discuss.'

'My province, I think,' snapped the Prioress, wondering how on earth she was to introduce the subject of Cecilia's tea service. 'I don't doubt you're doin' splendidly on the money side, but you may safely leave spiritual matters to me. Interestin' chap you brought to tea the other day,' she improvised desperately.

'Oh, but Reverend Mother, you should have told me you were unwell and I'd have put him off.'

'What?'

'A giddy turn, was it? I was *so sorry*. Never mind. In future, please don't hesitate to say if you're not quite the thing. I can manage very well in the visitors' drawing room – especially now we've got the Rockingham china – you know, that pretty stuff Sister Cecilia gave the Priory. You must come and see; it looks very fetching in the display cabinet.' She smiled, sank back a little and clasped her hands prayerfully. 'But we were discussing the religious aspect. You know, that's another thing I've found rather disappointing. When Catherine showed so little aptitude for the practical requirements of leadership, we suggested, and she agreed, that she take responsibility for improving our religious observance. It has proved an uphill task. I'm afraid I've had to ask Sister Beatrice to assist her. I know you will feel as strongly as I, because, as you said, spiritual matters are very much your concern. As a matter of fact, some of us have been considering how we can bring your role home to people – perhaps inaugurate a little ceremony in which you set us an example.'

'Example?' spluttered the Prioress fearfully.

'Sister Joan – such an inspirational thinker – came up with a touching suggestion. From your chair – we could move it to the centre of the chancel – you would ceremonially wash the feet of the postulants – perhaps one pair of feet would suffice – as a reminder to people of the virtue of humility, that however diverse the ways in which we are called upon to serve, no one is greater than the rest, for we are all equal in the sight of God.'

'Out of . . .' 'The question' were the words intended to complete her wrathful cry, but the Prioress's disobliging teeth prevented her from uttering them.

'Following Our Lord's example,' Margaret added, bowing her head. When she looked up, her eyes were moist. 'Moving, don't you think? Oh dear, is something wrong? Let me get you a drink.' She bustled to the sideboard, found a glass and filled it from a water jug. 'I should sip it slowly.'

The Prioress sipped it slowly. When she handed back the

glass she said plaintively, like a child, 'I need to rest. I do get rather stiff, you know.'

'Let me help you.' Tenderly, Margaret led her to the couch.

16

Outside, rain patting the window. Inside, the lulling hum and intermittent gurgle of water pipes. Sister Imogen, arranged in queenly state upon the seat of a large lavatory in her favourite cloakroom, required to empty neither bladder nor bowel. She required to think. Nevertheless, it was a naked haunch she had applied to the rosewood, for thus there could be no hint of duty evaded or of rest unofficially taken. Swift to denounce slacking in others, Sister Imogen could not have borne to admit the fault in herself, and with her knickers encircling her ankles, her conscience was perfectly clear as to the straightforward nature of her purpose.

Her thoughts, simmering incoherently, took some time to surface. She stared at a majestic basin, tracing the paths of veiny cracks, dwelling on a stain that no amount of rubbing with Vim would shift. 'Armitage Shanks,' she read thoughtfully, pondering the lettering above the overflow hole as if it were Holy Writ: 'Ar-mi-tage-Shanks.'

At length, the overflow hole and the inscription receded, were replaced loomingly by the face of Sister Clare. Sister Imogen glowered. Lately, Sister Clare had assumed a quite dominating position within the inner circle surrounding Sister Margaret. Allied with Sister Joan, she was chock-full of confidence, outlining and promoting their ideas. It was all very well for Sister Clare; she had the leisure in which to devise these ideas, having been given overall charge of the money-making departments, each supervised by a capable head of their own. Imogen's burden, on the other hand, could not be laid down so lightly. She was in charge of the 'consuming' departments – housekeeping and the general running of the place; there was no end to the demands upon these. And now Joan and Clare were set to win further accolades with their plan for the disposal of the old vegetable fields. But the production of vegetables for the house seemed to Imogen to impinge upon her territory – though Clare, in her quest for self-aggrandizement, was unlikely to be stayed by scrupulousness. How satisfying, then, thought Imogen, if she were to discover some crippling snag. Perhaps discussions with Sisters Martha and Fortuity would prove instructive. Encouraged, Sister Imogen rose, re-organized her clothing, and rinsed her hands under the basin tap.

* * * *

Over coffee cups in the office adjoining the kitchens, Sister Fortuity assessed the allure of home-grown vegetables. The type of visitor they proposed to encourage would expect no less from a tureen, she considered. Strengthened by this, Sister Imogen rose from her chair – but was detained.

'One moment, Sister . . . You know, I don't see why we shouldn't take on more regulars in the kitchen. It seems pointless relying so heavily on temporary staff, and it's not as if the work-load's likely to decrease. There's a particular sister I'd like to take on – such a keen little thing . . .' (Sister Fortuity had been unable to put from her mind the memory of Sister Kirsty pleading for a lowly position as if begging salvation.)

'It's not policy.'

'So you said. But I don't understand – not when the work's there to be done. Why rebuff those eager to do it?'

'To keep everyone on their toes. To make them see it's a privilege to have a permanent position. There was a lot of slackness, a lot of choosiness before. It's much better now, the attitude's improved, people are working harder and with no argument. And when Sister Margaret needs a good show in the chapel she can rely on it.'

'But it's causing great unhappiness.'

'Good grief! Here we are working day and night to put the Priory back on its feet' – Margaret's phrase came naturally to Imogen's lips – 'and people moan about unhappiness! If I weren't so busy I might get cross.'

Sister Fortuity sprang to her feet and began to stack the used coffee cups as if demonstrating the scarcity of her own leisure.

Imogen left, and made her way to the far greenhouse where Sister Martha proved even more enlightening than Sister Fortuity. 'Couldn't be done,' she declared, when the new plan was explained to her.

'But it works with the milk. We buy milk produced by cows grazed on our own land from the people who lease it.'

'Vegetables is different. Cows'll only give milk.' She waved a hand towards the vegetable field. 'That land'll grow owt. You can't tell your commercial grower to plant a few hundredweight of this and a few hundredweight of that. He'll plant a *field* of potatoes, a *field* of carrots. We can buy from what he produces, but to get a variety we'd have to buy from outside. You'll only get all home-grown if we keep a field for a kitchen garden.'

'I see,' cried Imogen.

Martha was surprised to see her take it so well.

* * * *

How to make the best use of her knowledge now engaged Imogen. She quickly rejected quiet words in the ears of Joan and Clare, lingered over the prospect of confiding in Agnes whom she rather admired; settled on the irresistible idea of an approach to the top.

Margaret, at first reluctant to relinquish Joan's brainwave, became anxious at the prospect of unsettling the visitors with vegetables of doubtful provenance. 'So Sister Martha thinks it can't be done. Well, she should know, and it's not as if she were protecting her own patch – her job has already changed. In fact, between you and me, I think the garden might do a lot better if Martha were head gardener and Lazarus deputy, instead of the other way round.'

'Or if Sister Lazarus gave up altogether,' Imogen put in daringly. 'She's got frightfully scatty lately.'

'Mmm. Not a bad idea. Look into it. Now, about the vegetables: I'll tell Joan and Clare to think again. And thank you, Imogen – that was a useful initiative on your part.'

Pink with pleasure, Imogen stole away to await developments, and, as a diversionary sideline, to propose retirement to Sister Lazarus.

* * * *

Clare was furious. There were too many 'Imogen says' in Margaret's new instructions. Joan, being used to the world's inability to accommodate theoretical ideas, gave in with an air of fatality. But Clare feared ascendancy passing to Imogen. 'I'm not at all convinced,' she declared.

Margaret was astounded. She was also, as ever, in a hurry. 'Fortunately, it's not necessary for you to be convinced,' she snapped from the doorway, 'just to do as you're told.'

As she hurried away to go over the accounts with Sister Veronica, a small doubt crept up on her. She took in the chief accountant's explanations, but with only half her attention. 'I don't know,' she suddenly burst out. 'Sister Martha's not one of the world's thinkers. Do something for me, will you Veronica? There's a problem about the disposal of the vegetable fields. I'd like you to investigate for me, on the quiet.'

* * * *

The potting shed housed a wild and wounded animal. Wooden slats, straining ironmongery, seemed unlikely to hold. Hearing the bellowing within, Sister Barbara looked fearfully across to

Sister Martha, who beckoned her to a further and safer distance.

Sister Lazarus was scarcely aware of being inside the potting shed. She was nowhere: a stranded creature. Tears poured from her eyes and ran into her mouth. She heaved air into her lungs in rib-breaking snatches to fuel convulsive, plangent howls.

When Sister Imogen had delivered the sentence, thoughts of her own ineffectualness hit her like blows. Standing like a found-out child before an accusing teacher, Lazarus had suddenly seen that while re-awakened disease had afflicted her limbs, only fear had paralysed her mind. A shot of courage might have saved her. Now it was too late; she was done for. She had stumbled towards the potting shed with her great weight of pent-up misery, and waited, trembling in the earthy dimness, for anger to bring her release. She pleaded for its arrival, enticed it with thoughts of Martha and Imogen, and when it came, gloried in it – pulled open drawers, hurled their contents to the wall; scuffed a row of pots from a shelf, beat them with a trowel to terracotta chips; grabbed a fork, stabbed open a sackful of compost, hurled dirt, sent the fork flying through the small window. And all the time howling, raging. Swirling earth mingled with effluence from her eyes and mouth.

The sound of shattering glass alerted other toilers. They joined Martha and Barbara. Warily, a small crowd approached the shed.

From among the scattered contents of the worktop drawer, Lazarus's hand alighted upon the budding knife. She opened the blade – and, as the steel flashed, opened her heart to a darting lust. Pain! She felt pain – others should feel it! Blood-red visions seared her mind's eye, of stabbings, slashings, gougings. She clenched the knife's handle and rushed from the shed.

At first she saw only Martha on the path; fat, open-mouthed Martha with her feet apart and her hand raised wardingly. 'Traitor! Scheming traitor!' shrieked a voice in her head. But then came a disturbance. Now she saw others – quite a crowd –

and Catherine pushing through. 'You,' she screamed, racing forward. And as she lunged with the knife: 'You should have *stopped her.*'

*   *   *   *

Faces, faces, peering faces; faces sorrowful, anxious, embarrassed.

Am I in Mercy's bed? Catherine wondered, raising her head. Mercy's or the one next to it, she decided, falling back on to the pillow. And did Mercy feel like this, an unprepossessing object in a showcase to be scrutinized, discussed and gratefully passed over? People visiting the injured, after some sympathetic preliminaries, fall back upon talk of themselves – not unnaturally, for the one in the bed has no energy to insist with voice or gesture: 'I am here, too. I exist.' In a way, I do not, thought Catherine; I am become, not one of life's participants, but an object that has had something done to it and requires counteraction.

Margaret's official face . . . 'Oh, how dreadful! But what a mercy it missed her eye. Tell me, Sister Luke, how is she? It's just shock, then, and the wound. How many stitches? I see. Splendid, splendid. One is relieved to find her in such capable hands.'

Angelica's face, urgent with concern . . . 'Catherine, oh, Catherine! I heard it was your eye – I was nearly sick – it didn't bear thinking about . . .'

Monica's anxious face . . . 'How awful for you, darling. Whatever came over the woman? She must be crazed. We couldn't believe it, could we, Cessy?'

Cecilia's face pinched with distaste . . . 'Going to be a nasty scar – right down her cheek. And it was Catherine's particular beauty – that unblemished look. I mean, it wouldn't be so catastrophic on a more mobile sort of beauty – like Beatrice's, for instance . . .'

'Cecilia! What a thing to say!'

What a thing, indeed, thought Catherine. Did Cecilia, in

123

some deep recess of her mind, imagine Beatrice wounded? And did this relieve the suspicion that Beatrice had betrayed her, that Agnes's surprising arrival during the tea party had not been accidental? Poor Cecilia!

And Martha's face, her sympathetic expression barely veiling an underlying complacency . . . 'For one mad moment I thought it were me she were after. But then she lunged at you – lucky, weren't it, that I managed to catch her arm, else she'd've had your eye out, 'cos that's where she were aiming. 'Course, thinking about it, it made more sense. Oh, I don't mean it made *sense* for her to knife anyone, but me – well, I'm her best friend, have been for years. She's come to depend on me, like – got shaky hands, y'know – drops things. Well, I shall stick by her – poor old Laz. I 'spect they'll more or less confine her from now on, but I'll see she don't want for comp'ny. I know how to handle her. 'Cos, between you and me, I've been carrying her, job-wise, for months. Oh yes; I've more or less run t'show. Now if Sister Imogen had let *me* put it to her – tactful, like – instead of coming right out wi'it . . .'

The dreary, self-satisfied voice droned on. Catherine experienced violent pity for Sister Lazarus, condemned to daily doses of it. It was no wonder she had gone mad. Oh! – the truth shone out like a beacon – it was *Martha* Lazarus had intended to wound. She, Catherine had jostled Martha, and Lazarus had been unable to redirect her passionate lunge. After all, she and Lazarus had had very little to do with one another, whereas the lives of Martha and Lazarus were inextricably woven together. Closeness does not always foster love.

It was an explanation which, for the moment, brought Catherine peace.

*   *   *   *

Catherine and Angelica crossed over the footbridge and entered the wood. ('Take someone with you,' Sister Luke had insisted, 'if go you must.')

Leaping ditches, dodging low branches and trailing briars,

choosing a route from a maze of criss-crossing paths, a lightness came over Catherine. She moved easily, dexterously among rooted things, the languorous odour of stillness touching her light, swift breath. They were moving towards Beechy Knob, a small hill near the wood's centre. Climbing the hill, Catherine imagined a bird's eye view, a breast-shaped mound of tree tops. At the summit there was a platform of well-drained ground, crumbly between the tree roots and full of cracks and gaps where unseen badgers dozed. She resolved to return one moonlit night, to stand still as a sentry and watch badgers' games.

'We came here in the snow. Was it last year?' Angelica asked.

'No. The year before.' (The year before, when there were merely hints of trouble ahead, but these easily dismissed, for the Reverend Mother and Sister Mercy had secured promises of funds from outside; the year before, when it was certain that life would go sweetly on, and Catherine would embody that unchanging continuity . . .)

'I remember,' Angelica was saying, 'that we climbed up here and stood looking through the trees. We saw a thousand white-topped branches like arms raised to the snow. And the stillness – it was a forest of petrified angels. Do you remember, Catherine? We gazed and gazed.'

'We were happy then,' said Catherine.

Angelica turned and looked at her, then quickly turned away. 'I don't see why we shouldn't be happy now,' she said, 'if we are sensible. All the things we love are still here to be enjoyed.'

'Not for everyone. How can we *enjoy* with misery in our midst – misery we can alter.'

'We can't alter . . . Anyway, I think you exaggerate. And I'm not going to argue about it.' She set off with a jolting downhill stride.

As the grey-clad figure descended, it struck Catherine – for a nun's habit confers anonymity – that it was herself leaving the wood and she, motionless and scarcely breathing, was rooted here eternally. Day and night, changing seasons, and still she remained, just being, with no possible power to affect events.

A bird flew startlingly from a tree overhead. Her heart leaped, she saw again the flash of metal, felt the blow, heard Lazarus's cry: 'You should have *stopped her.*'

Angelica had paused. She turned and called, 'Are you coming?'

'I've just remembered. Wait.' Catherine scrambled down, catching at tree trunks. 'I've remembered what Lazarus screamed. And she *was* aiming at me – I'd half thought she meant to attack Martha. "You should have stopped her" – that's what she yelled: she meant I should have stopped Margaret.'

Angelica frowned. 'Catherine – for your sake, for my sake, for all our sakes – will you please drop it?'

A draught cut through the trees. The wood turned darker.

'Come on, you've been out long enough.'

Catherine, feeling cumbersome, seemed almost to lumber after her.

* * * *

'How dare she?' Margaret fumed.

Beatrice looked in, observed Margaret's heightened colour, and made to withdraw.

'No, come in, Beatrice, and listen to this. Clare has taken it upon herself to circulate details of Joan's plan – you know, the one about the vegetable fields – among members of Council.'

'Cheeky,' Beatrice commented, joining Margaret, Agnes and Imogen at the table.

'And of course, the figures sound most attractive – far better than the return from letting the land for sheep grazing, for instance. But there's another side to this. If we're to serve our own vegetables – and we certainly are – we must hang on to that one key field, which puts the kibosh on letting the land for horticultural purposes, apparently. I put Veronica on to it, and it's all here in her report.' She passed a sheet of paper to

Beatrice. 'But if Clare's whipped up feeling, we're going to have to go over it all in Council. And they're so argumentative; and so slow to grasp the point – it's a wicked waste of time and effort. Blow the girl! I couldn't be more annoyed.'

'Show this to Clare.' Beatrice tapped the report. 'Better still, get Veronica to write one of those stiff letters she's so good at. "My dear Clare, I must caution you that should you persist in overstepping your brief . . ." '

'How would it be,' wondered Agnes, 'if Veronica's letter to Clare – containing a judicious ticking-off – somehow managed to circulate among Council members – sort of neutralizing our Clare's effort? Might save us a lot of grief.'

'Veronica wouldn't like it,' Beatrice mused, as if this were a further merit. 'She plays by the book.'

'We can handle it.'

'Oh, sure.'

Margaret rose. 'Well, I can see you have some excellent ideas. I shall ask Veronica to write to Clare – copies to me, of course. Then matters may proceed in your capable hands. You hardly need *me*,' she added with a self-deprecating smile, and slipped tactfully from the room.

'To the blind man, Imogen,' explained Agnes. And when Imogen still looked blank: 'A nod is as good as a wink.'

'Oh,' breathed Imogen. 'She meant "go ahead".'

'Right. Only she's got her position to think about. So: get your hot little hands on Veronica's letter, and take it from there. Off you go now, there's a good girl. I want a word with Beatrice.'

When the door closed, Beatrice swung her feet on to the table and settled back in her chair.

Agnes craned towards her and leered. 'Guess what I've been hearing.'

'Back off, will you? Your breath's particularly foul this morning.'

Agnes jerked away and looked fierce. 'I warned you about you and that Hope woman. She's started blabbing. You've upset her, it seems.'

'She'll calm down. I'm working on it.'

'Gossip. There is open gossip.' Agnes rapped the table. 'I may find I owe it to Margaret . . .'

Toppling her chair in her suddenness, Beatrice sprang to her feet. 'Go and boil your head, Agnes. I told you, I'm dealing with it.' With which she swept from the room.

17

Sister Veronica was a good and upright woman. It was not her fault if she had been placed on this earth minus an imagination or any other faculty capable of dealing with ambiguity. Faced with alternative explanations of some human or moral dilemma, she grew uneasy. 'But which is the *right* one?' was her cry. When the Priory's fortunes took a lurch towards disaster, she sought simply – but diligently – the most certain and rapid solution; and when this had come from Margaret (her then assistant in the accounting office) she had promoted it with courage and generosity, for there was nothing mean about Veronica. It brought her enormous satisfaction to see her erstwhile assistant as Directrix making sound the Priory's affairs. Any idea of plotting or deviousness behind the scenes was beyond her visualizing. Things were going well because – praise be to God – good sense and firm management prevailed. And when it was suggested that as a result some people had been made miserable and insecure, she accepted this as unfortunate but unavoidable; for as Margaret had said (and Margaret must know): 'There is no alternative.' Now the faithful soul was on her way to her one-time protégée's office, dutifully armed with copies of her letter to Clare.

'Veronica!' Margaret cried gladly, rising and walking across the room to a filing cabinet where she began to rummage through a drawer. 'Lovely to see you, but I've a thousand and one things to think about.'

'I've brought you the copies of my letter to Clare.'

'Mmm?'

'You asked for them, Margaret.'

'So I did. Thank you, dear. You're as meticulous as ever. If only the same could be said of others I have to deal with. Put them on my desk, will you?' She waved an arm abstractedly. 'Where *is* that report?'

Veronica laid the copies carefully on the desk. She stood back and regarded them doubtfully. 'You'll put them away?'

'Yes, yes. And thank you for being so prompt, Veronica. I'll try and pop in on you later; it's just that for the moment . . .'

'I know. You're busy. Well, I won't keep you. I hope this solves the difficulty.'

As she closed Margaret's door, she closed her mind to the incident, for her duty in the matter was done.

* * * *

Hope was clearing up in the Art Room. She rinsed and dried brushes and pens, rubbed at a stain on an easel, tidied cards and paper on a worktable. Now and then she took sly sideways steps to peep frowningly at her colleagues' work.

Outside in the dusk, Beatrice stood looking covertly in through the lighted window. She watched the scene intently, noting with interest her mounting dislike for Hope – it was a physical thing, like indigestion or an itchy scab. When Hope moved towards the door, she sped into action; ran inside and collided with her in the corridor.

'Hello stranger,' she said softly, gripping Hope's wrist with steely fingers.

Hope stifled a shriek.

'Get your cloak. We're going for a walk.'

'We are not!'

'How can I help you, if you won't talk to me? Your curtains are always drawn these nights, and I rather think you push your bed against the door. Now be a good child and get your cloak.'

'I've said all I've got to say.'

'But it's not as simple as you make out . . .' She paused and relinquished Hope's arm as a sister came towards them. 'Look, I'm doing my best; but we can't talk here.'

'Well . . . Oh all right. In two minutes. I'll meet you round the corner by the lilac tree.'

Waiting in the half-light, a feeling of depression came over Beatrice, for in truth she had nothing new to say to Hope. This was to be a final attempt to make her see reason. And if it fails, then what? she wondered. But no convincing solution came to mind, only vague and desperate notions.

'Shame for us not to be friends,' she remarked insincerely when Hope arrived.

'It's *you* who's not friends. If it were the other way round and you were the one pushed out of your job and made a fool of in front of everybody, I'd do something about it.'

'I keep telling you. There's nothing I *can* do.'

' 'Course there is. You're Margaret's chief aide. Margaret can do as she likes. Look, I'm not going to stand here arguing.'

'Let's walk, then.'

They began to walk down the path towards the back of the house.

'Let's get one thing straight,' said Beatrice. 'It wouldn't do either of us any good to bring Margaret into this.'

'It might. After all, it'd reflect badly on her if it got out, which it seems very likely to do. You and she have been friends for years; everyone knows that.'

'You're off your head.'

They had turned into the kitchen yard, and seeing the scullery door ajar and light flooding from the windows, hovered uncertainly by an outhouse.

'I hate it out here,' Hope said, shivering. 'Look, I meant what I said. Fix it so that I get my job back by the end of the week, or I'll tell everyone about us and how we tricked Sister Catherine.'

131

Beatrice controlled a desire to throttle her. Instead, she threw back her head and hissed: 'What was that?'

'What?' Hope asked sharply.

'That noise. Like a little creature scrabbling . . .'

Shrieking with terror, Hope gathered her skirts and raced from the yard.

Beatrice slipped into darkness behind the outhouse, out of sight of sisters running from the scullery to investigate. That was sheer self-indulgence getting you absolutely nowhere, she reproved herself, and lolled back against the wall, trying to summon constructive thought.

* * * *

The sisters clustered round Imogen were impressed.

'So you see,' Imogen was explaining, 'Sister Clare has overstepped the mark. Those figures she showed you were based on an inaccurate premise. It's all here in Sister Veronica's letter.'

'It's quite a ticking-off,' one sister commented, reading the letter and showing an understandable preference for its human rather than its statistical content.

'Mmm. Really puts her in her place,' said another, peering over her companion's shoulder.

'The point is,' Imogen said patiently, 'it'd be a waste of time hearing her going on about it in Council.'

'Quite. I say, Sister Anne, come and take a look at this. It's a really crushing rebuke from Sister Veronica to Sister Clare.'

'Yes, take a copy, Sister, and show it to the others in your department. If we can all agree in advance, there will be no need for Sister Clare to waste our time in Council.'

Anne, looking curiously at the sheet of paper pressed into her hands, ambled towards the door. 'My goodness, what a funny thing that Sister Clare is! If it were my letter, I shouldn't show it around,' she commented – and vanished, leaving behind her a rapt hush.

* * * *

Like all true budding powermongers (as opposed to those, like Imogen, who imagine they can secure a position at the heart of things by unswerving attention to their superiors' wishes), Clare had cultivated a following. Rather as the young Margaret had drawn Beatrice, Agnes and Joan, Clare inspired devotion in a group of young sisters and encouraged them to look to a time when Margaret would be Prioress and obliged in her turn to name a successor. Clare had spirit. 'Little Clare' was Margaret's affectionate term, denoting youth and energy rather than size, for Clare, in fact, was quite tall. She moved freely, almost impetuously, jumping up with excitement as an idea struck her, and spoke enthusiastically, whether in praise or scorn. Her eyes were blue, with a suggestion of a cast about them, her brows straight, her mouth wide, her chin firm. Clare was impressive, her close friends found.

It was one of these who brought her the news that Imogen was dispensing copies of Veronica's letter to all and sundry in the concourse outside the refectory. Clare and her friend went charging over there. Luckily for the peace of that neighbourhood, Imogen had gone, but a huddle of sisters remained, gleefully reading the letter.

Imogen be blowed, thought Clare. It was Sister Veronica, with her weighty authority, who had seriously undermined her. Clare dismissed her supporter and went alone to Veronica's office.

Veronica was utterly bewildered. It proved hard work conveying to her what had occurred. Then: 'There must be some explanation – an accident – a draught scattering Margaret's papers,' she conjured wildly. Her cheeks began to burn as the indelicacy of the situation struck her. 'I can only apologize, and assure you that it was entirely without my knowledge. In any case, I should not have approved. You have no doubt on that score, I trust?'

'No, not now. But what are we going to do? It can't just be left.'

'Indeed not. I shall investigate the matter at once.' Carrying her head high to belie her flaming cheeks, Veronica sailed off on a quest for enlightenment.

Sister Margaret was not available, a sister at the filing cabinet informed Veronica; she was escorting prospective visitors on a tour of the Priory.

'Then I shall wait for her,' Veronica declared, seating herself by Margaret's desk.

An hour later she was still there. Margaret came in and regarded her with annoyance. 'Not now, Veronica – I've simply masses of things to attend to . . .'

'This cannot wait,' Veronica said severely. 'The copies you requested of my letter to Sister Clare have been bandied about this Priory. I require an explanation.'

'Copies? Bandied about? I don't understand.'

Patiently, Veronica explained.

'Well, it's beyond me. I remember glancing at the letter on my desk – oh, and then I was called away. The pressure is quite daunting at times . . .'

'Then the copies were removed from your desk. I demand to know by whom. I intend to write again to Sister Clare expressing my regret for what has occurred, and I shall bring that letter to public notice. Furthermore, when the full circumstances are known, I shall insist that they also be made public.'

Margaret stared lovingly at the floor, waved her head sadly from side to side and said in a sincere low voice, 'Believe me, Veronica, I, too, am devastated by this impropriety. I shall investigate, and if I discover wrongdoing, the culprit shall not go unpunished. No stone shall remain unturned – you have my word on that.'

Veronica returned to her office to compose a second letter to Clare.

*   *   *   *

It was teatime in the Blue Sitting Room. Centrally seated were

134

Sisters Anne and Elizabeth who, between sips, were pronouncing as they found.

'Shocking,' said Anne. 'An appalling breach of good manners. And to think they pressed the thing into my hands!'

'How I feel for Sister Veronica. She is the last person to be associated with loutish behaviour,' Elizabeth declared.

Gradually, other sisters were drawn in, for Sisters Anne and Elizabeth knew how to behave; however tempted, they would never slide from their lofty code; and so, in matters of propriety, where hopes of being similarly well regarded were entertained, it was from Anne and Elizabeth (and Monica and Cecilia) that people took their cue.

'I must say, I went hot and cold when I heard about it.'

'Ghastly for Sister Veronica.'

'And for Sister Clare. I'm glad I didn't read the thing.'

'It's unheard of.'

'It lowers the tone. I just hope something is done about it.'

Agnes dropped four sugar lumps into her cup and strolled over to join them. 'Something the matter?' she inquired sympathetically, and was soon tut-tutting with the rest.

*   *   *   *

Later:

'But . . . But . . .' spluttered Imogen, drowning in Agnes's easy chair, 'you said, "A nod's as good as a wink." You said . . .'

'Oh dear me! I hope you won't go and jump off the Albion Tower if I recommend it,' Agnes said humorously. 'We're all grown up here; we have to take responsibility for our actions. Now I daresay *your* action may turn out, in the long run, to have done us a bit of good. And due credit will then be given, of course. In the meantime, it's put us in a bit of a fix. Susceptibilities' – Agnes pronounced the word wryly – 'have been affronted – people are such tender plants. So it's up to you to get us off the hook. You do see?'

'Perhaps if I say I misunderstood . . .'

'Not good enough, I'm afraid. You see, you and I are just cogs in the wheel. The thing that matters is the whole machine – and as we all know, only Margaret can drive that. So not a hint of this can be allowed to touch her. No, I'm afraid you must be a good soldier and take it on the chin – every bit of it.'

'But what . . . how. . . ?'

'Resign from the Forward Planning Committee – a token sacrifice. Make a humble little speech to the Council regretting your indiscretion – you can say your enthusiasm carried you away, if you like, so long as you make it crystal clear you acted off your own bat.'

'But it doesn't seem *fair*.'

'My dear Imogen; when was life fair? Chin up. In a few months' time it'll be forgotten, then we'll heave a sigh of relief and come begging you to help us again.'

Silence – while Agnes flicked out a lazy doodle (so relaxed was she), and Imogen clasped, unclasped and reclasped her hands.

'It's the only way,' Agnes said, peering kindly over her half-moon spectacles. 'But as I said, it's only a temporary setback for you. In due course I dare say Margaret will want to show you her gratitude.'

'Well, I suppose, in that case . . .'

'That's the spirit. We'll say Friday's Council meeting for your speech of resignation, shall we?'

Imogen nodded.

'Fine. Close the door after you, there's a good girl.'

A few minutes later, Margaret came in and sat on the edge of Agnes's bed. 'Well?'

'Imogen will take the blame. And as a token of regret she'll resign from the Forward Planning Committee.'

Margaret blew out her breath.

'The beauty of it is, we can still put a veto on Clare bringing up the vegetable field thing,' Agnes pointed out.

'And you think the fuss'll die down?'

'Over the letter? Yes.'

'Good.' Margaret slapped her knees and rose. 'Well done, Agnes.'

'Just a minute, Margaret. I should sit down again, if I were you.' Agnes had begun a more forceful doodle. 'I'm afraid there's something else.'

18

Beatrice, having recently returned to her room from her bath, sat in her shift brushing her long, damp hair. As it dried, her hair began to separate, to flow out in a pale gold mass. Eventually, she rose, hid the hairbrush in a boxful of religious pamphlets at the bottom of a drawer, and went to the window where, by drawing the curtain back a short way, she effected a looking glass against the darkness. She studied her reflection intently, drew her hair forward, tossed it back, turned this way and that. Then she raised her hands and loosened the neck-tie of her shift and pulled it down over one shoulder. Quite distractingly lovely, she thought, turning a little, raising the bare shoulder to her mouth. After a moment's further contemplation, she sighed and closed the curtain.

A knocking jolted her; she sped across the floor and jammed the door shut. 'Who is it?'

'Joan.'

'What d'you want? I'm not decent. I've just come back from my bath.'

'Well, make yourself decent and come to Agnes's room. Margaret's waiting for you.'

While Joan was gone in search of Beatrice, Margaret and Agnes found nothing to say to one another. Agnes leaned over some papers on her desk. Margaret watched her and wondered for how long she had kept this information about Beatrice to herself. For the difficulty was that one never knew how far Agnes was working for the general good (as Margaret thought of work done for herself) and how far for Agnes. It would be like her to ferret out information and then store it away for her own purposes. And yet Margaret clearly recalled asking Agnes to warn her should anything be discovered concerning Beatrice. That Agnes had her uses, Margaret would not deny. There was no one to touch her when it came to dealing with people and situations – just as today she had 'fixed' Imogen. Like herself, Agnes was stout in combat and no respecter of persons. (One had to admire the way she had deflated that snob, Sister Cecilia.) But whether Agnes was entirely trustworthy – ah, that was another question. 'I've never really cared for her,' Margaret reflected ruefully. One could not feel warm about Agnes as one could about . . . But here she searched rapidly for a substitute and, with relief, fell upon Joan.

Joan was a sweetie, and absolutely loyal. Furthermore, she had an intellectual capacity that one simply reverenced. Sadly, Joan was unreliable when it came to the practicalities of life – as Joan herself – bless her – was swift to admit. 'I shall just have to make the best of it,' Margaret decided; 'balance Joan with Agnes and Agnes with Joan.'

The conclusion filled her with alarm. It lacked some vital component. She became hot and prickly under her robe and would have comprehensively scratched herself were she alone. The irritation weakened her resolve and she began to consider with regret those indispensable qualities of Beatrice's.

Beatrice, she saw, was sometimes possessed of genius. It was she who had taught Margaret to deepen her voice to an authoritative level – a refinement that would not have occurred to Margaret or Agnes or Joan. It was Beatrice who had shown her how to flash her eyes when under attack, thereby implying a commitment beyond her inquisitor's comprehension and causing the attack to seem thoroughly impertinent. And Margaret recalled Beatrice's incomparable performances: her daring on the night of the Albion Tower, her disarming recitation of a prayer to safely conclude a tricky meeting.

Where Margaret and Agnes could argue and batten, Beatrice could weaken an adversary's will with the sheer magnetism of her presence. People longed to admire her. Now we might have something there, thought Margaret, seizing on the hope that Beatrice might charm even this difficulty away. Oh, if only she could, for she was truly irreplaceable . . .

Joan returned to them. 'She's dressing – from her bath. Don't suppose she'll be long. Look: do you really need me here?'

'Yes, Joan, we do. I know this is very unpleasant, but you may be able to help.'

'I can't see how. Absolutely beyond my understanding.'

'It's beyond us all. That's why it will take a concerted effort to deal with it.'

'I've never felt entirely comfortable with Beatrice,' Joan grumbled.

In her room, Beatrice had pulled on her robe and hidden her hair in her veil. Her heart had begun to knock. 'Keep cool, love,' she urged herself, putting on her shoes. She breathed deeply once or twice, then set off along the corridor to Agnes's room.

'Well, well – the old firm,' she commented, entering. It was such a familiar scene: Agnes sitting at her desk, scribbling; Joan hunched in her chair, the ribby veins in her forehead twitchy as landed fish; Margaret sitting composedly on the side of the bed – though her cheeks were pinker than usual. She grabbed a pillow and flopped down on the rug. 'What's to do?' she asked amiably.

'Beatrice,' Margaret said, then sighed and began again. 'Beatrice, I could certainly do without this piece of nonsense at the present time.'

'The Clare thing, you mean?'

'I mean on top of the Clare thing. I mean the – um – Hope thing.' And her cheeks grew even rosier.

'Ah. That's too bad. I've been trying to keep the lid on that one.'

'We are not surprised,' said Joan.

'The point is – is there any truth in these ugly rumours?'

Beatrice looked at her pityingly. ' 'Fraid so. Sorry Mags, old thing. I'm presuming' – she looked to Agnes and Joan – 'that Hope's been hinting at an affair between her and me?'

They did not trouble to confirm it.

'I suppose these things – I've no way of knowing, of course; this is an entirely uneducated guess – I suppose these things can't very well be *proved*,' Joan suggested, thoroughly flustered.

They looked at her.

'So I suppose Beatrice could deny it. "Woman off her head" sort of thing.'

Agnes shook her head. 'Too many rumours flying around. A denial won't put a stop to them or close her mouth.'

'Then if Beatrice confessed and resigned from the Council. . . ?' Joan wondered.

Beatrice plucked at the rug. 'Trouble is . . .'

'Yes?'

'Trouble is, there's a bit more to it than that.'

'More? You mean, worse?' Margaret almost squeaked, her deep voice abandoned in her terror at the prospect of further, unimaginable scandal.

Beatrice took up the pillow and hugged it to her bosom. 'Remember the Service of Dedication at the Albion Tower? How Catherine was seen at the window? Well, it was Hope who helped me to fix that up. And don't look at me like that – you must have realized I had an accomplice.'

'Rather an unfortunate choice, though, wasn't it?' asked Agnes, who prided herself on the management of her own coterie. 'You must be hard up.'

'The point is, she's threatening to blab about it.'

'This is serious!' cried Margaret.

'Yes. It'd put Catherine in the clear.'

'Then it's vital we silence this woman. There must be something we can do.'

'We can't bribe her, if that's what you mean. She wants her job back, and Sister Prudence would resign rather than give it to her. In fact, it wouldn't surprise me if the entire department threw down their paintbrushes. Hope's a damn good artist, but she's not cut out to be in charge of people.'

Joan gripped the arms of her chair. 'I think I've got it,' she cried. 'You say she's a good artist, Beatrice?'

'Yes, even Sister Prudence allows that.'

'Well, why not recognize it? Let her work on her own producing small paintings of the place – a corner of the garden or cloister, or the old courtyard, the little bridge into the wood – the sort of souvenir picture a visitor might like to purchase. Present the idea as a mark of her expertise . . .'

'Gosh, yes. I think she'd like that. It'd make her feel important.'

'And she'd be out of everyone's way. Brilliant, Joan!' Margaret boomed. (They could tell from her voice that she had recovered.) 'Put it to her straight away.'

But Joan looked doubtful. 'I'm rather an ideas person.'

'I'll handle it,' Agnes said. 'I'll make her understand the job's hers for as long as she keeps her mouth shut. So – it appears we can breathe again.'

'It's going to be a testing time. We must just tough it out. And Beatrice, because of the rumours I think you must resign. Make a speech to the Council – Hope's not a member?'

'No, no.'

'Thank Heaven for that. Admit only that you have inadvertently aroused – um – feelings, and propose to take a back seat as a mark of penitence – and to save me from embarrassment, of course.'

'Penitence,' repeated Beatrice, savouring the word. 'Don't worry. I'll do it beautifully . . .'

'And then, in the New Year perhaps, I shall reinstate you. As a mark of forgiveness I shall allow you to make a fresh start.'

'That's really big of you, Margaret,' Beatrice said, trying a new humble voice.

'And you really think we'll be all right?' Joan asked anxiously.

'If we keep our nerve. As I said – tough it out. Now, for goodness' sake let's get some sleep.'

19

'It was dreadful. I was ashamed,' confessed Anne.

'Quite appalling,' Elizabeth agreed.

'It is not the way we in this Priory behave.' Cecilia turned in her chair to look directly at Catherine. 'Go and speak to the Reverend Mother. It has been a hard job, I know, to capture her interest lately, but this news will jolt her. The Priory has been disgraced.'

Outrage was not confined to the Needlework Room; all over the Priory sisters were muttering or voicing disquiet openly, for nothing like it, they assured one another, had been known to happen before. They could recall the odd tiff perhaps, and an occasional breast-beating in public or resignation on the grounds of ill-health, but these had been single incidents occurring rarely and never to the detriment of Council (which was an orderly institution existing chiefly to confer the dignity of assent on decisions already taken elsewhere – by the Prioress, the Directrix and their close associates). Yet during today's meeting, within the space of one hour, two sisters had confessed to wrongdoing and tendered resignations (Beatrice and Imogen) and one (Clare) had stormed out in a huff.

'Yes, Catherine, I think you must,' Monica said regretfully.

'I'm not sure I can.'

'Oh, but . . .'

'You must! The feeling is tremendous.'

'And you are joint Directrix.'

'Sister Margaret must resign.'

'Sister Margaret, I am sure, will not resign.'

'Then the Prioress must dismiss her.'

'That is for the Reverend Mother.' Catherine rose to her feet, thinking, I cannot be seen rushing to take advantage of Margaret's discomfort. 'If I'm sent for, I'm ready,' she added. 'But you four have always been close to the Reverend Mother; if you feel strongly, go and tell her, it will be better coming from you.'

In the corridor outside the Needlework Room, Christa was waiting.

'We want to talk to you,' Christa said, seizing Catherine's arm and leading her away.

Six young sisters were crowded into Christa's room, perched on the bed or squatting on the floor or leaning upright against the wall. The one easy chair they had reserved for Catherine. She sat in it uneasily, feeling their eyes upon her.

'What,' Christa demanded, 'are you going to do? This is our best chance yet to stop her.'

The words, reminiscent of Lazarus's accusation, 'You should have stopped her', came as a shock. Unconsciously, she touched her scarred cheek.

Reading this as a sign of war-weariness, they rushed to be encouraging: 'Most people will be behind you now.' – 'They're outraged by the trickery and back-stabbing.' – 'Sister Margaret's really up against it.'

'Then I propose that everyone who feels strongly, says so – to the Reverend Mother, to Sister Margaret herself. When I'm required, the Reverend Mother will send for me.'

They looked at her in disbelief.

'Do you really imagine it'll be as easy as that?' Christa asked. 'You think Sister Margaret will yield without a gigantic fight? I can tell you, she'll have to be toppled. Pushed.'

Catherine stared at the crucifix on the wall. 'You see,' she began diffidently, 'I've tried. I've argued for a slower, more sensitive course. I've appealed to people's consciences, described people's suffering. As a result the Reverend Mother now entertains doubts as to my fitness. I can't "push" and "topple" as you suggest; it's not in my nature.'

There was a moment when they all spoke at once. Eventually, Christa's voice prevailed. 'The point is, *you* have an advantage over the rest of us. You are joint Directrix and have the power to do things.'

'To do what?'

Christa spread her hands. 'Call one of those briefing meetings – Sister Margaret calls them whenever she wants to rally opinion behind her. Why shouldn't you?'

Catherine was astounded. It was suggested that she seize her enemy's favourite weapon and use it against her. 'But these meetings were her creation . . .'

'So they're there to be used. Use them. Call her bluff. Announce a meeting to allow people to voice their dismay and decide what they want to do about it. It would be perfectly open and above board. Who could object? You are still of the same mind, I take it – that Sister Margaret's methods are causing distress and should be opposed?'

'Of course . . .'

'Well, then. *We* can't call a meeting. How can you refuse?'

Catherine saw she could not.

*   *   *   *

If I'm not very careful, Catherine thought, I shall fall between two stools. Cecilia and Co. wished her to rid them of ugly scenes and horrid behaviour; Christa, however innocently she presented it, was urging her towards a *putsch*. She walked through the night-filled cloister where a dry leaf scuttled in the darting wind, and imagined the consternation in Margaret's camp tomorrow when they learned of the meeting. Clare, Imogen and Beatrice would rally to Margaret, whatever the difficulties, and Joan and Agnes would gear themselves to be razor-sharp. Margaret would be full of fury, but would hide it well. I should not think of these things, only of the Priory,

Catherine remonstrated with herself. Even so, Christa was right to see that fallings out in the opposing camp gave them an opportunity. 'Let me use it well,' she prayed.

Music was coming softly from the chapel. Light shone in the organ loft. Catherine hesitated on the steps, leaned against the wall and closed her eyes. Her heart joined with the prelude's chorale theme – 'Jesu joy of man's desiring' – and she became lax with longing for amity and peace.

When the prelude ended she drove its echo from her ears, stiffened her resolve and continued on her way to her room.

* * * *

A day of rain. The sort of day, Catherine reflected, staring out at the courtyard where brimming puddles merged to form a shallow lake, when the story of Noah seemed not altogether fabulous. She turned from the window and went on towards the refectory, dreading the closeness of eighty damp nuns and the odour of faintly steaming serge; trying to repress the thought that, had fate been kind, the day would be bright and bracing.

Margaret was already seated in her usual dominating position on the dais facing the rows of chairs. I suppose I ought to sit up here when *she* has called the meeting, Catherine thought, learning the lesson tardily. She nodded to Margaret and pulled up a chair for herself.

'I do hope this won't take long,' Margaret said. 'My time is precious. This Priory does not run itself, you know.'

'Sisters,' called Catherine, and clapped her hands.

They shushed one another into silence.

'Many of you have expressed dismay over events at the last Council meeting. I think it would be healthy if we voiced our disquiet openly so that we can agree on future action. Now, who would like to speak?'

Sister Veronica made a short and dignified statement. She regretted what had occurred. She accepted Sister Imogen's apology. Above all, she exonerated Sister Margaret, whose behaviour had always been exemplary, and trusted that the unpleasantness would swiftly be forgotten so that Sister Margaret's good work might continue unhindered.

Margaret graciously inclined her head.

Well schooled, Sister Veronica, thought Catherine; and called, 'Anyone else?'

Sister Cecilia bobbed up. It was all very well for Sister Veronica, but some people looked back to a time when such things were unheard of. Before these new ideas of Sister Margaret's – which, incidentally, seemed to elevate financial considerations above all else – the sisters had always conducted their affairs with courtesy and integrity. How she deplored the new roughness of speech, the lack of deference to older colleagues, the brushing aside of cherished traditions. Why, when she was a young nun . . .

The point was eventually rescued by another senior sister, and a general deploring of present day behaviour broke out.

Sister Christa hovered between sitting and standing.

Not yet, Catherine's quick frown warned, for it would be unfortunate to frighten away the support of the establishment with a premature burst of radicalism. 'Well,' she broke in. 'I have noted your comments and will pass them on to the Reverend Mother. I am sure your anxieties are not lost on Sister Margaret . . .'

'Might I interject?' inquired Sister Agnes in her mildest manner. 'You know, Sister Cecilia spoke about a decline in our standards. She bases this decline, apparently, on one Council meeting . . .'

'I do not,' cried Cecilia. 'I complained about the general attitude – pushing people aside when they're no longer needed – treating senior sisters as if they were of no consequence – the bullying of the lay sisters . . .'

'Dear, dear. Are we to hear it all over again? If I might just get in a word? The point about the Council meeting is that those sisters who resigned did so after publicly admitting their fault. Now isn't that preferable to *hiding* one's faults and pretending to be blameless? How many of us know, for instance, about Sister Cecilia's little fault? Not many, I'll warrant, she took pretty good care of that. But for years and years she kept a very nice tea service belonging to the Priory for her own private use and enjoyment. Indeed, she would be using it still had she not been discovered. And I don't recall any public apology from *her*.'

The murmuring that had begun at the mention of Cecilia's 'fault', now grew bolder.

'I just think we should be careful before we start accusing one another of poor behaviour,' Agnes concluded reasonably.

Cecilia had turned pink. There was an uncomfortable shuffling. Catherine found herself at a loss.

Into the hiatus jumped Christa with a passionate denunciation of the system of allocating jobs. And when she paused for breath, Sister Kirsty wailed her agreement: 'You don't know where you are. It's awful. You don't seem to *belong*.'

'Not belong?' Margaret queried wrathfully. 'May I remind the young sister that she belongs to the Albion Priory? *This* is where she belongs. This is where we all belong. There can be no finer "belonging"!'

A burst of applause.

'Nevertheless,' Catherine insisted, 'within the community some people are less favourably placed than others. It has led to a new feeling of insecurity. While I acknowledge the firmer financial footing of the Priory, I do query that aspect of the new policy. It seems to me that when we come upon snags and disadvantages, we should make adjustments.' Cries of agreement. 'Furthermore, I'm disturbed that certain of us have been accorded quite unnecessary privileges. The system of the Blue and Green Sitting Rooms, for instance: they set people apart from one another, create divisions, distinguish the fortunate from the unfortunate as if good fortune were a virtue.'

'I must protest,' Agnes said.

But Margaret was already on her feet. 'I am sick and tired of people knocking success. Yes, there are problems. It would be wonderful if there were not. We are sorry if some people feel left out. But at a time when the Priory is fighting for its very survival, it is important to reward those who make a special effort. Have you *seen* the order book for our needlework? Have you *noticed* the massive increase in the work of the Art Department? Do you know that visitors are booking *six months ahead*? Can we please stop all this talk of problems and difficulties and start being glad that some of us are achieving things? Can we please applaud success?'

Members of the Blue and Green Sitting Rooms, who had begun to feel faintly alarmed, were happy to oblige.

Christa, red in the face, jumped to her feet and began to shout, stabbing the air with a forefinger to emphasize key words. 'Not a word, you notice, about *when* we shall do away with injustice. I doubt very much whether Sister Margaret *intends* to do away with injustice. I rather think injustice is part and parcel of her methods. What about the east wing? Sisters, the east wing is a scandal! I went there this morning and found water sheeting down the walls. It was damp, cold and quite disgraceful. Three lay sisters hospitalized already this winter – how many more, I wonder?'

'And we always prided ourselves on taking care of the lay sisters,' Sister Monica put in as Christa paused for breath.

'I think' – Catherine spoke directly to Margaret – 'you cannot ignore this feeling. Success is all very well, but worth precious little if it is got at the expense of our fellows. I put it to you – you must address the other side of the coin. If, as you indicate, we are prosperous, it is time to be generous. Many of us *do* see injustices – let's find a way of putting them right.' There were murmurs of agreement and Catherine, scenting victory, allowed her face and voice to relax. 'Now, I suggest we draw up a list of those items we feel we ought to tackle . . .'

Agnes, seeing that a diversion was required, jumped to her feet. 'Of course, Sister Catherine sees many things that are a mystery to the rest of us. Perhaps it does funny things to your eyesight watching others succeed where you've failed. And talking about generosity and nice feelings: where was Sister Catherine on the day of our triumph, the dedication of the restored Albion Tower? I'll tell you where. She was ill in bed. Not so ill, though, that her curiosity couldn't get the better of her. Several people saw Sister Catherine – too ill to join in our celebrations, mind – spying on us from an upstairs window. I think anyone as mean-spirited as that should think carefully before accusing other people.'

'Sister Catherine is *not* mean-spirited,' cried Sister Anne, her several chins quivering.

'And she was very ill that day,' Sister Luke confirmed. 'She was hallucinating. She thought Sister Megan had called on her for assistance . . .'

'I think,' Margaret said gravely, rising from her seat with a magisterial air, 'this has gone on quite long enough. There is work to be done, and I, for one, cannot squander precious time arguing. However' – she raised a hand detainingly – 'I have been attacked and' – her voice rose to drown a denial – 'I will defend myself. No,' she told a protesting Christa, 'you have had your say; please allow me to have mine. Sister Catherine said a very misleading thing – that we are now prosperous. We are not *yet*. We are working *towards* prosperity. If we falter now we shall fail. That is why I appeal to everyone: Summon the spirit we applauded on the night of the Albion Tower. We conquered adversity then. We shall do it again. Sister Beatrice . . . Where are you, Sister?'

Beatrice rose and hung her head.

'Hiding herself, you see,' Margaret pointed out unnecessarily but affectingly. 'Some of you witnessed her apology the other day – an apology for an *innocently* incurred mistake.' (Agnes gave Hope a hard look.) 'Let us not forget she was our heroine on that historic night. Sisters, words have been spoken in anger. I think it would be healing if Sister Beatrice now had the final word.'

'Thank you, Sister Margaret,' Beatrice all but whispered. 'Dear Sisters, there can be none so humble as I – a penitent – a sorrower. But I dedicate myself to this Priory, to the work that lies ahead; and I ask every one of you to join me. With God's help we shall succeed.'

'Amen!' roared Margaret, climbing down from the dais, going purposely to the door.

'Amen,' they echoed robustly, reluctantly or resentfully, according to their several tastes.

* * * *

'I can't tell you how I loathed it – loathed myself, almost. It offends my idea of *me*, all this arguing and scoring points.'

Catherine and Angelica were sharing the organ bench. Angelica had been playing a fugue. Catherine had feared to assume her former indulgence of being allowed to pull out the stops, for there was a forbidding quality about Angelica these days. Even so, she could not resist the chance to speak honestly to her closest friend.

'Why don't you give it up? If only you knew how unpleasant you look – how unpleasant you sound. It doesn't suit you. Do as I do – attend to your work. This is mine.' Lovingly, Angelica caressed the lower manual. 'I do a good job to the best of my ability. If everyone did the same there'd be less trouble.'

'You have a very rewarding job,' Catherine could not hold back from saying.

Angelica was silent. After a time she said in a tight voice, 'I understand you are responsible for our religious observance. Plenty to keep you occupied there, I should have thought. And so worthwhile.'

'Religion is more than observance.'

Angelica heaved a sigh and turned the pages of her music. 'There is no reasoning with you, Catherine. Now, please excuse me. I must practise this piece for my recital.'

A toccata poured out as Catherine went down the steps. Because it was late in the evening, Angelica chose light, thin stops, but the brilliance of the piece, the pattern of tumbling notes sharply and constantly punctuated by heavy dissonant chords, could not be muted. By the time she reached ground level, Catherine was absorbed, and turned into the chapel to hear it through. At one point Angelica broke off to practise a difficult passage on the pedals. Catherine marked her gathering expertise. Then the toccata resumed, pursuing climax and conclusion. Silence came joltingly. Catherine was about to steal away when a new piece began (she recognized it at once, for Angelica had composed it several years ago on the death of her teacher and predecessor). It was a quiet lament barely coating the stillness, an unaffected statement of grief. A middle passage rose to a pained crescendo, but soon returned to steadiness and the final farewell – a three-note phrase played again and again as though leave-taking were insupportable.

Sound merged imperceptibly with silence. Then, an abrupt clapping together of music books, the shutting of console doors; Angelica's feet clattering on the stairs, fading to nothingness.

We were such friends, thought Catherine. In the old days they would not have believed that difference could ever divide them, for their friendship assumed a coincidence of taste and view. Yet difference had grown as insurmountable as a prison wall. She imagined herself taking Angelica's advice – 'giving it up', becoming engrossed in perfecting the music and worship of the Priory. How easy it seemed. The idea drew her; she almost yearned for it, and saw that with practice her conscience need not be troubled, for what could be more estimable than working for the greater glory of God? And it came to her that were she not joint Directrix such a life could be hers at once. Suddenly, the prospect of defeat was alluring. In any case, she told herself, it was doubtful whether she could make a success of leadership, for it seemed an appetite for conflict was required, the sort of appetite enjoyed by Margaret and Agnes, that fired Christa's agitation. Margaret was the able one – let her be sole Directrix; let Catherine be free to pursue a path more suited to her temperament.

Having settled the future, she began to feel tranquil. But later, preparing for bed, doubt crept up on her. When she lay at last in the dark, she knew that Angelica was right to abandon her, for she could not give up the fight. An affronted sense of justice – as unwelcome to her as a physical affliction – would drive her on however hopeless and tasteless the task.

* * * *

Joan burst into Margaret's room clutching her head. 'That's torn it! The east wing's collapsed – the ceilings, anyway. Oh Margaret, I *begged* you to do something about it. Now we'll be blamed. And just as we've survived our greatest trial!'

'But this is splendid news – just what we needed!' cried Margaret, rising from her desk. 'I had begun to think the wretched place'd hold out for ever. This will get the lay sisters out. That wing is far too good for them – the best view in the Priory is to be had from those outer windows. Now we can do as we like with it.'

'But where are they to go?'

'I've got it all worked out. The rooms over the kitchens . . .'

'But they're in a dreadful condition . . .'

'It's a temporary measure. We'll turn them into proper living accommodation later on, once they understand they're not going back into the east wing. Now, I suppose people need rescuing?'

'It's chaos out there.'

'Quite. Well, come along.' Joan had sunk into a chair. 'Wait – I've an idea: fetch Sister Hope. She can do some sketches of the operation. Make sure she does one of me with my arm round some poor old dear. Pass me a blanket, Joan – I always think blankets look comforting. And you can write a stirring account of it for the *Bulletin* . . .' She was in the corridor now, and bursting into Agnes's room. 'Wake up, Agnes. The east wing's gone. Hurry. And bring Beatrice. This could be as good for us as saving the statue. What a godsend!'

PART THREE

20

'I don't feel I'm able,' protested the Prioress. 'These sharp winds play havoc with my sciatica.'

'Not if you're well wrapped up,' Catherine insisted, holding a cloak out in readiness.

'It'll do you good,' Cecilia said. 'You've been stuck in this room for weeks. Besides, what has happened to the lay sisters is truly dreadful, and how can you tackle Sister Margaret if you haven't seen it with your own eyes?'

'I can imagine it.'

'Really, Reverend Mother, you ought to come,' said Monica.

Grumbling to herself, she nevertheless allowed them to wrap her in the cloak and lead her into the draughty corridor. 'And the *stairs*,' she groaned when they loomed.

'We'll take them slowly,' Catherine said ruthlessly.

It was spring; the day bleak with a spiteful wind. The weather suited Catherine. Lately, her anger had grown like a cancer, nourishing not heat and passion but a bitter will to endure. She welcomed it, for it hardened her resolve. The soft temptations of a few months ago seemed remote as an infantile dream; now, a wide-awake world consumed her.

As restoration work on the east wing progressed, it became apparent that the heavy expenditure and elaborate refitting were not intended to compensate the lay sisters for past pain and inconvenience, but to lure yet more and even richer visitors. The abominable area over the kitchens now housing the lay sisters was treated to a coat of whitewash, an application of linoleum, the installation behind flimsy boarding of a couple of lavatories, basins and showers, and pronounced refurbished. 'It should be perfectly warm, being right over the Agas,' Margaret had said brightly.

'But a *dormitory*. There's no privacy,' Catherine and a few brave others had protested.

'When our financial position is secure we can consider a more luxurious arrangement. In the meantime it is absolutely vital that we live within our means.'

'But the huge sums being spent on the east wing . . .'

'Are an investment. The east wing will generate income which will allow us to do the things we would wish. But if we spend money like water now, we shall soon be back where we started. We must all make sacrifices.'

'Who must? The lay sisters?'

An impatient wave of the hand and she was gone. It was always the same; impossible to pin her down. Questions – 'Who?', 'When?' 'Why?' – were simply ignored. A daily issue of the *Bulletin* hammered out the right line and provided the well-placed and doing-nicely-thank-you with easy rejoinders to criticism. 'Throwing money at problems isn't the answer', 'These things take time', 'It's a question of priorities', the satisfied ones echoed gratefully.

* * * *

BULLETIN for the third of March.

'We are pleased to do our bit,' says Lay Sister Pauline.

'The dormitory is clean and bright and we are glad to be out of the old east wing,' Lay Sister Pauline said yesterday. 'Of course, it would be nice if we had separate rooms, but it is a question of priorities. Putting the Priory back on its feet must come first.'

155

It is good to hear that message getting through at last. And what a pity the whingers and moaners don't take a leaf out of Lay Sister Pauline's book! Do we want to go back to the bad old days of cadging our living? Of course not. We, the sisters of the Albion Priory, are made of sterner stuff. We intend to hold our heads high and earn our keep!'

'What a coup, Joan, getting a quote from that lay sister!'

'Yes, it was rather. She's a sensible sort. Agnes found her: she's put her in charge of the dormitory.'

'And it's an excellent piece of writing.'

'As a matter of fact, Margaret, Sister Verity wrote it. The *Bulletin's* become too much for me on my own . . .'

'You mean that stocky, fierce-looking woman?'

'I suppose she is a bit . . . But her heart's in the right place.'

'Indeed. I like her style – *committed*. We can use her, Joan.'

* * * *

The Prioress walked stiffly between the rows of beds. At the end of the room she looked back and grunted: 'Like a hospital.'

Cecilia shivered. 'Only, it isn't a hospital. This is where the poor things live.'

'Come and look at the bathrooms,' said Catherine. 'There are just two. Try the door.'

'Most insubstantial,' the Prioress found as the boarding trembled.

'And not enough room to swing a cat.' Cecilia waved her arms to demonstrate.

'And the draughts,' called Monica. 'Did you notice? Feel here.'

'And over here.'

Glumly, the Prioress felt. She had a nasty feeling that demands were about to be made. 'I hardly think Sister Margaret intends this as a permanent arrangement,' she said forestallingly.

'You will find she does. She talks vaguely of adding a few comforts, but with no indication of *when*. Personally, I find it outrageous that there are no plans for the lay sisters' return to the east wing.'

'Ah – now that may be impossible. I gather from Margaret that the rooms there are appointed in a very superior fashion, far beyond what is suitable for a nun – a bathroom attached to every bedroom, and there is a library, and a large sitting room . . .'

'Mmm. You see what she's done? She deliberately neglected the east wing so that it would collapse and an entirely new facility could be put in its place – one that fits in with her concepts. You do understand, Reverend Mother? She likes to preclude the tedious difficulty of opposition whenever she can.'

The Prioress detected an alarming note of sarcasm in Catherine's voice – alarming because out of character. She turned her face from the blazing eyes and recalled Margaret's hint about a certain irrationality in her co-Directrix's recent behaviour. Possibly, she had not exaggerated.

Cecilia prompted her, 'Reverend Mother, you will tackle Sister Margaret?'

'I shall talk to her, certainly,' she said huffily, and conceded as the cold penetrated her cloak, 'I am not heartened by what I have found.'

'We knew you could not be,' said Monica. 'This place would distress anyone of sensitivity.'

The Prioress made wings of her elbows. 'Now, if you would be so kind . . .'

Monica and Cecilia came forward to link arms with her and ease the painful journey back to her room.

*   *   *   *

'Well, I got her there,' Catherine reported. 'She was shocked, but whether she'll rouse herself to do anything . . .'

'Everyone should see it. There'd be an outcry,' Gabrielle – one of Christa's supporters – said.

'People will do their level best not to see it. If there's one thing I've learned it's that people avoid seeing what they don't want to see.'

'They should be made to see the dormitory,' Christa said.

'What do you suggest? We can't take the dormitory into the Blue and Green Sitting Rooms. And we can't drag their members into the dormitory. Of course, there have been a few honourable exceptions: the senior needlework sisters have visited the place – they're disgusted by it – so have Sisters Fortuity, Luke and Theresa; even Sister Veronica, I understand . . .'

They were walking in the garden, holding their cloaks tight to their bodies, oblivious of bravely flowering daffodils, of narcissus scent, of swelling buds and catkins overhead. They kept their eyes to the ground and envisaged the bleak dormitory scene.

Beyond the yew hedge and the greenhouses, Sister Kirsty stood gazing over the old vegetable fields. There I would be, she thought, cutting the first of the purple sprouting. She pictured herself bent double between the rows, her hands flying, her feet shuffling, her breath hot and wet on her face in the sharp March wind. Sister Beth working the far side of the field would call, 'Sticky going, isn't it?' or 'I'm just taking the centres out – side heads won't be ready for a day or two.' And every so often Sister Martha would yell, 'Time for us break. Come on, you two, or you'll fetch up like a couple of fish hooks.'

We were a team, thought Kirsty. Funny we didn't notice how happy we were.

'You with us, Sister, or what?'

Kirsty swung round. 'Oh – Sister Martha! I was just thinking: this time last year we were cutting the Purple Wonder.'

Martha came and stood beside her. 'So we were. Ah well, it's pastures new these days. Don't do to dwell . . .' She turned to Kirsty. 'I come t'ask you to go on planting them sweet-pea seedlings. I've gorra leave off for an hour – business indoors.' (A hollow feeling had attacked Martha; she felt in need of a restorative Blue Sitting Room tea.) 'You'll find stakes in t'shed.'

'Leave it to me, Sister. I say' – Kirsty caught Martha's arm to prevent her turning away – 'couldn't you ask again about me working permanent in the garden? You know you can rely on me. And Sister Beth, too. She's desperate to be settled again.'

Martha held up a hand. 'If it were up t'me, Sister . . . But it ain't. Don't ask me why they're agin it. I told Sister Imogen – you need proper gardeners in a garden, I said. Folks as know what's what. It wears me out having to stop and explain things to these newcomers every five minutes. There's some as don't know a trowel from a dibber, never mind a hoe from a rake. It's a blessed nuisance, Sister, I said.' Shaking her head at the inconvenience, she heaved her bulk round to face the house and screwed up her eyes to scan the niftiest route to the tea table. 'Have t'go or I'll be late. If I see Sister Imogen, I'll tackle her – but don't get your hopes up,' she advised, and went loping off along her chosen path. 'They want a flexible workforce, whatever that is when it's at home,' was the last Kirsty caught, but even out of earshot the flow continued from Martha's mouth.

By the garden wall, Kirsty discovered the sweet-pea patch marked out with lines of taut string. Nearby were boxes of seedlings and a trowel. On the far side of the garden, Sister Catherine and two other sisters were pacing. I wonder if she knows, thought Kirsty, then ran impulsively along the path.

'Sister Catherine – excuse me! – but I wondered if you knew we've got to move out of our rooms and into the annexe.'

'Who has?' Catherine asked, bewildered.

'All of us unattached ones. There's me and Sister Beth and five others in the north wing, and about a dozen in the south wing. Ten sisters with regular jobs are moving out of the annexe into the wings, which means we'll have to share two to a room.'

'But why? Who said so?'

'Sister Imogen told us this morning. She didn't say why, just that we've got to move our things after Evensong. It's going to make it really stick out – that we're the ones without a regular position. Why are they picking on us, Sister? I don't get it.'

'Oh, Sister Kirsty,' said Catherine, spreading her hands.

Gabrielle became alarmed for one of her friends. 'This'll affect Sister Rose – you know – used to be a cheesemaker.'

Catherine put her hand on Kirsty's arm. 'I'm going to look into it. Don't move your things until you've heard from me. The Reverend Mother said nothing about this when I saw her earlier,' she told Christa and Gabrielle. 'Come on, we'd better put a stop to it, or it'll be the lay sister saga all over again.'

Kirsty watched them go. 'If only she can,' she murmured wistfully.

* * * *

'Of course I agreed,' snapped the Prioress. 'A perfectly straightforward arrangement.'

She spat out the last three words, wild with herself for having adopted a ludicrous posture in an attempt to ease her sciatica, wild with Catherine for having discovered her thus. Painstakingly, the Prioress had built a wall of cushions upon the couch, in agony, had lowered her spine to the flat of the couch and raised her legs to lie over the cushion wall. (The tricky bit had been managing her skirt; she had gathered up a great knot of it and stuffed it between her knees.) All to no avail. Almost at once had come a knock at the door, and in her hurry to rise up, the cushions wall had collapsed and pain so seized her jolted limbs that she had fallen back unable to move a muscle. No doubt she presented a pitiful spectacle. It was so *unfair*. Tears pricked her eyes making her hot and watery. There was no end to the humiliation.

'How "straightforward"? Why should they move from their rooms to share accommodation in the annexe? What possible reason could there be?'

About this the Prioress was hazy. The chief thing she recalled from her interview with Margaret was a repetition of the proposal that she publicly wash some postulant's feet – a thing she wished fervently not to do. Passiontide would provide an appropriate opportunity for the ceremony, Margaret considered. By the Prioress's fevered reckoning that lay a mere three weeks away. The idea made her feel more than ever singled out for punishment and pain. 'I cannot recall her precise reason . . . As you see, I am suffering greatly. That excursion to the lay sisters' dormitory has inflamed my sciatica, as I warned you it would.'

Catherine ground her hands together and took in the scattered cushions. She bent to pick them up. 'Where would you like these?'

In her imagination the Prioress airily indicated that they might lie at the foot of the couch, rose to her feet with dignity and went to sit in her high-backed chair. Sadly, none of this could be enacted. 'Under m' knees,' she mumbled.

With some embarrassment, Catherine slid an arm under the bony limbs and inserted two cushions. 'Nothing under your head?'

'Perhaps one. A thin one.' For it seemed she was obliged to converse and would be at a disadvantage unless her head were raised.

'Is that comfortable?'

The Prioress grunted.

Catherine drew up a chair for herself and sat upon it. 'Now, whatever Margaret's stated reasons may have been, I should like to explain to you the consequences of moving the unattached sisters to the annexe.'

The Prioress sighed.

'All the sisters without permanent attachment to a place of work will now be isolated from the main body. They will lose the comforts – and the comforts are considerable these days – enjoyed by the majority. With the lay sisters, they will be set apart.'

'Margaret said nothing of that. Something to do with refurbishment . . . Or was it ease of organization?'

'Whatever. It really doesn't matter. The consequences will be as I have described, which, as Margaret is an intelligent woman, I think we must assume she intends.'

'But why should she intend any such thing?'

'I'll tell you. It is how her system works. She creates an unprivileged, helpless group at the bottom of the pile to keep others on their toes. Some of the Green Sitting Room lot would find themselves in that unfortunate position if, for example, she were to close down bee-keeping, or cut down the number of artists. And the more comfortable life becomes as a member of the Sitting Room, the more terrible becomes the prospect of losing it. So they praise Margaret to the skies to show their hearts are in the right place and reassure themselves by believing their privileges are thoroughly deserved. The more comforts they acquire, the more indispensable those comforts seem. The same goes for members of the Blue Sitting Room. She has built a pyramid of "success", with losers at the bottom to frighten people into line. People feel anxious to safeguard their own individual welfare, for it soon becomes clear that in order to improve the lot of the unfortunate ones, some of their privileges would have to go. People are no longer thinking of the general good, you see, but of what's best for themselves.'

In spite of her pain, the Prioress had listened. Indeed, so novel to her was Catherine's view of the status quo that for a moment she quite forgot her sciatica. And she found herself persuaded. After all, it explained the Sitting Room nonsense, and the strutting airs some senior sisters now gave themselves. The trouble was, the Prioress ruefully admitted, she would soon forget the reasoning behind it. She so quickly lost the thread these days. And anyway, what could she do – old, frail, pain-wracked? She had appointed Catherine to *do* things. 'What do you suggest?' she asked gruffly.

'That you forbid it. Prevent the move. Quickly. Now.'

Demands. Instructions. Do something about the lay sisters. Stop this move to the annexe. Make a spectacle of yourself washing some gel's great feet. Thinking of this last, the Prioress closed her eyes. It was the worst requirement because so glaringly public. She supposed she could bear to do something about the other – summon Margaret, perhaps; order her to think again. Well, no: it would forestall argument if she were to put her instruction in writing. But there would still be a fuss – uproar, even. Would the sisters obey their Prioress? Catherine, of course, would set an example, and Monica and Cecilia . . . Wait a minute! If she were to make Catherine sole Directrix there would be an end to Margaret's power. And Catherine, she'd wager ('Only a figure of speech, dear Lord'), would soon put a stop to tomfoolery with the postulants' feet. 'Do you know,' she asked, watching carefully for Catherine's reaction, 'they want me to wash the youngest postulant's feet – make a ceremony of it in the chapel?'

Utterly unexpected. Quite off the point. 'What?' Catherine cried.

'Margaret's idea. To symbolize how we are all equally great and equally humble in the sight of God – as if God needed to be reminded!'

'How typical!' Catherine exploded, leaping wrathfully to her feet. She began to pace about. 'She deliberately creates new inequalities, exploits those that already exist, then dreams up some sentimental symbol to pretend to the opposite. Talk about hypocrisy! You won't do it, of course,' she cried, returning to the couch and towering over it.

Fear showed in the Prioress's eyes.

'It's empty, meaningless, vulgar. In the present circum-stances it's a blasphemous lie.'

'She's trying to improve our spirituality . . .'

'Reverend Mother, I implore you – put a stop to this.' She fell to her knees and brought her hands down hard on the couch.

Jarred, the Prioress groaned. 'The slightest movement and I'm sick with pain. I can't *think* now. Perhaps . . . No; I couldn't stand the fuss, and I'm not sure they'd back us. Oh, how can I think when I'm suffering so?'

'Our Lord in His death agony thought of others.'

'Our Lord,' said the Prioress through gritted teeth, 'was divine.'

Catherine got off her knees and went to the window. In the courtyard below, groups of visitors were strolling. Two nuns hurried by, their heads bowed, their hands clasped in the manner demonstrated by Sister Beatrice.

'Please go,' said the Prioress.

'Will you tell Sister Margaret to stop this move to the annexe?'

'I shall pray for strength and guidance.'

Spent, Catherine left her.

21

'It's high time we isolated Catherine,' Margaret said.

Agnes had recently arrived in her office with details of Catherine's busy afternoon – how she had escorted the Prioress to the lay sisters' dormitory, aided and abetted by Sisters Cecilia and Monica; then taken part in an ambulatory conference with those hotheads and troublemakers, Sisters Christa and Gabrielle; and, finally, dashed to the Prioress's room where she had been closeted for nearly an hour.

'She's pretty isolated, already,' Agnes observed. 'Sister Angelica has very little to do with her – same goes for the Sister Precentor. It's just those two old needleworkers – and that radical lot, of course.'

With care, Margaret plucked a tiny scrap of fluff from her habit. 'I'm sure the threat she poses is minimal – more theoretical than actual, because the Reverend Mother wouldn't dare . . . All the same, she's a nuisance. She's become a rallying point for the malcontents. Without her they wouldn't have a hope. I'm tired of pussy-footing around the Sister Catherine factor. Let's get *tough*.'

*   *   *   *

Then most beautifully intoned the Sister Precentor: ' "Lighten our darkness, we beseech thee, O Lord; and by thy great mercy defend us from all perils and dangers of this night; for the love of thy only Son, our Saviour, Jesus Christ." '

Never had Kirsty sung 'Amen' so earnestly. 'Perils and dangers of this night' seemed particularly apt, for Sister Rose –the erstwhile cheesemaker, friend of Sisters Christa and Gabrielle – had proposed that they stage a protest. If Sister Catherine failed them (as seemed likely, for she had sent no message and Kirsty was almost sick with the struggle to repress her wilfully buoyant hopes) they would refuse to leave their rooms. And if their belongings were then packed for them in the laundry bags lent for the purpose by Sister Imogen, they would sit with their baggage in the north wing corridor and refuse to move to the annexe. With trepidation, Kirsty and Beth had agreed to the plan. None of the other disaffected sisters were likely to join them, for the thought of Sister Imogen's wrath was daunting; indeed, Kirsty secretly wondered whether her own courage would remain intact. During the hymn, she turned and looked hopelessly towards Sister Catherine whose lips seemed scarcely to move, so feeble was her participation.

Further prayers. Cecilia's knees creaked as she descended to her hassock. Not getting any younger, she warned herself, thinking of stiff joints and dodderiness – which put her in mind of the Reverend Mother. Not down for Evensong, she noted. Just as well, for the side pews were full of visitors, and ten to one the Prioress would ruin the atmosphere – drop prayerbook or spectacles, pronounce her part in the proceedings grudgingly. Much better that things be left to the Sister Precentor's deft mellifluousness. Cecilia put a clamp on her thoughts and began to concentrate, for this, the prayer of St Chrysostom, was her favourite.

' "Almighty God, who hast given us grace at this time with one accord to make our common supplications unto thee; and dost promise that when two or three are gathered together in thy Name thou wilt grant their requests:" '

(At this point, Cecilia usually allowed one or two small requests to hover discreetly in the forefront of her mind.)

' "Fulfil now, O Lord, the desires and petitions of thy servants, as may be most expedient for them;" '

(Pity about that last clause, Cecilia always felt.)

' ". . . granting us in this world knowledge of thy truth, and in the world to come life everlasting." '

'Amen,' warbled Cecilia, then waited with a beatific smile for the Grace.

The sisters, schooled by Beatrice, filed out charmingly.

Margaret took note of this and reflected that her friend had done a first-class job on them. At last, she thought, this Priory's getting to be an institution whose practices are becoming to God. The knowledge gave her deep satisfaction, for the establishment of those things which are pleasing to God had been her life's quest. Fortunately, Margaret had been blessed with an instinctive understanding of Godly preference. Not for her the breast-beating, heart-searching agony afflicting so many of the would-be holy. As a little girl she saw how she delighted her father with her obedient industry and calm good sense. Similarly, as an adult, she aimed to please her Heavenly Father, determined that when He looked down upon her it would be with untroubled eyes. All the more distressing, then, to discover her sisters in Christ less meticulous; their sloppy, self-indulgent habits had shamed her for her Lord's sake. Happily, she could now offer up another job well done – decorous, reverent conduct – she could almost glimpse the radiance . . .

But then, as she entered the cloister, she caught sight of Cecilia and recollected a more mundane task awaiting her attention. She hurried forward and took hold of Cecilia's arm.

Cecilia jerked back her head an inch or two, thus preserving that necessary distance between herself and a person of a lower social order. So ingrained in her was this habit that she performed it unconsciously, and few of those on the receiving end understood its significance, for her enquiries as to one's health or opinion of the weather were full of good-natured concern. Nevertheless, when poor taste on the part of the interrogated permitted a reply of some length, a blankness would veil her eyes shutting out her former interest, and her expression became severe. 'Dear, dear,' or 'Never mind,' she would interject firmly, backing away. Now, faced with a close-up of Margaret, she assumed a look of deep discouragement.

Margaret did not notice it. 'A word with you, Sister. There is a little job you can do for me – do, rather, for the Priory. Can you spare the time to step into my office?'

'I suppose I can,' Cecilia said reluctantly. 'Does now suit you? I've promised to visit poor Sister Lazarus later on.'

'Wonderful. Couldn't be more convenient. Come along.' Margaret led the way.

In her office, she waved grandly towards an armchair. 'Do sit down.'

Cecilia lowered herself cautiously.

Margaret arranged herself at her desk, leaned her forearms and clasped hands over it, craned forward. 'Yes. You have exactly the right qualifications.' (Cecilia's nose twitched suspiciously.) 'Our visitors come for peace and quiet, of course. Nevertheless, they do rather enjoy having a bit of a fuss made of them. I try to entertain them to tea at least once during their stay. Normally, I do the honours alone in the visitors' sitting room – sometimes upstairs with the Reverend Mother, but,' – Margaret lowered her voice confidingly – 'her *condition*, you know, and those rather unfortunate teeth. So I'm afraid the duty falls upon me. And the demands upon my time, Sister Cecilia, are simply endless. It suddenly came to me during Evensong. (Wasn't it a delightful service? The Sister Precentor has such an elevated tone – perhaps it was that put me in mind of you.) Sister Cecilia, I thought; the very person to relieve me of my little chore. No messy pourings-out from her! And, of course, she is used to handling the delicate Rockingham china. In Sister Cecilia's company the most retiring visitor will feel at ease, and the highest of the high quite at home. I shall make *her* responsible for entertaining the visitors to tea. What do you say?'

'Oh!' Cecilia feigned surprise. 'You are talking to me? I beg your pardon – I thought you were ruminating. Mmm. Well. It would have to be thought about.'

'Not for long, I hope. I can't stand indecision. Either the idea appeals to you, or it doesn't. It's a responsible position; I set great store on making our visitors feel at home. And naturally, it would mean membership of the Blue Sitting Room.' She paused for a full ten seconds, allowing Cecilia more than adequate opportunity to consider her proposal. 'Well, you disappoint me. I wonder whether Sister Monica would be interested?'

Cecilia's head began to wobble. 'I was about to get to Sister Monica. She and I are used to working together.' (Indeed, since their schooldays together, Monica had done much of Cecilia's work.)

Margaret clapped her head as if struck by a brainwave. 'Of course. The two of you. What an excellent idea, for sometimes there is quite a little crowd requiring tea. That's settled. You are both appointed.' She rose and went to clasp Cecilia's hand. 'And don't forget: this means you are both eligible for membership of the Blue Sitting Room.'

'As to that, I'm not sure we shall care for it,' Cecilia warned. 'Nasty thick china, I hear. Though I dare say we shall put in an appearance now and then – to be sociable, don't you know.'

* * * *

Cecilia's little feet scampered through the corridors. Just wait till she told Monica . . . Blow! Not in her room. Where was the woman? In the needlework room, perhaps.

Monica was indeed in the needlework room. She jumped guiltily when the door flew open, for she was engaged upon an illicit piece of work of her own – an embroidery depicting a milkmaid and her swain dallying in a flower-stippled meadow.

'Oh, you'll never guess, Monny!' Cecilia cried.

Monica rolled up her work and dutifully offered her friend her full attention. 'Then you had better tell me, Cecilia.'

Cecilia's face, flushed and shining, wore an expression

Monica remembered from their schooldays when Cecilia had wangled some treat or advantage for herself. And this was how she now presented Margaret's offer. She had crafted herself a victory. Her social poise, her classy superiority had been conceded and was to reconcile her with the beloved Rockingham china. 'In the end, you see, breeding tells. Apparently some of the visitors are more *our* sort of people. But I don't suppose the others will be too bad. In any case, *we* shall set the tone. Won't it be fun? I shall quite revel in it. And on the strength of our new responsibility we're to become members of the Blue Sitting Room – you can imagine how I let her know what sort of honour we think *that*. All the same, I shall enjoy breezing in and putting a few noses out of joint. That ghastly Sister Martha is forever throwing her Blue Sitting Room membership in my face. I dare say we won't mind it when there are no visitors to entertain. Oh, Monny – what a triumph!'

Oh dear, thought Monica, sensing danger in the proposal, hating to pour cold water on her friend's enthusiasm. 'It does sound rather attractive, but we shall have to go into it carefully. We'll ask Catherine first.'

'First? What first? I said we'd do it and that's that. Oh, don't worry – I know what you're thinking – but rest assured, I didn't show *eagerness*. Not at all, in fact I kept her dangling for quite a time. Ultimately I gave in, because we wouldn't have wanted her to change her mind, now would we?'

'You misunderstand me, Cessy. I suspect there may be more to this than meets the eye. Consider, dear, how we have urged people to go and see how the lay sisters are placed. We even took the Reverend Mother to the dormitory this afternoon. We have made an issue of it, and I don't suppose Sister Margaret is best pleased. This may be her way of buying our silence.'

'Rubbish!' Cecilia sprang to her feet. But Monica saw her eyes flicker with alarm and understood how her delightful new world had trembled. She watched pityingly as Cecilia marched upon the worktable and began to untidy a pile of paper patterns. 'I refuse to believe even Sister Margaret could be so devious. Really, Monica!'

170

When she turned and wandered back it was because, Monica guessed, some promising line of argument had occurred to her. 'No, I really believe the gel finds herself a little out of her depth, and she has had the honesty and good sense to pass the job on to those who are equal to every occasion. Give credit where it is due, if you please. Sister Margaret is a pain and a bore – I don't deny it; but in this I salute her judgement. It would be churlish of us to let her down. No, I am quite clear about it, Monica: it is our duty.' And she sank in triumph into her easy chair.

'Oh, Cessy!' Monica sighed, thinking what a burden it can be to know another too well. She had anticipated Cecilia's every thought, could have completed her every sentence. 'Well, at least let us tell Catherine what has occurred.'

'Tomorrow – or when we see her,' Cecilia said airily; then, bringing a note of vigorous virtue into her voice: 'Now we must go and visit Sister Lazarus. We promised.'

'So we did. And, dear one, do try not to talk *at* the poor creature. Be gentle. Try to draw her out.'

'But I do, Monica. I do my very best to be cheery and uplifting.'

* * * *

For the past two months, Imogen had entertained hope. Her longing to be taken back on to the Forward Planning Committee was so great she feared it showed in her face. She was afraid even to mention the Committee in case her voice cracked. When it was referred to in her hearing she went hot and lowered her head to hide her blushes. Recently, Margaret had congratulated her on her handling of the business of the lay sisters' accommodation. 'Your quiet good sense has seen us through what otherwise might have been a very tricky situation.' These were Margaret's very words. Imogen repeated them to herself every night on retiring and, when in need of a boost during the day, locked herself in her favourite cloakroom, sat on the rosewood lavatory seat and murmured them lingeringly. They must mean that forgiveness was nigh – forgiveness of her publicizing Sister Veronica's letter to Clare. They surely indicated how very much in Margaret's thoughts were Imogen's talents, and how sorely they were missed by the Forward Planning Committee. Thinking of this, Imogen stuffed her knuckles into her mouth to stifle an impatient scream. 'Soon; very soon, now,' she promised herself as she struggled to regain her composure.

But now, at half past eight on this Thursday evening in March, her hopes lay in ashes along the north wing corridor. At intervals on the brand new, blood-red carpet, Sisters Kirsty, Beth and Rose squatted with their bulging laundry bags, each outside what had been until an hour ago her room, and was now very definitely not her room but that of some other sister newly moved in from the annexe.

Sister Rose was their spokeswoman. Sisters Kirsty and Beth merely nodded or shook their heads and stared about them with fright-filled eyes. Sister Christa and others stood about in the corridor, lending their support. The sisters who had recently moved in from the annexe kept opening their doors, popping out their heads and indicating their willingness to return from whence they came.

'Stay where you are, and keep your doors closed,' Imogen commanded again and again.

But that did not budge the protesters. Whatever line she took, whether she cajoled or threatened, Imogen found they remained implacable. They would stay in the north wing corridor unless and until they were restored to their rooms.

'But your rooms are in the annexe now,' Imogen repeated wearily.

Not so, they insisted, and waited for Imogen's next move.

The redness of the carpet seemed to run and spread. The corridor rocked. Imogen expected the floor to give way, the walls to crumble, sulphur to seep in and choke them all; for Hell could not be far away. She was beside herself with impotent fury and dread lest Margaret should arrive and discover the impasse, when Sister Catherine appeared and began talking to Sister Christa in an undertone.

'Sister Catherine!' Imogen cried – and was relieved to hear the tight control of her voice. 'I trust you are here to lend your good offices to an immediate evacuation of this corridor. The sisters have accomodation waiting for them in the annexe.'

Sister Catherine, it appeared, intended to ignore her. She moved along the corridor to where Sister Kirsty was squatting, knelt down and questioned her.

Imogen, straining to hear, caught nothing. Near to her, Sisters Christa and Gabrielle were talking in rude, loud voices. Sister Catherine rose and went to speak to Sister Beth. At last she came to Imogen.

The corridor fell silent. Catherine looked hard into Imogen's eyes. 'They are doing as their conscience dictates. We must all do that,' she declared, and went quickly away.

Several sisters now disappeared into their rooms, and soon returned bearing rugs and blankets.

'Here you are, Sister Kirsty. Sleep on this.'

'And this'll do for you, Rose.'

'Sister Beth, take mine.'

'Good job we've got this new thick carpet on the floor.'

They were setting up camp like a bunch of eager Girl Guides.

Giddiness shook Imogen; she put a hand to the wall to steady herself, then turned and went to the end of the corridor, picking her way through the cinders of her dear, dead hopes.

* * * *

'All night?' You mean to say they stayed in the corridor *all night?*' Margaret was almost apoplectic. 'Whatever was Imogen thinking about? How could she allow it? And you say Catherine actually came and did nothing to stop it?'

'Gave it her blessing, more like.'

'Right. That does it. No holds barred from now on. I've been patient. I've put up with a lot of time-wasting nonsense. But now she'll discover what sort of fight she's got on her hands. Joan – the Bulletin. I want something – and make it crystal clear this time – to the effect that Catherine is stark staring mad.'

173

'Oh help, Margaret! I can hint at it – because I suppose approving of people sleeping in the corridor is hardly a rational response for someone in authority, is it? But I'm not a doctor. I can't state it as proven fact.'

'Oh, stop wittering, woman, and go and get Sister Verity. She'll know what I want. There are ways of saying these things. And Sister Verity says it with *punch*.'

Hurt and crestfallen, Joan went in search of Sister Verity.

'I must say, I'm disappointed in Imogen,' Margaret went on to complain to Agnes.

'There wasn't much she could do, apart from hoisting 'em over her shoulder and carrying 'em off to the annexe. Anyway, she had the presence of mind this morning to remove their belongings from the corridor while they were all at work. They'll find they have to go to the annexe tonight – unless they propose to stay in the clothes they've got on indefinitely.'

'It's most unsatisfactory,' Margaret said, unmollified.

Sister Verity arrived. She was a stocky, jowly creature with bulging brows and a pessimistic countenance.

'Ah, Sister Verity. You others may go. Sister Verity and I have a lot to discuss.'

* * * *

BULLETIN *for the tenth of March.*

Is this the behaviour we expect?

Three sisters spent last night in the north wing corridor rather than in their perfectly good beds in the annexe. Disgraceful, we hear you say. But we have even worse news to report. Our joint Directrix (not – need it be said? – Sister Margaret) actually encouraged *these sisters in their outlandish behaviour!*

Sister Catherine is becoming more and more strange. There have been whispers about her. There are even fears that she is losing her mind. If this is so, we pity her. But can we afford instability in a

174

leader? The answer is a resounding 'no'! For the sake of our Priory,
Sister Catherine must resign.

22

Catherine caught up with Angelica at the foot of the organ loft stairs.

'Don't know about yours, but my hair needs a trim,' she said, feeling foolish. (Most sisters paired with a friend to keep one another's hair to the regulation shortness, and she and Angelica had always cut their hair together.)

'Sorry. I'm expecting a pupil.'

'Oh, I don't mean right now necessarily. When you've time . . .'

'I should ask someone else. As a matter of fact, Sister Theresa and I cut each other's hair a few days ago.' Angelica ran up the stairs.

A pulse hammered in Catherine's throat. Misery seemed about to asphyxiate her. She leaned against the wall, taken by the thudding panic of bereavement.

When the organ sounded, she gathered herself and as soon as she was able, hurried away; for a hardened heart had not caused Angelica to play less affectingly – a mystery Catherine found too bewildering to fathom.

She decided to get the hair-cutting business over with at once.

The bathroom, a large white room partitioned into cubicles containing baths or barbers' facilities, was deserted. It seemed shameful, going in to cut her hair alone, the quietness more forceful than the normal noise of chatting voices. She prowled stealthily, collecting cape, scissors, comb, and gingerly removed her habit and veil as if dreading to disturb the silence. She sat in her shift on the stool and peered into the dingy looking-glass. A stranger stared back, or, rather, a familiar face unseen for some time. Terrible things had happened in the interim. The face had become gaunt, the skin lustreless, there were violet wells beneath large, over-bright eyes. A scar running vertically from left cheekbone to jaw, and dark clumpy hair threaded here and there with grey ('Grey, dear Lord!') reinforced an impression that here was an inmate of some prison camp. Horrified, she rose and went closer to the looking-glass, loosened the drawstring at her neck and slid the shift down to her waist. Bones jutted awkwardly. Collarbone and ribs protruded with the merest covering of skin. She could not bear the sight. She pulled up and secured her shift, draped a plastic cape round her shoulders and began methodically to slice away her hair.

When the job was done, a thought occurred to her. She approached the looking-glass again, this time removed it from the wall and propped it on the window ledge against the light. Pulling down her lower eyelids, she exposed no rose-red moons; as she suspected, the inner skin was bloodless. Anaemia, she thought, tidying up and gathering her belongings. She went into a cubicle to bathe.

Lying in the bath, a memory came to her. She and Angelica as postulants were bathing after cutting one another's hair. They called – joking, laughing – through the partitioning wall. Then she, Catherine, lay back in the water, stuck a big toe up each of the taps and feeling young and surrounded by comradeship burst into song. ' "Jesu, Lover of my soul," ' she sang to the robust, majestic tune, *Aberystwyth*. At the second line Angelica entered in harmony. They let their voices rip for the gathering waters, the high tempest; came together in unison for 'O receive my soul . . .' but were interrupted.

'Sisters! Sisters!' an elderly nun cried, rapping in outraged fury upon their doors. Silenced, hardly daring to breathe, they listened to her tirade, and only when it was certain she had gone did they wash, dry and dress, unbolt their doors and consult in whispers. 'Do you think she knew who we were?' 'No, hadn't a clue – I'm certain of it.' With great caution they peeped out into the corridor, and finding it empty, ran laughingly away.

The memory ran like a film through her mind. When it finished she was beset by loneliness. She stopped up her thoughts with action – washed briskly, towelled herself, dressed; then went quickly through the corridors and the cloister and ran up the Chapter House stairs to the hospital.

So run off her feet was Sister Luke that for a time Catherine forgot about her anaemia. A virus had attacked the lay sisters. Lying in their freezing dormitory, many of them had become very ill. Now the hospital was full to overflowing. 'And only one extra pair of hands would Sister Imogen allow me,' Sister Luke complained.

'You should have sent for me,' cried Catherine, rolling up her sleeves, putting on an apron.

Many hours later Catherine sank into a chair and mentioned her own indisposition.

'I shan't bother the doctor, Sister, but let me have some iron tablets, there's a dear.'

'Oh, but I think you should. You've looked pinched for months.'

'Later on maybe. In the meantime, see what you can find.'

Just before supper-time she left the hospital, promising to return in the morning.

'There you are,' Christa cried, as she hurried through the cloister. 'I've been looking for you. Sister Imogen took their belongings to the annexe this morning. Rose intends to camp again in the corridor, but Kirsty and Beth seem to be weakening.'

'They must do as they think best.'

'Hang on. The other thing is . . . Well, you'd better come and see for yourself.'

Christa led her into the concourse outside the refectory. On the noticeboard was the latest *Bulletin*. Catherine discovered that she was advised to resign. She read the piece slowly, then read it again, aware of curious glances towards her as nuns went in to supper.

'Cheek, isn't it?' Christa asked.

'I think I shall draw up a dossier and pin it up beside this. I've plenty to say and shall say it strongly. One can at least learn from one's enemies.'

'Great idea!' Christa was encouraged by Catherine's resilience. She really is coming on, she thought, recalling how Catherine had required prompting and urging in the past. These days her blood was up. She clapped her on the back. 'If you need any help . . .'

'Thanks. Let's go and eat.'

*   *   *   *

Catherine sat at her desk. Christa leaned over her. Behind them, Gabrielle lolled in the easy chair.

'As a result of the ill effects of their atrocious accommodation, two-thirds of the lay sisters are ill, many so seriously that they are confined to the hospital,' Christa suggested.

'No, no,' Catherine said. 'We must think how *they* would write it.' She put her head in her hands.

'Don't forget to mention the annexe business,' Gabrielle put in.

'Shh.'

Catherine began to write.

When she paused, Christa took the paper from her and read what she had written aloud:

' "At our wit's end," says Sister Luke.

It was a grim scene yesterday in the hospital. Sister Luke and her staff were exhausted. "Every bed is taken, and many more are sick in the dormitory," she said. "Two sisters have pneumonia. Most are too ill to do a thing for themselves."

This state of affairs is unprecedented in the recent history of our Priory. We demand to know *why*.

179

'Gosh, yes, that's really good.'

'It's hateful. But that's the way it's done. Give it back. I'll list the faults of the dormitory next, then ask why they put the lay sisters there in the first place.'

'Then the annexe business,' Gabrielle reminded her again.

'No. I think a different topic each day. One sheet of the dossier put up at a time. More of an impact, don't you think?'

'You're right. Come on,' Christa said to Gabrielle. 'We'll go and give Rose moral support.'

'And Kirsty. I managed to persuade her to stay in the corridor for another night, too. But Beth's dropped out, unfortunately.'

Catherine looked up. 'Don't put pressure on Sister Kirsty. She's unhappy enough as it is.'

Late that night while her sister nuns slept, Catherine crept through the corridors to the art room. She flicked on a light, found a lamp on a desk and switched it on, and extinguished the light overhead. Paper, indian ink, pen. Painstakingly, she wrote out a sheet of her dossier, then, to save herself trouble on future nights, copied out two more – one dealing with the compulsory move to the annexe, another entitled 'What is the Purpose of this Priory?' In a desk drawer she found a box of drawing pins. Taking these and her finished work, she left the art room, went back along the corridor, but instead of going on to her room, turned right and went into the cloister.

The wind had dropped. There was only freezing stillness. As she tiptoed between wall and open arches, afraid almost to let her breath cloud the air, the independence of the place struck her. For in this unpeopled time, stones ooze dampness, dust consolidates, and secretive spores bloom shyly in the grass. She started as a black shape swooped across the pale navy of the quadrangle. A bat, she thought, straining to see; but it darted into the dense hollow between two pillars and was obliterated. When she reached the door she was glad to end her trespass.

On the noticeboard outside the refectory, she pinned sheet one of her dossier by the side of the *Bulletin*. In her exaggerated wide-awake state she could not leave it, but read it through compulsively again and again. At last she turned away, went through the corridors to her room and soon lay with her racing thoughts in bed.

23

Agnes burst into Beatrice's room. 'My God! Has she seen it?'

Beatrice, who was lying on her bed with her eyes shut, chose her words carefully. 'If I said "incandescent with rage", would that answer you?'

Agnes groped for a chair.

'You'd better watch out. I thought you were supposed to be her eyes and ears. 'Fraid you've rather slipped up, Aggers.'

'That blasted Catherine . . . I'd like to pin her to the proverbial wheel . . .'

'What a shocking thing to say!'

'Damn it, she must have got up in the night and put the thing on the noticeboard. Clare says it was there first thing.'

'Clare, eh? And she didn't come running to warn us? You'd think she'd try to earn her passage back – like good old Imogen. Now if it had been Imogen who'd spotted it, she'd have ripped it down and come panting like a good doggie to lay it at Margaret's feet. Sweet, I always think, the way poor Imogen tries.'

'The point is, should I go and talk to her or keep out of the way?'

'Depends how strong your stomach is this morning. I'm feeling a bit queasy myself.' And no wonder, she thought, recalling her interview with Margaret.

Beatrice had been the unfortunate bearer of the news. 'S'pose I should've kept my face straight,' she reflected. The trouble was, she had rather enjoyed Catherine's spunk. It was so unexpected. A worthy paragraph describing the lay sisters' woes and a heavy-handed rebuke aimed at authority were the sort of the things one would have anticipated from Sister Catherine. Instead, she had cheekily imitated the opposition's style. It was possible, Beatrice conceded, that she had allowed a degree of amused admiration to colour her account of the dossier outrage. Whether she had or had not, old Margaret had fairly hit the ceiling, positively *popped* – leaped from her chair, arms flailing, eyes swivelling – had been all for marching on the noticeboard then and there and ripping it down. 'But Mags, old girl,' Beatrice had protested, 'that'd be so undignified – completely lacking in confidence. Ignore the thing; disdain to even look at it . . .'

'Shut *up*,' Margaret had yelled. 'Don't you understand? I . . . want . . . it . . . removed. Now!'

Beatrice had felt quite shaken. It was the first time Margaret had rejected her advice – and with such unpleasant passion! 'Well, don't look at me,' she had said huffily.

'Clear off, then. Go on, scram! Where's Agnes? – it's her job to prevent things like this. Send Joan to me – p'raps she'll talk *sense.*'

Margaret, Beatrice recalled with a shudder, had been as imperious and as unlovely as a Chinese emperor.

Agnes saw that she was unlikely to get any further information out of Beatrice. She left her and set off cautiously along the corridor.

The door to Margaret's office was open. Joan was standing in the doorway, wringing her hands. From within Margaret's voice roared: 'Ridiculous suggestion! You're losing your touch, Joan. Send me Sister Verity.'

Joan seemed not to see Agnes as she lurched past her in the corridor.

Think I'll go and sound out Clare, Agnes decided, turning back. Don't like the sound of things here.

Soon, Sister Verity came plodding to Margaret's door.

'Come in. Oh, thank goodness it's you, Verity. Have you heard?'

'Heard what?'

Steadying herself, Margaret told her. 'And what do you think we should do about it?'

'Rip begger up oh, pardon – plain-speaking woman, me . . .'

'Quite understood. And then?'

'Hit back.' She punched a fist into the palm of a hand.

Margaret breathed out with relief. 'My feelings exactly. Do it at once, Verity. Then come back here and we'll work out our strategy. By the way,' she called as Verity went to the door, 'I've decided to make you my Communications Secretary.'

* * * *

Catherine's anger was like an engine. *She* did not power her legs, this force drove them – on, on, on. The dislodged remainder of her body floated above them in a haze of indignant disbelief. Light-headed, she burst open Margaret's office door. Her eyes, too, were supercharged, for they pounced upon the dossier (*her* dossier) in the wastepaper basket, and reported other images in sharp detail. Blood-filled veins spoilt the whites of Margaret's eyes, and her hand, stilled by her surprise, hovered like a hawk's talon; Verity, whose nose was stippled with open pores and whose dinted cheeks hung loosley in folds, was caught with her upper lip curling from her teeth in the manner of a whinnying horse.

'*There* it is,' cried Catherine, swooping on her brutalized handiwork. 'How dare you remove it? How *dare* you?'

'How dare *you*?' Margaret countered. She rose and leaned across her desk. 'How dare you write such stuff, accusing me, blaming me?'

'That's rich. You had the nerve to ask me to resign.'

'I? I had the nerve? I do not write the *Bulletin*. You, on the other hand, produced that scurrilous sheet yourself.'

184

'Whether or not you personally write what goes into the Bulletin, it gives your point of view.'

'Because my point of view, dear Sister, happens to coincide with the best interests of this Priory. It is I who have set this Priory back on its feet. You and your nasty broadsheet seek to undermine everything we've built up. That is why I had it removed. Quite simply, it is against the Priory's interest.'

'I see. So freedom of speech is expendable . . .'

'Don't talk to me about freedom,' yelled Margaret, by now very red in the face. 'The day we get trial by broadsheet is the day that freedom dies. You are the one threatening freedom, stirring up discontent, accusing and blaming those who work day and night . . .'

'Are you saying,' Catherine quietly interrupted, 'that you will prevent me from putting my point of view on the noticeboard?'

'Certainly – in the interests of the Priory.'

'Right. Then I shall call a meeting and explain the situation to everyone.'

'We won't fret about that,' Verity put in. 'Folks know which side their bread's buttered. They'll back us, you'll find.'

'Yes, call a meeting,' Margaret agreed, after a slight hesitation. 'You can put your side and I shall put mine. Then we'll call for a show of hands and that must be an end to the matter. I won't allow us to be diverted by dissension. There is work to be done around here, and I intend to see that it's done.'

* * * *

Margaret was beginning to relax. She did not enjoy argument; it had been a necessary preliminary to gaining her position and power, but now she had earned the right to abandon the pursuit, for, as all right-minded and unprejudiced observers of the Albion scene would concede, practice had proved her contentions correct. So it was with impatience and some resentment that she now debated with her co-Directrix. Perhaps 'debated' was inapposite, for though she was ready and willing to launch upon her own set piece, she hardly listened to her opponent, merely took in key words here and there which usefully triggered her own pet phrases. The word at the moment was 'freedom' – actually, 'freedom' preceded 'of speech', but Margaret intended to ignore the secondary words as they did not quite fit what she intended to say. 'Freedom' was excellent. She focussed on it and felt the ground grow firm beneath her feet.

It was her turn to speak. 'Catherine talks of freedom,' she began, stating the truth inadequately. (There were no protests.) 'Shall I tell you what is the best guarantee of freedom? It is success, material success, for if the Priory fails, where is our freedom then?'

She was away, heading for the safe ground of just rewards for the hardworking, and as she touched down on this she sensed an exhalation of relief from the audience. Catherine's remarks had unsettled the sisters and they wished to be made comfortable again. It buoyed Margaret up, this knowledge of their underlying support. 'There is nothing wrong with making our Priory wealthy,' she said soothingly. 'Wealth allows choice. It is what we choose to do with our wealth that is important.'

But suddenly, to Margaret's chagrin, Catherine bounced to her feet and did not wait for Margaret to give way.

'But it also matters *how* our wealth is created,' she shouted (rudely, Margaret thought). 'It matters very much when it is created at the cost of some people's poverty and distress. Our so-called success has been achieved by deliberately excluding some members of this community. Can the lay sisters choose to return to the east wing? Can the sisters in the annexe choose to do the sort of work that is well-rewarded? They cannot. They are denied choice. An inferior mode of living is imposed upon them. So where is *their* freedom?' she demanded, sitting down.

Margaret was angry. It was time to tell a few home truths.

'I shall speak plainly,' she announced. 'The fact is, there is *no regular work* for the lay sisters and the annexe sisters. This Priory had become inefficient. Too many things were undertaken merely to keep people occupied or to indulge inclinations. We

could not go on in that fashion. We needed to work purpose-
fully, to *earn* our living. To that end, some areas of work had to
go. Others had to be made lean and fit. Some areas, the
profitable ones, were expanded – needlework and art, for
example. More people were needed to do housekeeping and
cooking to cater for our many visitors, but as I am sure you are
aware, the number of visitors staying with us at any one time
varies considerably. Therefore it is necessary to vary the
number of people working to serve them; which is why we need
a *flexible* workforce.

'But I must be frank with you. In spite of the visitors, we still
have sisters whose labour is surplus to our requirements. In
other words, they are *passengers*, because the rest of us – those
doing necessary and profitable work – are obliged to carry
them. Now, I put it to you: would it be equitable if these
passengers were placed in exactly the same position as those who
earn their privileges? Of *course* it would not.

'You know, I think a sense of gratitude wouldn't be too
much to ask. I have been disturbed to hear that certain sisters
who should properly reside in the annexe have refused Sister
Imogen's request to go there peaceably, and have set up camp
in the north wing corridor. Sisters, I find their behaviour
inexplicable and quite disgraceful. How *dare* they complain
about their circumstances? Do the sisters who are obliged to
support them complain? I say to Sister Rose and Sister Kirsty:
stop this outrageous behaviour now! Be grateful for the
generosity of your peers; show respect for authority. Above all,
try to be worthy of the name of Albion!'

Applause broke like thunder upon a tense, close atmosphere.
Catherine was obliged to bellow her request to be heard.

'Wait! Listen! I admit the old regime was flawed. I admit
the need for reform. Not only because we were inefficient, but
because we were self-indulgent, too. We prided ourselves on
being good to the lay sisters, but we never gave them their
proper due. Our "goodness" sprang from random charitable
whims; there was no sense of the duty we owed them as a
community. Let us not compound these flaws. Margaret's way

has improved our lot materially, but it has not addressed our other failings. Let's find a success that everyone can share. It must be wrong to create barriers for some and then to punish them; yet that is what we are doing. Let us agree to make the lay sisters and the so-called annexe sisters participants in our good fortune. Can't we give up a little – our new sitting rooms perhaps, those new offices and bathrooms? Will you agree to forgo a few luxuries for the sake of others? Let's vote on it,' she cried, flinging out her hands.

Margaret, scenting danger, got hastily to her feet. 'I was about to suggest a vote, myself. For I am sick and tired of going over and over the same old ground. Let's put an end to the argument, once and for all. You are voting,' she warned them sternly, 'on whether you wish the Priory's affairs to continue in my hands. Do you wish to consolidate the progress we have achieved, or risk losing it for the sake of Sister Catherine's notions? Those who wish things to continue as they are with *me* in charge, raise your hands.'

Catherine, strained and pale beside the rosy one, had never seen such a flowering. She thought of plants shooting after heavy rain, of a tufted field transformed overnight into a meadow of foot-high grass. She had not suspected Margaret's power to nurture this near unanimity.

Evidently, Margaret was not altogether satisfied. 'Is that all? It is interesting to see who is behind one . . .'

Cecilia, who was holding her hand in the air, kicked Monica's ankle. 'Put yours up,' she hissed.

'But you heard what Catherine said . . .'

'Do you want us to lose the tea-party job? Put your hand up, Monica, or I shall never forgive you.'

Miserably, Monica raised her hand.

Elizabeth was experiencing a similar difficulty. 'Please, Anne,' she whispered.

'Oh, I don't know . . .'

'Please. You'll be out of the Blue Sitting Room – the only one of us not a member.'

'Oh dear,' moaned Anne, slowly lifting an arm.

'That's better,' Margaret said, as half a dozen tardy arm-raisers complied. 'Over to you, Sister.'

Catherine's face was as grey as her habit. Against her pallor, the scar on her cheek and her dark eyes stood out shockingly, giving her a fanatical appearance. But her voice did not betray her. She spoke quietly, evenly. 'So be it. You want Sister Margaret to remain in charge. But will you ask her to moderate her policies? Are you willing to forgo some of your privileges for the sake of the less fortunate? Raise your hands, please, if you agree so to do.'

Christa and her friends now raised their hands for the first time. One or two of the annexe sisters – including Rose and Kirsty, their cheeks still flaming from Margaret's rebuke – daringly voted in their own interests; but most of these were too embarrassed to raise their hands, conscious that it was not they who were called upon to make sacrifices. (The lay sisters, of course, were not eligible to be present.) During these initial moments there were rustlings, murmurings, head-turnings.

'Don't dare,' Cecilia whispered sharply to Monica. 'I meant what I said.'

Monica had raised her hand, but only as far as her mouth. She bit on her knuckles and thought how dearly she loved Catherine, and then how dearly she loved Cecilia. Between these two loves there was no room for the issue at stake. In the end it was Cecilia, her friend and companion since childhood, who won the contest of her affections. She lowered her hand to her lap and bowed her head.

Anne knew that Catherine was right – as Jesus is right, and the Scriptures. If she were telling a morality tale she would make Catherine triumph. But there was also to be considered her dearly prized membership of the Blue Sitting Room. Blow it, she *enjoyed* the Blue Sitting Room. Was that so very wicked? It was plain there would be no consensus to forgo it. Why should she be holier than the rest? And as Elizabeth's sidelong glance now warned, if she were to defy Margaret and raise her hand, sure as eggs were eggs she would find herself somehow excluded. Tears sprang to her eyes as she thought of Elizabeth,

Cecilia and Monica tripping merrily away at half past three, and herself left solitary in the needlework room. She put her hands between her knees and waited tensely for the moment to pass.

Silence fell like a blanket. Thoughts were smothered, an agonizing prickle of suspense filled mouths and nostrils. They could hardly breathe.

Margaret broke the stillness. 'I think we've waited long enough. Pretty decisive, wouldn't you say?' She turned to Catherine.

But Catherine was running from the room.

* * * *

Margaret contemplated Verity with affection. The pleasure of victory was more intense because she had secured it without assistance from Beatrice, Agnes or Joan. Hitherto, all matters of strategy had been planned with them; it was assumed their contributions were indispensable. Now Margaret knew she was omnipotent. She would call the others in eventually, for she knew how to be magnanimous. For the moment though, Verity's forthright attitude suited her mood.

'To all intents and purposes,' she mused, 'that vote should have settled the issue of the succession. I'm sure it has as far as Catherine is concerned. Did you see how she scuttled away? It's just a matter of bringing it home to the Prioress.'

'Done any work on that?' Verity enquired.

'Yes, lots. But I'm about to bring matters to a head. Did I ever tell you about the new ceremony we're to have; the washing of a postulant's feet?'

'Go on.'

'It's part of my campaign – mission, I suppose, is a better word, because that's how I feel about it, Verity – *mission* to deepen our spirituality. And I thought how fitting it would be if our spiritual leader were to follow our Lord's example when He washed the disciples' feet.'

'All of 'em? Take a dickens of a time.'

'No, no. One will be enough – it's the symbolism we're after. I had thought the youngest postulant's feet, but I've discovered she's a great buxom thing. Little Sister Fay will suit the part to perfection, so I shall say "one of the postulant's feet" and in fact see that Sister Fay is chosen. We'll have the ceremony in the chapel where the visitors can watch. I think they'll be impressed.'

'But the Reverend Mother won't like it, you reckon?'

'The Reverend Mother, Verity – now don't be shocked – is a thoroughly lazy woman. Believe me, it was a painful business finding myself drawn to that conclusion, but it was inescapable – she likes the Priory run with the minimum trouble to herself. What a tragedy it is that those who bear responsibility for our religious life take their duties so lightly! I may be primarily concerned with our material welfare, but I do care deeply for the spiritual side. I shall insist on the Reverend Mother pulling her weight. She shan't get out of it.'

Verity attempted a grin, but as always on these rare occasions her weighty dewlaps proved a handicap and limited her effort to a cheerful sneer. 'You reckon she'll have a darn good try, though – make you her successor and tell you to get on with the feet-washing yourself?'

Demurely, Margaret fluttered her eyelids. 'Not *necessarily*. Rome wasn't built in a day. No, it'll test her commitment – for I shall make it plain that more, much more will be expected of our spiritual leader in the future. After all, as we grow materially stronger it is vital to have a corresponding growth in our spiritual development. This little ceremony is but the start of things. Now, come on, Verity. Mustn't waste time chatting. The *Bulletin*. I'm keen to keep up the pressure. We both know Catherine is a spent force but it needs to be said again and again until the Priory makes it official.'

24

Catherine went across the crowded concourse holding her thumb against the back of a drawing pin which was pressed through the second sheet of her dossier. The pin's point protruded at the ready. She held the sheet of paper half an arm's length from her body and strode sharply, her head unnaturally erect, her eyes fixed on her goal.

It had cost her a great deal to come here at this busy time of day, but if she had come at a quieter time, early this morning or late last night, the prompt removal of her dossier would have ensured ignorance of its existence. They would remove it in any case, she had no illusions about that; but its arrival and removal would at least be noted by this preprandial throng.

No doubt the sisters gathered here would think her foolhardy in the light of yesterday's verdict. However, there was such a thing as bearing witness, she had told herself as she sat on the edge of her bed gathering courage. The cost of her present effort was evident in her unnatural gait, her set expression, her unswerving gaze, for it was not muscle but willpower that propelled her.

Unknown to Catherine, her strange appearance gave credence to sentiments expressed in today's issue of the *Bulletin*. ('We are alarmed to note Sister Catherine's marked eccentricity of late.') The sisters making way for her to pass, fell awkwardly silent. When the dossier was in place, Catherine turned on her heel and strode away. They let out gasps of relief. How embarrassing if she had paused to read the *Bulletin*!

Catherine had gone into the kitchen. But the meals she intended to collect for hospital patients were not yet ready. 'I'll come back in quarter of an hour,' she promised, backing away from a jet of steam and the appetite-quelling stench of food cooked to death in vast quantities and incongruous variety – glutinous meat and sweet steamed pudding, onion, jam sauce, boiled cabbage. Almost retching, she went into the yard and walked aimlessly, gratefully breathing the fresh sharp air.

At that moment, Sisters Rose and Kirsty arrived outside the refectory.

'Doesn't look as though they're ready. What's the matter with them in the kitchen?' Rose grumbled, and turned away to push through the crowd to the noticeboard.

Kirsty followed her, not because she wished to read the notices, but because the public scolding from Sister Margaret had made her nervous. Rose, who was friendly with Christa and her crowd, was so sure and strong she made Kirsty feel safe.

'I say, Kirsty, come and look at this.'

Reluctantly, Kirsty looked. It was the piece written by Sister Catherine, and it was about the plight of the annexe sisters. It made Kirsty glow to read it. 'She really understands,' she said to Rose. 'Though I don't suppose it'll do us any good. Still, it's nice to know someone's bothered.'

'Oh, my goodness. Look here.' Rose pointed to the *Bulletin*.

Kirsty grew hot. She hoped Sister Catherine would not see it. Then, reading further, her heart lurched to a standstill. 'The two annexe sisters still camping in the north wing corridor are becoming a couple of pests.' As her heart raced to make up for its missed beat, a particular word caught her eye. For a moment it transfixed her. Then she gave a cry, turned, and ran until she found herself in the open air.

'Whatever is it, Sister?' asked Sister Fortuity, who was coming across the yard.

Kirsty leaped into the shed and jammed the door shut with a sack of potatoes. Then she gave vent to her indignation and fear

– bawled, drove clenched fists into her stomach, bent over, straightened, bent over again.

Fortuity pummelled the door. 'Open it, please. Sister Kirsty . . .'

Hearing the commotion, Catherine came running.

'Sister Kirsty has shut herself in. She sounds dreadfully upset.'

'Sister Kirsty! It's Sister Catherine here. Please tell me what is the matter.'

Kirsty became exhausted. She slipped to the floor and leaned back against the potatoes. Sister Catherine's voice, imploring her, made her hold back her tears. If anyone deserved an explanation it was Sister Catherine. 'Scroungers,' she blurted. 'It says we're scroungers.'

'What does? Where?'

'The *Bulletin* on the noticeboard. It says there's no proper work for us and the rest have to keep us. That we're scroungers moaning for better conditions.'

Fortuity broke the silence. 'The poor thing! You know, they really do go too far. It's not the fault of these sisters. It's the way things are run nowadays . . .' Her voice trailed away as Catherine turned to stare at her.

'I didn't notice your hand raised in their support,' she observed shortly. Then, as Fortuity paled: 'I'll stay with her. I expect she'll come out in a minute. Will you get someone to carry the trays to the hospital? I was about to do that myself.'

'Of course.' Fortuity gave the shed door one last hopeless look, then hurried away.

When her tapping footsteps were no longer heard, Kirsty heaved away the sack, opened the door and looked out. 'I was a bit upset. It was the shock. Sorry,' she said shamefacedly.

'Let's go and talk somewhere quiet.'

* * * *

'I used to come here a lot,' Catherine said, going into the deserted cowshed.

'Is it all right for us to be here?' Kirsty wondered nervously.

'I'm sure they won't mind. It's a couple of hours yet before milking.'

'Did you milk the cows?'

'I helped out when they were short-handed. That was how I got to know Sister Mary John so well.'

They sat on bales of hay.

Out of the sharp, keen air, it was soporifically warm. The cowshed was not quite silent, but faintly hummed and stirred. It was a lulling place, simple, uncorrupted; hay as fodder, hay as dung scented it reassuringly. A cat stole from the shadows, arched its back, mewed, then pressed against them in a languorous passing by. 'Come back, puss, come,' Catherine called, putting out her hand. The cat returned and jumped into her lap where it nestled and began to purr.

After a time: 'Can you weather this, do you think?' Catherine asked Kirsty, who looked blank.

'Oh, you mean the nastiness? Well, I don't know. When I go into the north wing corridor I have this awful feeling of not belonging. I sit down outside my old room and think how I used to come and go. But it still feels as though I've walked into someone else's house and just plonked myself down – sort of intruding. I hate doing it. But then again, I hate the thought of giving in like Beth. If I start sleeping in the annexe I shall end up like them, feeling small, as if I don't count, and I shall go around hanging my head. I'm frightened when Sister Margaret and the Bulletin say things about us, but doing things with Rose I still feel I'm me. I've got my pride, you see.'

'Oh yes, I see. I think you're very brave. But I suspect it'll be a long time before things get any better. If sticking with Sister Rose feels right to you, then I should go on doing it. Sister Christa and Sister Gabrielle will always be behind you. They're strong-minded women. I suppose they're the hope for the future.'

'Oh, but Sister Catherine! You can change things. After all, you're as high up as Sister Margaret; it's just they don't seem to listen to you.'

'I doubt whether I can ever affect things here. I'm no match for Sister Margaret – never have been. In a way, I'm part of what was wrong with the place and allowed Sister Margaret to gain her toehold. I shall go on trying, but really I'm just banging my head against a wall. Sister Christa's the next generation. At first I rather distrusted her, but I've come to respect her, you know. She's got this ability to distance herself from the bruises – essential if you want to win battles. 'Fraid I'm not the right stuff for waging war.'

Kirsty glanced at Catherine and recalled the unpleasant remarks about her in the Bulletin. 'I shouldn't bother reading things on the noticeboard, if I were you, Sister,' she hinted anxiously.

Touched by her solicitousness, Catherine laughed. 'You've given me back my appetite. Come on. Let's go and see if there's anything left to eat.'

25

It's a pity I'm so fond of these, thought Anne, helping herself regretfully to a second cream puff.

When she had eaten it she detected no feeling of repletion or content. You see, she reasoned, hoping the lesson would be remembered for future occasions, a second one is no use. You could go on and on. Think how much happier you'd feel if you knew it was in you to resist temptation.

The knowledge that it was not in her made her gloomy, and she began to dwell on the vote taken at yesterday's meeting – another occasion when she had succumbed to the temptations of the flesh. Full of cream and sugar and self-disgust, she shifted in her chair and said belligerently to her neighbours: 'We voted out of sheer selfishness yesterday, you know. Selfishness and greed. It wouldn't hurt us to forgo this sitting room and all these disgusting cakes to help the annexe sisters and the lay sisters.'

There followed the kind of silence born of a social lapse. There was then a rush to dispel it.

'Oh, *Anne*,' said Elizabeth, conveying distaste and disappointment.

'What does the gel say?' Cecilia demanded of Monica, having concluded that her ears had misled her.

Monica was saved from replying by Sister Martha's outburst. In any case, Monica could not have borne to repeat Anne's words for they rang alarm bells in her own conscience.

'Stuff and nonsense! – sorry, but I've never heard such a load of rubbish. Sister Margaret's doing a right good job, and as far as I'm concerned, what she says goes. I'd back her to the hilt. Don't get me wrong – I'm sorry as the next person for t'annexe sisters; in fact, I've done me darnedest for Sister Kirsty, and I don't mind telling you I felt proper let down when I heard about trick she's been playing. Just goes to show how you can't help some folk.'

'Pooh!' Anne said loudly, jamming a cushion into the small of her back. (These low soft chairs played havoc with the digestion – a lump like a rock had grown in her chest.) 'You can comfort yourself all you like, but the result's the same – we hang on to our little luxuries. We're fooling ourselves if we say self-interest doesn't come into it.'

Sister Faith drew herself up. 'I don't think we should lower the tone.'

'Quite so,' Martha said. 'But I still think Sister Anne's talking poppycock.'

'Shall we change the subject?' asked Sister Joy. She turned pointedly to Sister Elizabeth (who was mortified that her friend should earn a reproof from such as Sister Joy or Sister Faith). 'Have you heard about the visitors expected today – two sisters from overseas?'

'I hadn't heard, no. How interesting. Do tell us about them, Sister.' And Elizabeth set an example by sitting up straight and raising her teacup daintily.

It seemed to jolt them into good behaviour. They sat up and assumed expressions of rapt interest. Sister Joy endeavoured to pack her tale with fascinating detail.

Only Anne looked cross, a martyr to her ruined digestion.

* * * *

Beatrice stopped staring out of the window, breathed upon it and with her finger drew a grid in the condensation. She traced noughts and crosses with the aimlessness of a boy kicking a can through the gutter, and with a similar purpose – the relief of tedium. For she was bored; seriously, dangerously bored. Lately, life had gone flat. The fun of grooming Margaret for power was over. (It was possible she had done the grooming too well, for Margaret behaved like an autocrat with no sense of gratitude; indeed, that she had ever been groomed seemed now to escape her memory.) There was no fun to be had these days. She missed the feeling of life being transacted beneath the surface – intrigue, danger, the glorious business of fooling people. No one had guessed about Margaret, for example. There had been no cries of astonishment at the miraculous and instantaneous metamorphosis from bright but deferential nun into masterful creature with a ready-made plan to save the Priory's fortunes. People were like sheep: so accepting. Yet if it had not been for Beatrice spotting the genius of the plan (originally Joan's, but argued for more cogently by Margaret) and painstakingly turning its proponent into a powermonger, where, she would like to know, would the Priory be today? And where would Margaret be without Beatrice's secret work on her behalf – stage-managing the briefing meetings, planning trickery and getting the better of Catherine?

Unlike Margaret who liked to wield power openly, Beatrice yearned for the secret side of the craft. It was as the hidden agent that she excelled, influencing events and determining outcomes with a deceitful sleight of hand. Secret power was the greatest thrill. She loved its paraphernalia – the late-night plotting, the deadly rivalries; loved its never-to-be-spoken-of-knowledge, and holding other lives in the palm of her hand while she looked into uncomprehending eyes and thought, Little do you know, but I've cooked your goose. When her pulse raced and her nerves sang, these delightful physical sensations became part of what must be covered with a comfortable expression and steady hands. And I'm so darn good at it, thought Beatrice, impatient with the wasting of her talents, for Margaret in her new arrogant mood appeared to have no need for undercover work. Or could it be that someone else was now providing that service – Sister Verity, perhaps?

Frowning, she wandered down the corridor, a corridor on the first floor of the south wing. When she came to the wide landing, she paused – for the rasp of charcoal upon paper rose from the bottom of the stairwell – and cautiously peered over the banister.

It was Hope making a sketch of the old courtyard – a favourite scene with the visitors – as viewed through the ornately carved window. A board with paper attached was propped on her knee. She stared out of the window, drew rapidly, looked up and stared again. Beatrice observed her for some moments. Then a smile crept over her face, and she raced back silently to where she had played noughts and crosses and where she had seen upon the windowsill a large dead bluebottle. She collected the fly and returned to the top of the stairs, leaned over the banister and extended her hand to where she judged it to be directly above Hope's drawing. The effect of relinquishing the fly and its soft ping upon the paper was predictable. A scream, a scattering of clipboard and charcoal, a tumbling chair, a vanishing Hope.

Now Hope would be in a quandary, thought Beatrice. She could not abandon her work, nor could she summon assistance for so nebulous a cause. Chuckling to herself, she pictured Hope in some corner below, trying to squeeze up some courage. Sure enough, when Hope crept into view, her jerky chicken's head described her fear with every timid step. Beatrice was about to cast around for a second missile when she was distracted by noise outside: an unbearable throbbing and a whirring as of giant wings. She gazed in anticipation through the window. Below her, Hope also gazed.

Dust blew up in the courtyard. A helicopter descended and neatly came to rest. Then Margaret stepped up. She stood patiently, waiting to greet the airborne visitors.

Beatrice recalled Margaret speaking to her about these visitors.

'I shall want you to help me entertain two nuns who are coming from overseas, Beatrice. You can be very charming when you put your mind to it. A good impression is vital because their organization may be interested in putting money into the Priory.'

'Good Lord, Mags! You're not planning to sell us off?'

'Don't be ridiculous, Beatrice. Possibly they will invest in us, that's all. But I'm talking about a very considerable sum.'

'Mags, you *are* planning to sell the Priory!'

'Just do your stuff this afternoon. Understood? You can leave matters of finance to me.'

Beatrice had gloomily anticipated a couple of worthy *religieuses*, fat, squat, bespectacled, even – such was her luck these days – moustached and bearded. But now – oh my God – take it all back! Could these be they; these slender wonders clad in gold-coloured tunics and *trousers*? And with hair, unless she was very much mistaken. Yes, there was definitely hair showing under their veils which were little more than gold-coloured headscarves. One sported shiny black curls against cheeks and forehead, and from under the head-covering of the other jutted a Pre-Raphaelite auburn frizz.

She waited no longer. Raced down the stairs (nearly causing Hope to suffer a heart attack), along the corridor to the door, paused for breath, then swung out on to the gravel path with a dazzling smile.

'Ah, here is Sister Beatrice. Sister, I should like you to meet our visitors from the Convent of Eternal Enterprise, California. Sister Diane, Sister Betty-Lou.'

'Delighted. Charmed,' said Beatrice.

Sister Diane extended her hand. 'Hi, Beatrice. Sure is good to know you.'

'Certainly is,' confirmed Sister Betty-Lou.

* * * *

It was late. Elizabeth and Anne were in the Needlework Room stretching a newly completed tapestry to save time in the morning. Monica and Cecilia had looked in to keep them company.

'What did you think of their get-up?' Cecilia asked. It went without saying that the get-up she referred to belonged to the Californians.

'Narsty cheap clorth,' Elizabeth said through a mouthful of drawing pins. 'Pull harder,' she exhorted Anne.

'I thought it a rather becoming style of dress,' Cecilia said in a faraway voice, 'at least, on them. They have the figures to carry it off. A get-up like that would go rather well on Sister Beatrice – she's so tall and dashing. It would have suited Catherine once, before she lost her looks.'

'Oh, not Catherine,' Monica protested. 'No, no; it would never suit her, not at all. Catherine has always been . . . otherworldly.' Her voice had become choky. She had remembered catching Catherine's eye during Evensong. Candlelight on her sad face and a fleeting smile had sent a wave of *déjà vu* over Monica, rekindling a sense of irrevocable loss she had once experienced as a child.

'We have to move with the times,' Cecilia said complacently.

This was a startling announcement coming from Cecilia who was a stickler for tradition and a great decrier of modern manners. Even Anne, kneeling over the damp canvas with her bottom in the air, twisted up her head to look at her.

'Progress,' Cecilia said, waving an arm. 'Oh, yes. One of the guests at tea the other day – an *entrepreneur*' (she pronounced the word firmly in French) 'made me see it all – a most enlightening conversation.'

Anne snorted.

Elizabeth said: 'Well, I thought it most unsuitable attire. And I must say, that's a bit rich coming from you, Cecilia.'

'Stop talking and hurry up. My knees are going to sleep.'

'You know, Anne,' called Monica unsteadily, 'I've been thinking. There was something in what you said this afternoon – about us voting for selfish reasons.'

Elizabeth groaned. 'Not that again, please.'

Cecilia looked closely at her friend. Was she becoming senile? Senility ran in the family, she mused, recalling Monica's spectacularly demented Aunt Tilly.

'But I think there may have been *something* in what Anne said . . .'

'My goodness, I wish you'd get a move on, Elizabeth,' Anne grumbled. 'The blood's gone to my head.' It was not blood to the head but bile to the throat that truly concerned her. Those horrible cakes, she thought. Never, never again.

26

'Mad' was in vogue – 'mad', 'deranged' and 'eccentric'. And once, coming into a room and finding it charged with the magnetic pull of a slanderous conversation, Catherine caught the word 'crazed' – swiftly followed, of course, by an appalled silence. She almost chuckled at their embarrassment, but foresaw in the nick of time that a chuckle would confirm her reputation.

The Bulletin continued to express concern for her state of mind, and this encouraged the speculation, for when a thing is written it acquires the stature of truth. Perhaps I *am* mad, she found herself wondering late one evening when her morale was low, but then she recalled how her sense of humour was intact and decided she was sane enough.

Neither the gossip nor a sense of futility deterred her. When impelled to speak out, she spoke out, for she no longer cared what people thought about her.

One day, Christa said, 'Do you know they hiss at Sister Hope?'

'Hiss at her?' Catherine was horrified.

'I don't know how long it's been going on, but I was walking behind Sister Rachel and Sister Michael on the sloping lawn by the sycamores when they suddenly gave out like snakes. I suppose they hadn't heard me behind them on the grass. I couldn't think what was going on until I saw Hope at her easel.

She started, then hung her head. Later, I tackled her about it, asked her if it had happened before. She wouldn't talk; just shrugged and coloured up. I got the impression she'd grown used to it.'

'But how very unpleasant! And how unfair. Everyone's been so forgiving to Sister Beatrice.'

'What do you expect? They made Sister Hope the villain of the piece. She entrapped Sister Beatrice was the official line – though it takes a bit of believing when you come to think about it.'

'It's blaming one rather than the other that's at the root of this. Something ought to be done.'

She had gone to Margaret's office to demand an investigation. 'If two or three impartial senior sisters look into the matter and find, as I suspect they will, that Sister Hope was unjustly condemned without a hearing, a statement to that effect might put an end to this persecution.'

Margaret's reaction was instantaneous. 'Utterly disgraceful,' she cried, meaning any questioning of authority's verdict.

'The hissing? I quite agree. But if we hold an enquiry . . .'

'*Your suggestion* is utterly disgraceful. It's lucky for that girl she's still here! I find your remarks offensive and insulting. You had better go.'

So now Sister Hope was added to the list of wounded. Understanding her impotence to change the course of events, Catherine set herself the task of protecting and comforting the casualties.

I let Mary John down, she brooded, leaning over a gate to watch Mary John's friends munching the new spring grass. Her heart ached at the sadness of it. Doing battle with Margaret, she had neglected her friend. If only she had glimpsed the depths of Mary John's despair, she might have persuaded her to go on with life. Self-importance blinded me, she told herself, vowing never again to be so neglectful.

*   *   *   *

'What now?' Catherine asked, peeling off her rubber gloves.

She felt most useful in the hospital. It was not especially congenial to her, for she was easily sickened by malodorousness, by sudden contact with stickiness, by the relentless necessity to deal with human waste. But her weakness could be controlled, she had discovered, and knowledge of her usefulness more than recompensed the effort.

'Oh, you've done the sluicing. How kind!' Sister Luke exclaimed. 'Well, you could give Sister Lazarus some attention. You're so good with them, Sister Catherine.'

'Them' referred to the officially disturbed – Sister Lazarus and Sister Grace. 'See?' she exhorted herself with a grin, 'you have a natural affinity with the condition.' But as she approached Lazarus's door, her face straightened. The disturbed were not all the same. Sister Grace was a sweet vague woman, Sister Lazarus was not. On good days Lazarus was lucid or withdrawn; on difficult days she was excitable or seething with incoherent rage. Have I still some lingering fear of Sister Lazarus? Catherine wondered, as a nerve jumped in her scarred cheek.

'She might go out later,' Sister Luke called down the corridor. 'See if you can persuade her. You'll need help, though. I can spare Sister Megan for half an hour later on. But if you do go out, keep away from the garden.'

Of course. The garden, as a place and a topic of conversation, was treacherous ground for Sister Lazarus.

She knocked on the door and opened it.

Lazarus narrowed her eyes as one of Martha's spies came in.

'How are you today, Sister?' Catherine asked.

I'll show her how I am, thought Lazarus, and shot out her hands. 'See?' she cried. 'Steady as a rock.'

'Yes . . .' Catherine's voice quailed. She stared solemnly at hands that might have been electrified, so convulsively did they jump and twitch.

That's given her something to think about, Lazarus thought.

Catherine racked her brain for news – oh yes, the trouble getting this year's Palm Crosses, and Sister Winifred finding a bird stuck in the old library chimney. As she talked, she went over to a table on which books, skeins of wool, a handkerchief, orange peel and other items were jumbled together, and began methodically to sort them.

There she goes, thought Lazarus. Soon as she came in I knew Martha had sent her. Well, she won't find it, let her turn the room upside down. She was perfectly confident about this, for she was unable to find it herself. What precisely 'it' was, Lazarus could not have put into words, for she had forgotten a long time ago – knew simply it was a highly desirable thing of her own she had once treasured. Whatever it was, it had slipped from her grasp, due, no doubt, to the unreliability of her fingers. But at least Martha had failed to get her hands on it – why else did she come looking?

Martha's visits gave Lazarus a desperate time. She sat tensely on the edge of her seat while Martha sank into an easy chair and thrust out her legs and let her hands hang over the chair arms. 'How goes it, Laz?' she would ask, and without waiting for an answer launch into one of her word-spewings. 'I'm feeling peckish, Laz,' she might interrupt herself to say after a time. 'What've you got?' And Lazarus would hold her breath as Martha sauntered to the table and poked through her belongings, then opened a drawer or the bedside cupboard door. 'Ah, them apples look nice. Ribston Pippin, ain't they? You want one, Laz?' But Martha would keep her back turned to Lazarus, grab up her skirt and give the apple a rub. Then it would be munch-munch through her words and all the time her fat hands rifling, searching.

She never found it, though. Martha's visits were torture, but afterwards Lazarus found comfort in that.

Then, of course, Martha sent her spies. They had no luck either. This one couldn't even find the Nice biscuits. 'They're in the cupboard,' Lazarus said slyly.

Surprised, Catherine lost the thread of her newsy chatter. In any case, it had been talk for talk's sake, talk to cover a malevolent silence. She opened the cupboard door. 'These? You'd like a biscuit?'

'Not I,' Lazarus said stoutly. Oh no, she was not to be caught out like that.

'The packet's been opened, I see.' (Not by *me*, thought Lazarus.) 'I'll try and find you a tin to keep them in. Are you sure you won't have one?'

What's her game? wondered Lazarus, and retorted craftily, '*You* have one.'

'No thanks. I've given up sweet things for Lent,' she said lightly, putting the biscuits back in the cupboard and closing the door.

She came slowly back to Lazarus, thinking, I must stop this inane chatter, stop shying away from the silence – if I give her a chance perhaps she'll speak. She sank to her knees in front of Lazarus's chair, and slid her eyes casually over the chair back, the wall, the floor.

Nothing. Not a word.

After a time, Catherine said, 'I've seen the weaving you started.' Someone had kindly made a simple loom for Lazarus in the hope that her fingers might manage a shuttle though they failed with a needle and knitting pins. 'Wouldn't you like to spend more time in the work room with Sister Grace and Sister Ellen? It'd be company . . .'

Lazarus shuddered.

'It doesn't appeal to you?' Catherine asked softly, taking hold of her hands.

Her face was very close to that of Lazarus, and about a foot lower. Lazarus freed one of her hands, reached out and shakily explored the scarred cheek. 'There's something on your face.'

'I know. It's nothing.'

A wave of incontinent feeling shook Lazarus. She felt herself darkly confined, sweating, panicking. Then daylight rushed at her; there was a flash of metal . . . 'Oh! I . . . I . . .' she stammered.

There was a smell like vinegar. Catherine swallowed and made herself stay still. The convulsive hand in her own gripped tightly, tighter.

' . . . lost it!' Lazarus got out.

The door opened and Sister Megan put her head into the room. 'Are we ready for our walk?'

'Shall we go out? Get some fresh air?' Catherine asked Lazarus.

'We daren't.' (Lazarus knew now that this was not one of Martha's spies after all, but Sister Catherine. Sister Catherine had a mark on her face, which was fortunate for it made her easy to recognize. In future she would not be alarmed by Sister Catherine.) 'They might come in and find it while we're gone.'

'In here? Ah, I see . . . I know what we'll do. We'll ask Sister Luke to let us have the key to this room, then we can lock the door behind us.'

'A key?'

'Yes. Then everything will be safe while we're gone. Will that do?'

Lazarus nodded, and Catherine went to the door to speak quietly to Sister Megan. 'Sister Lazarus has wet herself. I think she'd rather you saw to her.'

'Right you are. We'll be dry and sweet in a couple of shakes.' Catherine went in search of Sister Luke.

'Key? Oh dear, let me think,' said that lady, flustered.

'If you can find it, I think it might persuade Sister Lazarus to leave her room more often.'

'I know. Just a minute.' She rummaged through a drawer. 'It'll be one of these. Go and try them. That was clever of you, Sister, finding out what the problem was. I wish you could be with us more often.'

Ten minutes later, Catherine, Lazarus and Megan set off arm in arm along the corridor. Carefully, they descended the Chapter House stairs, and at the bottom Lazarus freed her arm from the chatting Megan's and felt her skirt pocket and the key safely inside. Oh, she thought, such peace of mind!

In the cloister a group of nuns fell silent as they approached. When they had gone by, the nuns stared after them, watched the gaunt wild ones and the gabby Welsh nurse go slowly by the arches, passing alternately through shadow and pale watery shine.

27

'You asked to see me, Reverend Mother?'
'Yes, Sister Catherine. Come in.'

The room was full of April sunshine. The Prioress was sitting by the window, in her hands a square of canvas, a needle, a length of pink embroidery silk. 'I've got some work on the go.'

When the Prioress or Cecilia and her friends talked of work in a possessive tone of voice, they referred, Catherine knew, to a piece of embroidery, for decorative sewing was the only work a lady allowed herself – and gardening, of course, though somehow gardening, being an outdoor pursuit, was not work but recreation. 'That's good.'

'Yes, I think it's coming.' She held it out at arm's length. It was a conventional flower spray worked in *petit point*, the Prioress's favourite stitch, for it covered the ground with gratifying speed so that one's work seemed to grow before one's eyes. 'I'm trying to stir myself. This last winter rather got on top of me. There is nothing like work for clearing away the cobwebs. Mmm, and er, I've come to a decision.'

'Oh.'

'Yes. Sit down. Not over there – bring up a chair. I'll just finish this row, if you don't mind. Tch, tch – blow it! Mmm.'

The succession, thought Catherine. It must be that. Ah well, I have been expecting it.

'There.' The Prioress took a pair of scissors from a stool by her side, snipped the thread and jammed her needle into the back of the canvas. 'Of course, it's only for a cushion – I'll get Elizabeth to make it up for me and stuff it. I was much more ambitious in my youth. I worked that fire screen, you know.'

Catherine did know very well, but turned her head and murmured politely.

'That was done when Jacobean embroidery was all the rage.'

Finding nothing more to say about it, the Prioress frowned, and thought how very peaky – no, worse than that – *overwrought* Catherine was looking. Her appearance did not inspire confidence. No wonder everyone had plumped for Margaret. Even Catherine's former supporters – Cecilia, Monica, Elizabeth, Anne, the Sister Precentor and Sister Angelica – had all regretfully concluded that Margaret and not Catherine should replace Sister Mercy as sole Directrix and Prioress-in-waiting. Anne and Monica had fallen over themselves to qualify their opinion. 'I think Catherine is not well,' had said Monica, twisting her hands, and Anne had declared sarcastically, 'Catherine was really up against it – trying to persuade us to go against our own self-interest.' (This last had annoyed the Prioress, for she had clearly ruled out discussion. 'I just want a straight answer – Sister Margaret or Sister Catherine?' she had told each sister summoned to her side.)

The decision, once arrived at, had released in her a surge of energy. She started some work – and it must have been nine or ten years since she last took up a needle. She renewed her interest in the chapel proceedings (to the annoyance of the Sister Precentor) and found she had to hand it to Margaret, for there had certainly been a pulling up of socks – no milling round the door after service, no ill-disguised yawning, no dashings in at the last minute, but everything calm, orderly, dignified.

She told no one of her decision. Keeping it to herself gave her a sense of power. It occurred to her that there was no need to squander this by making it known and allowing it to be the end of the matter. No, no. She could hug it for a while and think carefully of the consequences, make sure she secured the right *terms*. And there was nobility in her role: hers to dispose and withhold, hers to deal justly, hers the chance to ensure a measure of mitigation for the loser (and everything as she wished it for herself).

Margaret had forced the issue, of course. She knew – for the woman was no fool – that the Prioress viewed her role in the coming foot-washing ceremony with distaste and dread. What a *shame* about the Prioress's sciatica, had said Margaret with her head sympathetically on one side, for sadly there was to be much leaning forward and bending down. Never mind. *Next* year, when the question of the succession would undoubtedly have been resolved, the Prioress-in-waiting could relieve the Reverend Mother of the chore. Unfortunately, it seemed that *this* year she must make the best of it, for spiritual leadership was indispensable to the role of foot-washer. Margaret had gone on to describe the enviable conditions in which a semi-retired Prioress would find herself – oceans of uninterrupted time for contemplation, reading and prayer – the *important* things, Margaret had added, wistfully.

Message understood, m'dear, the Prioress had thought, waving a gnarled hand impatiently towards the door.

But Margaret had dutifully clasped the hand and drawn it to her lips. 'Do think it over,' she murmured.

The Prioress had thought. She had consulted. The decision was always inescapable. But there was heartache in remembering Catherine as she once was and her hopes for her. She shan't be made to suffer. I won't have her belittled, she vowed. Over her sewing she considered the matter. As roses spread salmon-pink across the canvas, it became clear that she must make a sacrifice.

'I think we'll have a nice cup of tea.'

Wearily, Catherine rose and went into the little pantry where there was a sink and a kettle. When the tea was made she left it to brew and returned to the sitting room to set out a tray. Then, sensing that nothing would be said until they were fortified by a sip or two of strong Earl Grey, she sauntered to the fireplace above which hung a portrait of the Prioress's predecessor.

Hooded eyes stared down into Catherine's. Breeding is the thing, the great lady seemed to sneer, and I doubt very much whether you modern young things possess it. Oh dear – might not her scrutiny be misconstrued, Catherine wondered – might it look as though she entertained false hope? Blushing, she hurried back to the teapot.

'Here we are.' She held the tray while the Prioress helped herself to milk and sugar. 'Now' – she sat down – 'I think you have something to tell me.'

The Prioress puffed away the steam and drew carefully from her cup; then, jerking back her head, said gruffly: 'I've decided to name Sister Margaret my successor – and sole Directrix, of course.'

'Yes,' said Catherine, and sighed.

'However, I shall see that you are not embarrassed. I shall keep the decision to myself for a month, which will give you time to find a position that is congenial and becoming. When you are quite sure about it, come and tell me and I shall make it a condition of my naming Sister Margaret. You have four weeks to make up your mind.'

'But Reverend Mother, there is no need for it. If I'm allowed to, I shall work in the hospital. If they think otherwise I shall join the annexe sisters and go where I'm bid day by day.'

At the word 'annexe' the Prioress jumped and slopped her tea.

Catherine ran for a cloth and blotted skirt and carpet.

'You'll do no such thing! I won't have it. Think how bad it will look. Think how it would have upset poor Mercy!'

Her teacup rattled violently on its saucer. Tactfully, Catherine relieved her of it and put it down on the stool.

'I didn't mean to upset you.'

'Well, you succeeded. I have steeled myself to make a great sacrifice for your sake, Catherine. If I were to name Margaret at once, I shouldn't have to go through with this washing-the-feet malarkey. Sister Margaret would do it herself – she good as told me – providing she were named successor before the ceremony.'

'Reverend Mother, I wish you would save yourself the trouble.'

The Prioress's eyes glittered. Her head trembled. She had not braced herself for martyrdom to have it thrown in her face. 'You want to be a living reproach to us – is that it?'

'Certainly not.'

'Well it sounds suspiciously like it. Sounds like sour grapes to me.'

'Reverend Mother, I will do as you ask. I will talk to Sister Luke . . .'

'And to the Sister Precentor and Sister Angelica. I'm sure they'd be delighted to have you working with them . . .'

'They'd be embarrassed. Truly. My fault, but there it is. You know, there's so much ill-health at the moment – the lay sisters, and now the stress on the annexe sisters – it would be a blessing for Sister Luke if she were able to gain another pair of hands.'

'I suppose the hospital would do – if we can think of a suitable title. How about "Sister Almoner"? "Almoner" has a substantial sound. But I'm sure you're quite wrong about the Sister Precentor and Sister Angelica – they're your friends. And it was always your natural place, the chapel. Anyway, think it over. Come back in four weeks and tell me.'

'All right. I will. And thank you for your kindness, Reverend Mother. I'm sorry about the ceremony. I wish . . .'

'We won't talk about it. Drink your tea.' She took her own cup from the stool and tasted the contents. 'Bah! Stone cold. Let's have some fresh.'

Catherine collected the cups, and the Prioress took up her sewing.

'I wonder,' she mused. 'Elizabeth said I should work the background in beige, but I'm rather inclined to blue. Always such a cautious one, Elizabeth. I think blue might lift it. What do you think, Catherine? Shall I be adventurous? Yes, I've made up my mind. A nice bright blue.'

28

There was a spring in Margaret's step. Bounce, bounce, she went through the cloister, smiling, inclining her head. The nuns passing by felt especially favoured, for Margaret's customary style was to bustle as if time were of the essence and to set her face in an expression designed to discourage those hoping to waylay her. When Sister Imogen met Margaret's sunny countenance, she caught her breath. But there were further wonders to come. Margaret, having passed Imogen by, suddenly turned and called after her: 'Oh, Imogen – just a moment – something I've been meaning to say.'

Imogen hurried to her side.

'I was so pleased to hear those tiresome annexe sisters have given up their silly protest at last. Your doing, I'm sure.'

Margaret referred to Sisters Rose and Kirsty who, having become worn out with lack of sleep, had taken to their beds in the annexe – actually, to recover their strength and plan further protests, though Imogen and Margaret were unaware of this.

'You know, Imogen, it's high time you came back to help us on the Forward Planning Committee.' She spoke as if Imogen had been taking an unreasonably long vacation.

Imogen's heart began to race. 'Yes, yes,' she stammered.

'Good. Well done. Then we'll expect you at two o'clock today. We need all the best brains – something big in the air.'

Imogen could not speak. Her heart was swelling to such a

size that already it jutted into her larynx. As Margaret bounced away, she folded her arms and brought them tight in against her ribs to prevent a messy explosion.

A minute later, Clare came across her still rooted to the spot in the cloister. 'You all right, Sister?' she asked curiously, for Imogen was very red and had her arms pulled into her waist. 'Got the jip or something?'

Imogen shook her head and looked secretive. Poor old Clare, she was thinking. Still out in the cold. Whereas I, I . . . She lurched forward and found her legs were wobbly. She needed a little sit down.

On her rosewood throne in the cloakroom, she let out her breath. Happiness curled up inside her like a warm dog; water chuntered in the pipes; the sun peeped in. Oh blissful day that had restored her at last to the Forward Planning Committee!

* * * *

So Margaret needs to muster support, thought Beatrice, seeing Imogen at the table. What's she up to?

Margaret bustled in and opened the proceedings. 'Things are moving,' she announced, and darted a look at Verity (a look registered jealously by Joan and Beatrice, wryly by Agnes). 'I, er, happen to know that the Reverend Mother has been taking soundings. However . . . ,' she paused and looked thoughtful, 'it seems the feet-washing ceremony will go ahead this evening as planned. Now,' she became brisk again, 'I've had a letter from our Californian friends. They were very very impressed with our set-up here. For some time they've been looking for a chance to expand, and are now convinced they see an opening. They propose to build a branch of their convent in the grounds of Albion Priory. The point is, Sisters, where to put it? Any ideas?'

'I should have thought,' Verity put in promptly, her face empty of expression, 'the old vegetable fields would fit the bill.'

'Splendid, Verity! All that land lying idle. How satisfying to find a use for it at last.'

'I presume we gain some advantage from this?' Agnes enquired.

'Very considerable advantage.'

But Joan was uneasy. 'Hang on. I see a snag. If we're not careful we'll compromise our own interests. We can't afford to jeopardize our autonomy.'

'Can't afford to turn up our noses at good offers – they don't grow on trees,' growled Verity.

'But Agnes!' Joan turned to her in appeal. 'What about Clare's new plan?'

'Clare?' Margaret cried with annoyance.

'Yes, she's been working on a new project. Sounds promising, doesn't it, Agnes?'

'I hardly think it would measure up to *this*,' Margaret retorted, jabbing her pencil into a sheaf of correspondence.

'But Clare's new project wouldn't be so risky. After all, you're talking about foreigners actually occupying Albion territory – could lead to all sorts of trouble. I think we should hold back.'

'Consider each option on its merits,' Agnes said judiciously.

'Bet Clare's is worth peanuts,' scoffed Verity. 'Whereas this . . .'

'Is worth millions!' cried Margaret. 'If we let it go too cheaply, someone else'll reap the benefit, for mark my words: whatever the controls and restraints, that land will find its price. You can't buck the market, Joan.' (Joan groaned and put her head in her hands.) 'Can we agree to look into it further? One of us will have to go over there. That reminds me, Beatrice: Sister Betty-Lou sends her regards and says she hopes to return your kindness in California.'

What a turn-up! thought Beatrice. She beamed round at her companions. 'Surely no one's going to object to simply exploring the idea?'

'Much too good a chance to miss,' Imogen declared stoutly, earning herself an approving smile.

'Everyone agreed? Good.' Margaret gathered her papers

and rose. 'We'll get on with it, then. Come along, Verity – things to do.'

* * * *

The ornaments of the chapel – altar crosses, statues and portraits of the saints – were draped in the mourning cloth of Passiontide. A feeling of suffocation attacked Catherine. It is all the black stuff about, she reasoned, trying to stave off her panic.

Before a congregation of nuns and visitors, Margaret was explaining the symbolism of the ceremony about to take place. She had a special voice and manner for religion, and she achieved it by making her mouth small, her face still, her eyes wide and directed downwards. Catching herself with these critical observations, Catherine heard in her head the Prioress's comment: 'Sounds like sour grapes to me.' (At that moment the Prioress was making a more pertinent comment in her own head, for soon the Sister Precentor would lead her to the throne-like chair placed in readiness at the top of the chancel steps.)

Catherine could not banish her critical frame of mind. She thought of other ceremonies peculiar to Albion, revered and handed down from generation to generation, springing from what they truly believed about their community which was why they were precious and not embarrassing. But perhaps it was only she who was uncomfortable with the present proceedings. She looked cautiously to her companions on either side. Blank faces gave nothing away.

Cecilia was thinking: If the Reverend Mother slops the water I shall die. I shan't dare look for fear of catastrophe.

At her side, Monica was wishing that the Reverend Mother would look less cross.

Fiddlesticks! thought Anne, listening to Margaret, but Elizabeth's eyes had misted with tears.

How wonderful Margaret is, marvelled Veronica in her pew half way down the nave. Not only has she the brain and willpower to put us back on our feet, she has the spiritual imagination to create this moving ceremony.

I'm glad I went before I came out, thought Imogen, who, from the front pew, had an unimpeded view of the water waiting in the big china bowl. I just hope they had the sense to make the water good and hot for that poor girl.

Martha was covertly watching the attentive guests. Makes you right proud, she thought, this ceremony and all them posh folk clocking us. Then a feeling of inner subsidence disturbed her and she recalled: Tea were a bit thin – wonder what's laid on for supper.

Beatrice was imagining herself beneath a Californian sun, clad in gold, her flaxen tresses hanging a good six inches beneath her jaunty veil.

I shall catch my death, worried Sister Fay waiting barefoot at the bottom of the chancel steps.

It was time. The Prioress struggled to her feet. 'For pity's sake, may it be got over quickly and safely,' she prayed.

Catherine closed her eyes. The thing that was about to happen seemed more terrible, because it was false, than the sisters voting and the Prioress deciding in favour of Margaret. She was oppressed by a sense of irrevocableness and feared that in a moment distress would physically overwhelm her. As a safeguard she blocked out her sight and held instead to the music. She listened to the organ's fluting with avid concentration.

Angelica had chosen well. Notes rippled evenly and without emotion over a sustained anchorage. There was no hint of modulation or dissonance, no massing in chords; all was light and airy and innocent, and endless effortless flow. Unconsciously, Catherine smiled, for the tinkling sound had transported her. She glimpsed into heaven and saw cherubim and seraphim dance.

Suddenly, the bass note, the foundation of the music's harmony, crept up one tone and plunged the notes above into dissonance. Heaven lurched; desire stirred in the bowels of angels. There was a sliding and a tumbling as note pressed against note, squeezing, resisting, yielding ... Catherine leaped to her feet and stumbled into the aisle.

Nothing is what it seems, she thought, leaning heavily on Beatrice (who, with presence of mind, had caught her and led her from the chapel and was now supporting her to her room). Scratch an angel and it will wink and leer. Put up an image and people will cheer while the substance lies dead in the ground.

Beatrice turned the handle and kicked open the door. She pushed Catherine on to the bed and went to fetch a glass of water.

'Drink,' Beatrice commanded on her return. 'Come on. You must be feverish – your skin's burning.'

She struggled to sit up. The water solidified in her chest. 'You poor thing. I suppose the trouble is you're feeling it's all up,' Beatrice guessed. 'Well' – she sat on the side of the bed – 'don't be too hard on yourself. You were up against a champion; hadn't a cat in hell's chance.'

'Oh, come on,' she protested as Catherine looked at her wonderingly. 'You surely didn't underestimate Margaret? Did you? Look, she's just as sincere as you about wanting what's best for the Priory. Probably with more conviction. I bet you're the self-questioning type – am I right? – hesitating, letting everyone have their say? Well, you won't catch Mags dithering. She knows what's right and she goes for it.'

A fit of coughing racked Catherine.

'Drink some more. Come on. Oh well, have it your own way. Gosh though, you do look green. When the service is over I'll get someone to look at you. Hey – you're not going to pass out, are you?'

With an effort, Catherine opened her eyes.

'Didn't mean to upset you – just trying to cheer you up. You see, even if you had been a match for Margaret, you'd still have lost. Want to know why?'

Catherine threw back her head and sighed.

'Because she held the ace of spades. Her ideas made most people better off. Well, they weren't going to say no to that, were they? And of course, Mags's stroke of genius was making 'em feel good about it. Though it's an easy enough thing, I suppose, making people feel deserving. When you come to think about it, that's what religion's all about.'

Catherine gasped. 'Christ,' she got out, 'was hardly about succouring the better-off.'

'Oh, *Christ*,' Beatrice said dismissively. 'I'm talking about religion. Ask yourself: what does religion do? You can't get away from it, it does what it's always done – supports the status quo; makes the division of spoils legitimate. True, there's usually a bit of hand-wringing over the poor from time to time – but not too much, otherwise people get shirty. They know the church is for *them*, the respectable, decent, well-ordered folk. Mind you, I did think you could've bolstered your case by bringing Jesus into it more – the eye of the needle and so forth; and Paul – "the greatest of these is charity". Not that it would have done any good. People take all that with a pinch of salt. It's God, the old man in the sky, who matters. They know in their guts that He's on their side – fond of law and order and the profit motive.' She hesitated, took on a dreamy look and confided, 'Personally, though, I've always looked to Jesus' – she was thinking of her particular peccadillo and of Jesus forgiving Mary Magdalen. 'But we all cling to what suits us, I guess – it's human nature.'

Catherine had closed her eyes. Beatrice leaned over her and administered a friendly shake. 'What I'm saying is: cheer up, it wasn't your fault. Margaret had it all – the magic hand – able to make a Good Thing out of improving the lot of the majority. I mean, you can't lose with the majority behind you – stands to reason. Do yourself a favour. Play your cards right and you can still carve out a nice little niche for yourself; after all, you've got prestige, and between you and me, Margaret's a bit of a sucker, on the quiet, for prestige.'

Outside there was a faint stirring. Beatrice went to the door and looked into the corridor. 'Chucking out time,' she reported. 'I'll send Sister Luke or someone.' And she added as final encouragement, 'Do buck up now. Take a tip from Auntie – okay?'

Going cheerfully towards the cloister, she wondered whatever had come over her, she had been so pleasant. It could only be that the very thought of California had had a mellowing effect. Well, she could certainly afford to be generous. Life was looking up, there were goodies in store: sun, travel, glamour; Sister Betty-Lou . . .

29

The bluebells were out in the wood. For the past few weeks Catherine had monitored their progress from tight green flower-heads to the first peeping of blue and finally this intensely coloured flower-burst. As she came over the foot-bridge their perfume tugged her, and enveloped her as she went under the trees. She marvelled again at their comradely scent, undetectable in a single flower, yet potent and heady from a massed effusion. She went slowly along a winding, overgrown track and when, ahead, it dipped under muddy water, took a semi-circular diversion through vegetation. At close hand the depth of colour was striking, each flower so violently blue that colour seeped like a bruise into the bending stem. In the distance the blueness was softer, milky in the slanting light. Between the trees, over banks where briars prepared to shoot, and in flat clearings, waves of bluebells went on and on. Trees canopied greenery above them, moist greenery bedded them, and through them jutted stiff young ferns with uncurled tips, formal as bishops' crooks.

The climb to the top of Beechy Knob made her puff and blow. She sat on a log, listened to the rustling, singing wood, scanned the sky-coloured floor below and idly wondered whether prolonged exposure to the unremitting blue might prove hallucinatory.

Her enforced holiday was nearly over. ('You must take a long rest,' the Prioress had ordered. 'Sister Luke tells me you are unwell. She will be glad to have you working with her in the hospital, but not until you have recovered your strength. Until I settle matters with Sister Margaret you are to do absolutely nothing at all.') This evening she would become Sister Almoner and Margaret would become sole Directrix and the Prioress's successor. Catherine was glad. The way ahead was straight-forward; she had only to be herself – a small part (a tiny thorn in the flesh of authority, perhaps?) but she would play it faithfully.

She had been sitting so still that a rabbit emerging from a briar patch nearby, paused to sniff the air and ponder. Unconcerned, it leisurely loped away.

Then Catherine rose and climbed down between the smooth trunks of the beech trees. At the bottom of the Knob, she turned along a path leading through sycamores whose trunks spurted from the ground in clusters like giant tufts of grass. Their leaves were yellow-green in the sun. They trailed and brushed against her face as she ducked and weaved her way through them.

Arriving back at the wood's edge, she heard the chapel bell. Its sound came unevenly on the breeze. She stood still and listened, for the bell's ringing brought the Priory to life in her mind's eye – the sisters about their work, thronging cheerfully in the refectory and decorously in the chapel, going singly to their rooms or in groups through the cloister; and hidden beneath their everyday demeanours a remorseless undercurrent of thought and emotion. Now, here, pressed to an ancient oak, the moist exhalation of plants on her skin and breath, the Priory world seemed remote and quite impossible. But even as she thought this she moved away, set off across the footbridge; and soon she quickened her step as if fearing to be late.

*   *   *   *

'I am up and down,' said the Prioress, turning her head to look bleakly out of the window. 'The winter was lowering. Spring was so late. Those nice few weeks we had at the end of April were a tonic, but lately there has been so much rain.'

224

'The sun is glorious today,' Margaret said briskly.

'I am not the woman I was,' the Prioress concluded sadly.

Ah, thought Margaret. Are we getting somewhere at last? She crossed her legs and smoothed her skirt. 'There is no need for you to exert yourself, Reverend Mother. You have earned a period of contemplation – indeed, I am sure the Priory will be the better for your prayers and thoughts. As I pointed out . . .'

'Yes,' said the Prioress irritably. 'Well, I've come to a decision.'

Silence fell in the room. Sounds from outside buzzed faintly, joined with the floating dust and faded fabric to cast a pervasive muzziness.

'Sister Catherine has been unwell.'

Margaret pulled a sympathetic face.

'She has overtaxed her strength, I fear.'

A bubble of annoyance rose in Margaret.

'I have spent some considerable time thinking about it, trying to decide what is best.' She stared at the cushion she had recently embroidered. 'It came to me that Sister Catherine can no longer endure the onerous role of joint Directrix. However, some position must be found for her.' (And here the Prioress leaned forward and peered at the very rose she had been stitching when reaching this conclusion.) 'After all, Sister Mercy chose her for her assistant. That must count for something. There is the dignity of the Priory to consider.'

'I am sure . . .' Margaret began, but was put off by the Prioress suddenly jabbing with her finger.

'Pass it to me, will you?'

Margaret stared at the empty chair beside her. 'Oh – you mean the cushion?' She got up quickly, preparing to apply it to the Prioress's aching back. 'Where would you like it?' she asked solicitously.

The Prioress snatched it and closely examined her work. 'Oh, what a relief. Must have been a trick of the light. Thought I'd missed a stitch.'

'You made it?' breathed Margaret.

'I worked it. Sister Elizabeth made it up for me.'

'It's lovely. If only I had the patience.'

'Do you think so?' the Prioress asked curiously. She herself was no longer convinced of its merit. Ready to defend her choice of a blue background to Elizabeth – who had lamely suggested beige – she had been taken aback by Cecilia's frank disparagement. (Unlike Elizabeth, Cecilia could not be accused of liking to play safe.)

'Oh, that nasty shade of blue, Reverend Mother!' she had cried. 'Whatever possessed you? Were you trying to use it up?'

'Certainly not,' the Prioress had cried. 'Elizabeth suggested beige, but I thought blue would make a better background for the salmon-pink.'

'Dear Reverend Mother – that cruel blue makes the salmon look quite gorn orff! Beige, I grant you, would have killed it. But green . . . Now if you had chosen a pale sage green it would be an altogether different story.'

At once the Prioress had known she was right. It had ruined the cushion for her. Now she was wild to use up the rest of the salmon-pink with some nice green thread she had discovered in her workbox. She regarded Margaret thoughtfully. 'If you really like it, you can have it. It would be fitting in a way, for while I was working it I decided to make you sole Directrix and Sister Catherine . . .'

She got no further. Margaret's hand shot out and claimed her present. She clasped it to her breast, genuinely moved. In years to come she would point it out to guests: 'That cushion was worked by our former Prioress; she made it especially for me, her chosen successor.' Just a minute, though; the Prioress had not quite said she was her chosen successor – not yet. 'Forgive me, Reverend Mother, I interrupted you. I was touched, quite overcome.'

This surprised the Prioress considerably. However, she recollected herself. 'Yes, as I was saying, my successor must guarantee Sister Catherine's position. I am very firm about that.'

'Oh – absolutely. Something fitting . . .'

'She wishes to be attached to the hospital. This is a surprise, but there is no dissuading her. "Sister Almoner" is a suitable title, don't you think? She has no nursing qualification, and Sister Luke says her particular forte is soothing the patients down. Apparently, a great many patients these days require some soothing down.'

Almoner? Margaret flinched from the word with distaste. It sounded suspiciously like 'social worker', a complete waste of time – and didn't it cast a rather doubtful aspersion on the Priory? Still, if it satisfied the Prioress it would do for now. There was no saying what any particular sister would be doing a few years hence, for the changes had hardly begun. As that dynamic Californian nun would no doubt put it: they ain't seen nothin' yet. 'That sounds perfectly satisfactory,' she conceded graciously.

'Good. It's settled, then. I shall name you my successor tonight, by the way. Before Evensong. It'll be the usual thing. I shall say my piece while you wait outside. Then the chapel doors will be opened and you will walk down the aisle to the chancel steps and say something suitable to the congregation. And I shall mention Sister Catherine – thank her for her work for the Priory, describe her new position.'

At last! And so casually alluded to! Margaret, her one hand clutching the cushion to her breast, fell on her knees at the Prioress's feet. 'I shall do my utmost to prove worthy,' she murmured, her free hand pulling gnarled and reluctant fingers to her lips.

'Of course. Well, I'm rather tired.' The Prioress hoped now to be rid of her.

Margaret went dreamily to the door.

'And if you see the Sister Almoner, tell her I'd like a word.'

* * * *

Catherine came in.

'You are out of breath,' the Prioress remarked.

'I was in the wood. I came back and ran into Sister Marg . . . I mean, the Directrix. She said you wished . . . Can I help you, Reverend Mother?'

227

Evidently, the Prioress was turning out her sideboard drawers. Assorted objects were heaped on the sideboard top; several had fallen on to the carpet. Catherine began to collect items from the floor.

'I've been looking . . . Drat! Why is it always the last thing one comes across? And now it's stuck.' She tugged at a package caught in a crack between drawer end and drawer bottom. 'Got it.' (There was a tearing sound.) 'Never mind – it's only the wrapping paper. Yes, here we are.' From the wrapping she withdrew a book and pushed it at Catherine. 'For you. Take it.'

Catherine was astounded. She turned the book over in her hands. It was a Book of Common Prayer splendidly bound in cream leather, the title wording inlaid with mother-of-pearl.

'The Prioress – that is, my predecessor – gave it to me before she died.'

Then Margaret ought to have it, Catherine thought, and wondered how to suggest this inoffensively.

The Prioress seemed to read her mind. 'I gave the Directrix a thing she fancied,' she said gruffly in the tone of a child making a lame excuse, 'so I'd like you to have the prayer book.'

Relieved, Catherine allowed herself to possess it. She turned the tissue-thin pages edged sharply with gold – they had a clean, crisp feel, yet gave off a delicious mustiness. 'I love it. It's quite beautiful.'

The Prioress grunted. She had no doubt as to the merit of the prayer book. Then her face fell as she took in the mess. Hotly pursuing a gift for Catherine, she had disregarded the growing dishevelment. Now it filled her with gloom. She placed her forearm along the sideboard and scooted a heap of objects into the drawer.

'Oh, let me. I'll make it tidy,' cried Catherine, putting her prayer book to one side.

The Prioress brightened. 'Will you, m'dear? That is kind, for I admit I am uncommonly tired. And when you have done we'll take a small glass of wine – it will buck us up no end.'

Later, going down the stairs, Catherine felt the Prioress had dissembled in the matter of Margaret's present, had given her a

228

thing she did not value, or, more likely, a thing she valued greatly to make up for not letting her have the prayer book which, taking the succession into account, should probably be hers; but since she could not deny her delight in the gift (and here Catherine smiled and put the prayer book to her lips), it would be hypocritical to pretend to care.

*   *   *   *

Though there was no one to see her (save her Maker), Margaret stood to attention outside the closed chapel doors. It was a solemn moment. The organ had ceased playing. The Prioress, unheard by Margaret, was now acquainting the congregation with her decision. When two awe-covered postulants opened the doors, Margaret did not hesitate; she had rehearsed every step, every look, every word.

She went briskly down the aisle. (Delay would have been inappropriate, for if ever an honour came tardily, it was now.) Her smile, however, was forgiving. The muscles of her throat were flexed and ready to emit exactly the right sound of becoming sweetness and underlying authority.

Her words were also well-prepared. There was to be no triumphant speech, no hectoring look at the future – these would keep for another occasion. Magnanimous in victory, she proposed to strike a conciliatory note. It had come to her in the quiet of her room as she sat on her bed with the Prioress's cushion in her lap, that she could do no better than repeat the charming prayer she had uttered at the time of her appointment as joint Directrix. It might also serve as a reminder that a great deal of trouble would have been saved had she been created sole Directrix and the Prioress's successor in the first place.

She had reached the top of the chancel steps. Turning, she faced the assembly, put her head slightly on one side, and began: 'Sisters: in the words of Saint Francis of Assisi:

229

"Where there is hatred, may we bring love;
where there is discord, may we bring harmony;
where there is doubt, may we bring faith;
where there is despair, may we bring hope;
where there is darkness, may we bring light;
where there is sadness, may we bring joy,
for Thy mercy and truth's sake." '

AMEN